A Lady's Honor

Honor at Heart, Book 2

Caroline Warfield

Merlin's Owl Press

Formerly entitled Dangerous Works. The new edition is fully edited and enlarged with new material.

Cover design by DAR Albert

To Greg, still the hero of all my works,
now and always.

A Lady's Honor

She may be skirting scandal in the opinion of some, but Lady Georgiana has her own code of Honor

A little Greek is one thing; the art of love is another. Only one man ever tried to teach Lady Georgiana Hayden both. She learned painfully, a young age to keep her heart safe. She learned to keep loneliness at bay through work. If it takes a scandalous affair to teach her what she needs to complete her work, she will risk it. She is determined to give voice to the ancient women whose poetry has long been neglected.

Some scars cut deeper than others. Major Andrew Mallet returns to Cambridge a battle scarred hero. He dared to love Georgiana once and suffered swift retribution from her powerful family. The work she offers risks his career, his peace of mind, and (worst of all) his heart. Can he protect himself from a woman who almost destroyed him? Does he want to?

Chapter One

Cambridge 1816

Books be damned and women with them.

Andrew Mallet lay on a narrow bed while Harley—former batman, loyal servant, insolent bastard—massaged the twisted muscles of his back with ruthless determination. Through a door Andrew could see his friend, Jamie Heyworth, slouched in the battered leather of a well-worn chair, oblivious to the exquisite Tudor roses and honeybees carved in the finely waxed walnut mantel that crowned Andrew's study.

He ignored Jamie's drunken stupor, eyes focused with angry resentment on two small books resting innocently on his worktable. In a room filled with books, two more should have had little impact. Andrew, however, one-time soldier and would-be scholar, couldn't just leave them at the bookseller's. The walk there inflicted wrenching agony on his back and hip, and he immediately regretted it.

"What you need is a woman. Warm your bed and serve a better table." Jamie's voice managed to sound emphatic even though he slurred his words. Andrew ignored him.

A woman? Hardly. His bookstore foray had thrust him into an ugly scene. He tried not to think about the woman who had set the bookseller off. Her pretense of scholarship set the old misogynist off on a rant. *The damned bookseller behaved like a pretentious fool.*

"Watching that brute of yours manipulate your back isn't my idea of an evening's entertainment, Mallet, I must say," Jamie rambled on.

"Perhaps you should find someone else to visit." Andrew turned his face into the bedding and let soft linens muffle his words.

Jamie heard him anyway. "Unkind. You know I worry about you. A woman. One would do this household no end of good."

"You think my injuries don't provide me with enough discomfort? You want to inflict a woman on me as well? What I need is work." He groaned in response to one of Harley's more vigorous movements.

"Work? What is the point in that? You're a nabob. The army left you well enough off. I can see where keeping your father's little house has some appeal, even if it is too cramped in here for company, but damn it, Andrew, you could afford a proper staff. That ham-handed ruffian is no one's idea of a proper anything."

Harley cast him a baleful look, finished his ministrations, and left the room with a basin full of towels.

"Are you angry because Harley left you for me? You liked him well enough as your batman in Portugal." Andrew rolled onto his side, faced his visitor, and flashed his odd, lopsided grin.

"True enough. He would've left me for you sooner, though, if you were in camp more often. Too busy running the hills with the partisans to stay for long. He preferred your pretty face."

"Ah, Jamie, you malign me. He preferred my abstemious habits." Andrew ignored the reference to his face and watched his companion fill his glass again. Jamie was four or five rounds in.

"You weren't so abs...abst..." A loud belch punctuated his sentence. "Abstemious about women. And they all liked your pretty face. That's for certain. Remember Colonel Stafford's wife? A beauty, that one." Jamie Heyworth flashed a grin full of pure wickedness as only he could, drunk or sober.

"Not my fault!" Andrew took the teasing with good humor. Jamie's habitual conversation bristled with sharp needling but never with cruelty. Andrew swung his feet around, sat up, and stuffed his shirt into his trousers. "I explained that to you before. She bribed poor Corporal Collins, who kept my things, to get into my bed. I tossed her out."

"Didn't hurt your reputation none. The great, dark, mysterious Major Mallet, all the more interesting for being so difficult to catch. What happened to the corporal?"

"Stripped of his rank—back to private. Back to the infantry. Don't know after that." An uncomfortable silence followed that remark. Both men knew well what the infantry endured in the last years of the war.

"Still, a proper gentleman needs a proper staff to run a proper household. Glad I'm going back to London tomorrow where it is civilized."

"Where you can bunk in with Glenaire, you mean."

"Of course!" A swift wink punctuated Jamie's words. "Keeps a fine cellar, our Richard does. He can afford me. Rich as Croesus is the Marquess." He raised a glass in mock salute.

Andrew cringed. He once held Richard Hayden, the Marquess of Glenaire, as one of his closest friends, bound by school ties and shared adventure. Jamie had no idea what had caused the rift between them, and Andrew didn't plan to enlighten him.

"Rich as Croesus," Jamie repeated, "And generous to his friends." He downed the contents of the glass and poured another.

Glenaire remained loyal in his way, but Andrew didn't plan to let him or any member of the Hayden family interfere with his life again. Glenaire's entire clan had made Andrew's life a misery, particularly the Hayden he encountered in Groghan's bookshop that afternoon, Glenaire's sister.

Jamie mumbled into his glass, less coherent by the minute.

Andrew brooded against the doorjamb, staring at sparks flying up his chimney. He'd earned his peace after eleven bloody years and intended to enjoy it without interference.

"I've had my fill of the damned Haydens," he snarled, "and I'm not about to tolerate interference from Richard."

Jamie ignored him. "Still, a wife would do you good. Don't look like you wish me to the devil! Mistress then. Clean you up a bit."

Andrew pushed himself upright. "I need cleaning?"

"'Spose not. You're fastidious enough. Meant this place." He waved an unsteady hand in a gesture that encompassed the entire room.

"No clutter here but my papers. A man needs something to work on."

"Scholar like your father? Are you going to tutor the careless sons of privilege, browbeat 'em into learning like he tried to do to me? Write pretty poetry? What?"

Andrew shrugged into the dressing gown. "The world has enough bad poetry. It isn't my gift, and I haven't the patience for teaching. I've a notion to try my hand at translating, just something to keep my mind and hands busy."

Andrew kept his need to create something clean and good after eleven years of war to himself. Guilt regarding his father crippled him as effectively as his scars. He couldn't explain his driving need to do something–anything–the old man would have been proud of, not even to Jamie.

"Sounds deadly dull to me. If a woman can't clean you up, she might cheer you up. Visiting you is like visiting a mausoleum. Find some jolly girl with laughing eyes."

"Her eyes wouldn't laugh at the sight of me." A subtle but unmistakable change transformed Andrew's tone.

"That's it then? The face? Don't bother me none. Would think some kinds of women would find it romantic."

Andrew thought Jamie believed what he said. The line that sliced Andrew's face in two didn't revolt him as it did others. Jamie looked Andrew directly in the face, but few respectable women did the same. He knew his features attracted women before; not so now. The revulsion, the swift look away, told him what he needed to know. Then again, when Jamie suggested a woman, he probably didn't mean the respectable kind.

"I'm surprised half the unmarried women in Cambridge aren't here already," Jamie went on, "bringing calves' foot jelly and tisanes to cheer you. Most of the married ones, too."

"They can keep their pity. Think what would happen if they got past my face. They'd have to see the rest of me." He didn't want to find out what it would feel like to see revulsion on a woman's face at an intimate moment. He limped into the study and dropped into a soft armchair with a loud groan.

"You walk a far sight better than you did right after Waterloo. I thought the fancy physician Richard found fixed you right and tight."

"He helped. I'm on my feet at least, but army surgeons set the left leg badly to begin with and not quite even with the right. Richard tried to send me on to a surgeon in Edinburgh, but I preferred to come home."

"Richard let you come? He's like a dog with a bone. If he thought you needed more—"

"Even Richard Hayden—exalted damn Marquess of Glenaire—can't keep an Englishman from his home if he wishes to be there." *Particularly one who missed his own father's funeral.*

When no reply came from the other chair, Andrew grumbled. "He may have been right, though. Damn him."

"Isn't he always?" The slurred words faded out at the end.

Andrew continued as if Jamie hadn't spoken. "Something isn't healing. When I move the wrong way, it still feels like the very devil."

Silence greeted that statement. Andrew reached over and removed the glass that dangled precariously from Jamie's hand. The man was dead asleep.

Andrew sunk deeper into the soft leather and looked up at the beams of his ceiling. His study—he still thought of it as his father's study—provided his only sense of home. Books lined the walls. Bookshelves ran over doorjambs and around the diamond-paned casement window that opened over the lane below. Books filled small stands, ingeniously wheeled so they could be pulled up to the worktable or pushed back for space. He came here for healing and to pick up the strands of his disjointed life, but today contentment eluded him.

Jamie's talk of women and Richard Hayden raised unsettling memories. The confrontation at the bookseller's raised even more.

Images and voices swirled up from dark places where he locked them away—a broad flagstone terrace stretching out to a garden filled with the scent of lilacs and the deep darkness of a moonless night. For a moment he hovered there in the April night, a woman warm in his arms—Georgiana Hayden, young and shy, responsive beyond his boyish dreams.

Then there was Georgiana today. He rammed a fist down on the arm of the chair to stifle the memory. *What was the blasted woman doing in Groghan's bookstore?* Groghan catered to the Cambridge elite, the fusty crowd of male scholarship and ego. *What misbegotten quirk of fate sent her there the one time I decide to pick up my own orders?*

"Some'un sent a message." Harley's growl startled him, but he welcomed the distraction.

"Bring it then." He reached for the thick package of folded vellum sealed with the Hayden family crest. Painfully familiar handwriting covered it, and it smelled of lilacs. *Hell and damnation.* Andrew Mallet harbored many nightmares. The memory of sweetness and lilacs caused misery to well up in him as violently as other buried memories: a French prison cell or the noise and blood of Waterloo.

She had risen up today at Groghan's, filled with aristocratic outrage, and demanded service from a business that rarely saw a woman cross its threshold much less expect to order books. The sight pole-axed him. *Really, Georgiana, Greek?* Old Groghan about had apoplexy, and for a moment, Andrew thought he would refuse to hand over the books she requested. He took her coin, however.

When the woman turned and faced Andrew, his mind had fogged at the sight of her. In shock and unable to think, he pretended he didn't know her. *Damned fool! I ought to have guessed she wouldn't let it be.*

Jamie snored loudly, oblivious to what had been happening around him. Andrew let out a long breath and tore the message open.

. . .

Dear Mr. Mallet,

It has come to my attention that you suffered the loss of your father some time ago. I regret that I was unable to express proper sympathy at the appropriate time and wish to extend my condolences now.

Yours Sincerely,

Lady Georgiana Hayden

She chose to ignore his rudeness. Her perfectly proper and impeccably formal message sounded inoffensive, but he knew better. *She wants something. Blasted aristocrat. What the hell does she want?*

Using one hand to push himself up, he swayed a bit before he staggered toward the hearth. He held one corner of the vellum to the fire and let it burn in his hand. The final piece dropped into the fireplace at the last possible moment.

"Will there be a reply?" Harley's long-suffering voice exhibited neither respect nor fear of reprimand. Their long relationship made the first unnecessary and the second unlikely. "The man that brought it here is waiting."

"No reply."

Silence, apart from the low rumble of Jamie Heyworth's drunken slumber, lay thick in the room; firelight flickered in the hearth; shadows embraced the corners. Andrew felt Harley's eyes fixed on his back, but he stared, without wavering, into the fire. Neither man moved. Mallet looked back over his shoulder, annoyed.

"That will be all. If Lady Georgiana wishes a reply she will be disappointed."

He turned his damaged face back to the fire and studied the silent embers. He still heard no movement behind him.

"Harley, leave me. Now." With an exasperated sigh, Harley did what Andrew told him.

What is that blasted woman up to now?

Chapter Two

Maidens of the river, who always walk with rosy feet..."

Georgiana frowned, picked up her pen, and tried again.

"...river maidens who—who what?" *Andrew would know.*

"Walk? Tread? Amble about? Ramble?" None sounded right to her. "And did they always do it? Did they do it continually?"

Georgiana ran her thumb over the black stains on her index finger. She succeeded in removing the stain no better than she succeeded in translating the fragments of poetry by a woman named Moero. Whether they walked or tread was the least of Georgiana's problems anyway. She had precious little from this poet and no context to give it meaning.

Andrew would... She squashed the thought. *The toad didn't even acknowledge me at Groghan's. What was it that made me believe he could help?*

"Eunice, what do you think?"

"My lady?" Eunice Williams blinked up from her incessant stitching with the wide eyes of a frightened doe. She sat, as always, in the farthest corner of Georgiana's upstairs sitting room, as far from her mistress's writing desk as the dainty room allowed.

"Listen. 'Nymphs of Anigrus'—whatever or whoever that may be—'river maidens who tiptoe with rosy feet these, these...'depths, I think."

Eunice darted eyes left and right as if seeking a place to hide. "I...I...," she stammered.

"Come, come Eunice. I know it is crude, but does any of it make sense to you? Rosy feet? Pink feet? What do you think?"

"I'm sure I don't..."

Don't have any sense? No, Eunice, you don't. Andrew would know. He always understood. She could hear him say, "Close Lady Georgie. Accurate, but you might try..." He always had a suggestion. His schoolboy grin accompanied every word. Though two years her junior and only fifteen when he discovered her secret, he still beamed like a proud papa every time she solved a problem.

Georgiana allowed a deep sigh to escape her. Andrew had ignored her. First, he pretended he didn't know her and then he sent no reply to a perfectly proper and perfectly innocent message. *Had he changed so much? Drat the man. If he had replied I might have had an excuse to call on him.* She pushed him out of her head again.

"Perhaps...that is," Eunice stammered on. "Perhaps your little poem needs the attention of a scholar."

Georgiana glared and watched the color drain from Eunice's face. She knew that Eunice meant the attention of a man. Eunice ducked her head and applied herself to her endless needlework.

Georgiana tamped down her anger. Eunice might be little company and less help, but none of it was her fault. Custom drove Georgiana to accept their "companionship." Poor Eunice was forced into it by economic necessity.

"Eunice," Georgiana called, causing the woman to jump as if she feared a sudden attack. "Fetch Chambers and tea, the good China tea."

Eunice scurried away, relief on every line of her face.

Chambers, austere in butler's black, opened the door with a flourish fifteen minutes later. Eunice, who floated in behind the tea cart on a flutter of ruffles, asked in her reedy voice, "Shall I pour, my lady?"

"Yes, yes," Georgiana said with an impatient wave toward the tray. She glanced up to see the butler backing toward the door.

"Chambers!"

"My lady?" He stopped at the door and stared at the wall behind Georgiana's left shoulder.

"I wish to show you something. You had schooling, didn't you? You have some Greek?"

"Greek, my lady?" he said through tight lips. "Of very little use in my current position, I fear, but yes. I studied as a schoolboy."

Local vicar no doubt. Even a boy destined for service got that much—more than any girl, even a Duke's daughter, she thought bitterly.

"Very well," she said holding up a piece of parchment. "Take a look."

He hesitated, eyes fixed on the wall.

"Come, come, man. It won't bite."

Chambers took the paper between two fingers and held it as if it would indeed bite him.

"Well?"

"It appears to be a poem, my lady. By a person named Moh-rho."

"Moero. Correct."

"I'm not acquainted with that writer. We didn't, that is, I have not had the privilege."

"I'm not surprised. She isn't much read."

"She?" His face remained impassive, but distaste was palpable in his voice.

"She," repeated Georgiana. "Now look at the Greek and listen to this: "Nymphs of Anigrus, river maidens, who, who, always? Forever? Still? walk with, with rose colored feet on the deep, greet and hail and save Cleonymus who set these fair pictures—statues probably—to you, goddesses, beneath, beneath something, some sort of tree?"

Chambers stared at the paper still pinched between his fingers.

"Well?"

"What is it you wish, my lady?"

"Your opinion, man. Is it adequate? Nymphs are goddesses, are they not?" That much at least she knew; though, how they looked was beyond her. "Do they walk? Glide? Tread? That's more formal. What do you think?"

"If this is your translation, I'm sure it must be correct just as it is," the old man said through lips so tight she feared for his tongue. She ought to let him be.

"Do you care for it Chambers? In Greek or in English, either one?"

"Care for it, my lady? It is not my place." He raised his eyes from the poem only to look back at the wall, avoiding eye contact. "I have no opinion."

An unholy urge to goad him came and went. Infantile gestures never satisfied.

"Will that be all, my lady?" The voice betrayed no emotion.

Georgiana set down her quill. "You may go, Chambers."

She sank back in her seat and lifted her cooling tea. Her butler was a gray cipher of a man with no more interest in her poems than Eunice had.

There were twenty people on Georgiana's staff, and not one of them so much as looked her in the eye, much less engaged in conversation. To expect more was ludicrous. Differences of class aside, not one person had taken any interest in her study of Greek in the eleven long years since Andrew left.

Andrew cared, at least he did once. She squeezed her eyes shut. Andrew again. The man's horridly scarred face—and the untouched face of the long-gone schoolboy—haunted her, had done so since she saw him at Groghan's store. Thoughts of that face left her unable to get any work done.

She replaced her cup in its saucer with a slap. The clang of crockery made Eunice jump. Everything made Eunice jump.

"Stay put, Eunice. I'm just gathering my references."

Georgiana rose on a swish of silk skirts, tossed the cup and saucer onto the tray, and pulled Liddell's Lexicon and a handful of others off the shelf. She spread them on the desk and began to flip absently through them, checking various words. "Nymph" was clear and consistent. "Anigrus" didn't appear and was likely a proper noun in any case, but she wondered what or who it was. Any man with a half-decent education probably knew.

She resented her own ignorance. She didn't know how the nymphs moved. Walk was the simplest translation, she suspected, but she wanted to know how they walked, what sort of movement the poetess was trying to depict. Lack of knowledge frustrated her.

She picked up a shabby little book from the scattered pile and ran a finger over it affectionately. *Stewart's Advanced Greek for Young Scholars*, her oldest and dearest friend. She smiled at the odd conceit. Her oldest Greek reference perhaps, though she had few enough friends. She opened the cover. A neatly copied inscription covered the frontispiece.

To Lady Georgiana, with wishes for success.
Respectfully,
A. Mallet

She was seventeen when he found her lurking behind the palms in her father's conservatory, contending with an abbreviated passage from Plato. Andrew acted as though it was perfectly normal for a girl two years his senior to struggle alone over material he had mastered many years before. Fear of discovery and her mother's bile had made her very careful. Only Andrew knew, and he never revealed her secret to her parents. Two weeks after the encounter, an anonymous parcel arrived. It contained *Stewart's*.

Andrew didn't think like the others. She savored his suggestions. He helped her through Pindar. He helped her through Paul. He told her she did "amazing work." She refused to believe that life had changed him, no matter what passed between them in the end. A glimmer of hope sparked back to life in her. She rose abruptly.

"Call for the carriage, Eunice. We're going into Cambridge."

The placid face didn't alter. Eunice seemed quite used to her mistress's sudden odd starts. "Yes, my lady. Shall I bring a basket for goods? Are we going to the bookstore?"

"Yes, bring it, but we probably won't need it. Fetch my parasol. Once we get there, we're going for a walk."

Andrew Holden may not want to further our acquaintance, but he will. Oh yes, he most certainly will.

Chapter Three

"I don't care if it is the Duchess of Devonshire or Prinny's latest flirt. I said I am not in!" the voice roared. "And stop pushing that posset in my face. It doesn't help, and it tastes like hell."

Georgiana felt heat rise in her face. She sat ramrod straight. Her rigid shoulders didn't touch the back of the narrow wooden chair in Andrew Mallet's front parlor. Her mood, dark and growing blacker, contended with the sunny little room; its whitewashed walls hung with seascapes, its windows with blue chintz.

Her mother's voice echoed in her head, "Who would receive you, Georgiana, you great awkward oaf, you with your freakish starts?" She heard that voice often enough. Indeed, she heard it still whenever custom or her parents' dictates forced her to endure her mother's presence.

She heard the manservant—Harley, she remembered—muttering to himself while he descended the enclosed stairs. "I'm not your bloody go-between." It was obvious that she didn't need a go-between. She heard it all for herself.

Harley rounded the last step and looked her over with an impertinent glare. She thought she knew what he saw. At thirty-five, she was no longer young, and she believed she would never have been described as pretty. She hoped she at least projected dignity and culture. Her attempt to freeze him with a look failed. The man didn't freeze.

"I inquired like you said. He ain't in."

He knew her story about a walk along the River Cam and coming upon Little Saint Mary's Lane for the foolish tale that it was. He tried to warn her. "Mr. Mallet ain't in," he said, but she insisted he "inquire."

She lifted her chin another notch and rose from her seat in the single graceful movement her mother so ruthlessly taught her. "I regret that Mr. Mallet is not at home. I will take my leave."

An imperious gesture to Eunice produced a calling card. She extended her graceful, fawn-gloved fingers and offered it with the proper gesture. "In case he should wish to contact me," she said.

Harley stared at the card with a grimace of distaste, but he took it with two fingers and tossed it onto a silver tray with the rest of the mail and correspondence. She distinctly heard him mutter, "No chance o' that," under his breath.

She needed to escape before this fiasco spun further out of control. She reached the doorway at the foot of the narrow stairs when movement caught the corner of her eye. She looked up at a dark shadow, the shape of a strong and imposing body leaning heavily on the door frame. The shadow did not speak. She imagined his eyes, cold and distant.

She swallowed the urge to leave quickly and raised her voice, pitching it so that it could be heard upstairs while she looked directly at Harley. "You have my card, Mr. Harley. Should he wish to reach me, you know my direction."

Harley looked directly back. She watched the expression in the old rascal's deeply wrinkled face change. Where there had been impudence, she saw calculation—and something else. Georgiana's heart skipped a beat. The man's expression registered compassion.

"He ain't well." Harley turned his shoulder, lowered his voice, and leaned toward the open door so the sound wouldn't carry up the stairs. "Irascible he is when the pain is on him."

Her posture relaxed, and she darted another glance up the stairs. A question formed on the tip of her tongue, but she thought better of it. The door closed behind her. Just before it swung shut, she heard a gravelly old voice mumble, "Now what made you say that, you damned old fool?"

"It is getting worse not better." Lady Georgiana's voice faded away. Two days after her humiliation in Andrew Mallet's parlor, she endured a worse one.

Dr. Wetherby disregarded everything she said. The foppish physician sent down from London by the Duke and Duchess could never quite conceal his distaste, no matter how much her father paid him. She considered voicing her outrage, but that would require more energy than she possessed.

"My dear Lady Georgiana," Wetherby intoned, tenting his tiny fingers in front of his corpulent frame. "A delicate woman such as yourself must expect certain, um, complaints from time to time."

Georgiana narrowly avoided an unladylike snort at his description of her as "delicate." Whatever her weakness, no one but he would describe her as delicate. Her great height ensured that.

Wetherby continued without a break, absorbed in his own words. "When a lady hasn't been blessed with offspring, one's, that is to say, the womanly, ah, equipment, builds ill humors. If you would just let me bleed you again?"

She rolled her eyes in disgust. "I bleed almost to death as it is!"

"Yes, but in between, to prevent the buildup of—"

"In between?" Her weak voice made it less than a shout. "I bleed for a week, as though to death, and I'm exhausted for another. I have only two productive weeks before it starts again. Do be serious! You can't expect me to let you drain me in between."

"Perhaps, if I might suggest, your efforts to be 'productive' are at the root of the problem. Such labors draw off humors needed elsewhere. If you could but accept a woman's nature—"

"Out."

"I beg your pardon, my lady?"

"Out. We're finished. This is foolishness. It gives me no relief."

The man stiffened. "Are you dismissing me? You cannot. His Grace–"

"I know what my father ordered." She held up the crumpled piece of paper and waved it in his face. "I am aware that I am ordered to cooperate. I will not. You may be assured my intransigence won't be held against you. My father will assuredly pay you. You can continue to report my failings to my mother, but I wish to hear from you no more. Out."

He summoned his dignity, stalked to the door, and departed with a baleful glare for his patient.

Georgiana squeezed her eyes shut, husbanded her strength, and breathed in the sweet sound of silence. *Gone at last.*

She unfolded the crumpled paper in her hand and reread the message that the physician brought with him. It commanded her to cease burdening the estate with her health problems. *He sends no fatherly affection, I see.* She tossed the paper aside and picked up another.

Her mother's missive reeked with rose scent and depressed her even more.

GEORGIANA,

His Grace insists that you see Dr. Wetherby and orders you to cooperate with his recommendations. If you will not abandon your odd starts and fits on your own, do attempt to seek a cure for your ills. Marianna comes out this spring, and given your circumstances, it is better for you to remain in Cambridgeshire under his care. The family demands that you rest in seclusion in your little house and not parade yourself about in the region.

Wilhelmina Sudbury,

Your mother

GEORGIANA GRIMACED. The Duchess wrote "your mother" as though Georgiana might forget that fact. *Don't worry, Mother. I won't embarrass you or ruin your golden child's chances.*

Georgiana agreed with the Duchess on one thing: She preferred to stay in Cambridgeshire, far from interference and abuse. The house belonged to Georgiana, a divinely inspired gift from an eccentric great aunt, but she depended on her father's largesse for everything else from food to the salaries of her servants. Buried here, at least she could work. Work gave her life meaning; nothing else did.

A third letter lay unopened on the table. It arrived separately, just before Wetherby came smirking and preening to disturb her peace. She fingered the seal. Her brother Richard, the Marquess Glenaire in his own right, franked it himself. It wouldn't have been subject to parental scrutiny. She opened it carefully.

"My Dear Georgiana," it began. Once he might have written "Dearest Georgie." At thirty-three he became more like their father every time she heard from him. She frowned and read on. She hoped she'd at least find some affection here.

MY DEAR GEORGIANA,

I trust this missive finds you in enjoyment of good health. Our lady mother reports some concerns. Since she is vague and hushed, I am unclear as to the nature and extent of your complaints. I know Simon Wetherby by reputation, and so, I took the liberty of making some discreet inquiries. Should you find yourself in need of the most modern medical assistance, you might pursue one of the references you will find enclosed. Should you need funds for this endeavor, you need only ask me.

. . .

She glanced at the extra page. Two of the gentlemen were located in Edinburgh. The third lived and worked in Cambridge. He was both physician and surgeon. This was highly unusual. She didn't doubt that the names on the list constituted the very best. Perhaps her friend Mrs. Potter knew something about this physician-surgeon, Dr. Peabody. If he lived in Cambridge, Mrs. Potter would know of him. She picked up her brother's letter and continued:

As to your inquiries, I do remember Andrew Mallet, but I admit to some surprise that you would recall him. Mr. Mallet, I believe, is returned from several years' military service. His service left him considerably richer, and I don't believe he has the need to take up his father's profession or take on students. Though he hasn't ascended to the peerage, he could, I believe, conduct himself as a country gentleman should he choose. In regard to your description of the gentleman's physical state, I must say such observations are somewhat indelicate in a lady. Be that as it may, I believe, given his reputed performance at the late events at Waterloo and other circumstances, it is likely that the gentleman you describe is he. I am given to believe that he wishes no contact with former acquaintances, and you would be well advised against pursuing the connection.

Again, I send wishes for your health.

Your dutiful brother,

Richard, Marquess of Glenaire

What other circumstances, damn it? What left Andrew so scarred and dimmed the lights in his eyes? Richard knew more than he said. He always did. He certainly knew exactly where Andrew lived.

Andrew didn't need money, and he didn't need to seek employment as a tutor. Her initial plan to hire him now seemed unlikely to meet with success.

Georgiana didn't know any more now than she did when she wrote to her brother except that Richard wanted to warn her off. She would need to keep her actions out of Richard's notice in the future—if she could.

Chapter Four

Edwina Potter—the vicar's widow, grandmother of a University fellow, and Georgiana's one true friend in Cambridge—lived in a whitewashed home with a sturdy slate roof and deep blue shutters lying cheek by jowl with similar houses on Peas Hill. It shared a wall with its neighbor to the south. Window boxes sprouted with a glorious display of late summer flowers, and curtained windows welcomed visitors from all ranks and circumstances.

Georgiana approached Mrs. Potter's door slowly, impeded by a sharp wind. She pulled her pelisse around her, lowered her head, and held her bonnet firmly in place. Near her destination, two pairs of gentlemen's boots, festooned in the first stare of fashion, came to a halt at her feet. Two faces, one hard and cruel, the other slack-jawed and dandified, looked at her with derision. Both wore the robes of Cambridge students.

"I beg your pardon." She tried to pass.

"Well, you should beg our pardon." The hard-faced one said. Neither moved. "Cambridge streets aren't a place for a woman alone."

Insolent puppies! Georgiana regretted her decision to leave Eunice at home. She left her coach at the end of the street so she wouldn't inconvenience the residents or her coachman. He could maneuver down such a narrow lane only with great difficulty. She believed she could walk the four or five doors to Mrs. Potter's house with ease. She had been wrong.

"Move. Now! Out of my way!" She projected her best thundering aristocratic outrage. The bullies were immune to it.

The dandy looked amused. "Well, now, why should we give way to your lot? Perhaps you should make yourself more agreeable. Don't you think so, Murchison?" He looked to his companion for confirmation.

A cruel smile grew on the other's face. "A woman on our streets. Yes, she could be agreeable. Indeed, my friend Harrison, she could."

Neither gave way, and Georgiana knew better than to try to move past them in the confines of the narrow lane. She turned to call for her coachman, but a figure in black blocked her view. His cape billowed in the wind, and his scarred and battered face formed a mask of wrath.

"Andrew," she whispered. He looked past her.

"Let the lady pass." His voice fractured their smug smiles.

Harrison moved enough to permit her to pass. Georgiana heard Mrs. Potter's door open just feet from where she stood, but she stayed riveted to the spot, her eyes filled with Andrew Mallet.

She fled his house a week ago believing he was ill, yet here he stood like an avenging angel. *Should he be out like this?* His movements looked ungraceful and slow. *Is he well?*

The thunderous expression of her tormentor alarmed her.

"Do be careful, Mallet," Murchison growled. "The entire town knows that this one doesn't know her place. She approached Lawrence Watterson. 'For assistance in translation,' she said! She may be a duke's daughter, but she can't approach a University Fellow unpunished. Watterson dined out on that story for a month."

Harrison snickered. "Of course, gentlemen wouldn't want all women banned from the lanes of Cambridge."

"Gentlemen wouldn't accost a lady on a public street. You two are barely men." Fire burned deep in Andrew's black eyes.

A look of fear flashed across Murchison's face, quickly replaced by resentment and cunning.

"You wouldn't want your reputation tarnished by such a relationship, Mallet," he whined. "People respected your father. You wouldn't want to give them the wrong idea about the son. Not if you wish to be a part of things in Cambridge."

In one quick movement, Murchison found his arm bent behind his back. He yelped in pain when the silver-tipped walking stick pressed into the back of his skull.

"You will walk away now, and I will pretend I didn't hear your pathetic attempt at a threat. If you don't, I won't waste words with empty threats. My next assault will be swift and direct."

They were gone in an instant. Georgiana felt the very breath leave her body. She regretted rescue almost as much as she hated dependence, but she thought he was magnificent.

"It is young Mr. Mallet! Andrew! How delightful!" Mrs. Potter, blue eyes flashing beneath snowy white hair and elaborately beribboned lace cap, beamed at him. Her energy hid her years. Georgiana wasn't sure how much the old woman had witnessed. She expected Andrew to turn on his heels.

Instead, he smiled past her at Mrs. Potter. "Mrs. Potter? Can it be? You haven't changed in fifteen years." He relaxed against his staff.

Georgiana glanced from one to the other, filled with curiosity. She wondered how Mrs. Potter knew him, but then remembered that Andrew had spent his boyhood in this place.

"Scamp! I don't remember you being such a liar as a boy." The old woman's face glowed. "It is good to see you. You have been gone far too long."

Georgiana felt like an intruder who couldn't formulate a clear sentence. Good manners bade her keep quiet, but she longed to ask about his health. She ought to thank him for his help. She wanted to berate him for his previous behavior. Above all, she yearned for an opportunity to seek his help.

A withered hand touched her arm. "Lady Georgiana Hayden, let me make you known to Mr. Andrew Mallet. He is newly returned from the wars, our very own war hero!"

"Mr. Mallet. Good day to you. I owe you a debt of gratitude."

Georgiana wrapped both arms around her waist as if to protect herself and waited for the inevitable rebuff. None came. No welcome materialized in the deep black eyes either.

"The lady and I are acquainted," he said with a slight bow.

Andrew, Georgiana saw, addressed Mrs. Potter and avoided looking at her directly. She tried to step back, but Mrs. Potter's hand tightened like a clamp on her elbow, holding her in place. The old woman's small bones, short stature, and kindly manner concealed shrewd intelligence and steely determination.

"You oughtn't to spread nonsense about 'heroes,' you know. Each man does the duty presented to him," Andrew said.

"Rascal. I read the papers." The old woman spoke to Georgiana. "His father was so proud. At Waterloo—"

"Yes, well, many good men died." Shutters came down behind his black eyes; he closed the door firmly on the subject of war and his father. "Tell me, do you still make the best ginger cookies in Cambridge and knit the worst scarves?" Georgiana saw the corner of his mouth turn up in an echo of his once irresistible smile. That smile fascinated her, as did the thought of Andrew Mallet and ginger cookies.

"Please don't tell Lady Georgiana tales!" Mrs. Potter leaned closer to Georgiana and dropped her voice. "Once, just once, when his father told me he needed a warm scarf, I foolishly leapt into the breach, knit one, and sent it off to his school. It unraveled in a week." She turned to Andrew with a laugh. "You never let me forget it."

His laughter reverberated through Georgiana. She felt it echo against her chest and forgot again to breathe. Their banter made her feel like an outsider, in spite of the withered hand holding her firmly in place. When her heart drummed in her throat, she thought she knew how a frightened rabbit must feel. She didn't like it.

"I see there is no pretense of not knowing me this time," she blurted out, as much to stifle her own unease as to join the conversation. She felt her neck warm, but she held her chin high and squared her shoulders to fend off a blow.

Mrs. Potter beamed like a proud mother hen. Georgiana felt a push in her back. The old woman was urging her to continue.

"Lady Georgiana." Mallet sighed deeply. His voice dropped to a hoarse whisper. "No. No pretense. I apologize for my lack of proper manners at Groghan's and just now. I'm not quite myself. I didn't expect to see you." He looked at her as if he reached for something else he wished to say, but it eluded him. Instead, he nodded at Mrs. Potter. "Now, ladies, if you would please excuse me."

Georgiana put out a hand to stop him. Her heart still beat erratically. She feared his rejection, but she would not let him end the conversation. "If I might have a word?"

He stood, hat in hand, wishing to pass, but he waited for her to continue. His face remained blank. Mrs. Potter's smile gave her encouragement to go on.

"I have a business matter, actually, that I would like to discuss with you. Perhaps later, at your convenience. If you might call on me. At Helsington Cottage."

Georgiana knew she was babbling and resented him for causing it. She clamped her jaw shut and willed herself to wait for an answer.

"I am afraid that is impossible," he replied. "As you have unfortunately been told, I'm not well. I don't go out often. I wish—I need—to be left in peace. Good day."

"Good day," she whispered, watching him pass.

"Andrew!" He stopped at Mrs. Potter's call. "I can well understand the need for peace after so many years of war, but surely that doesn't include friends. My grandson, Geoffrey Dunning, for example?" Andrew nodded but looked puzzled about her meaning.

"Geoff dines with me on Sunday evenings. Would you join us Sunday next?"

For a moment Georgiana thought he would decline.

"I know I impose." Mrs. Potter's voice quivered with the weakness of age. "A lonely old woman craves good conversation and old friends, and I miss your father's company."

The old fraud! As if she couldn't have her pick of company in this town!

Andrew frowned. He fingered his staff and spoke with resignation. "If you wish, Mrs. Potter. Sunday next. Ma'am, Lady Georgiana. Good day." With a slight nod, his awkward gait took him away.

"Perfect." Edwina Potter's eyes twinkled with glee. No trace of age or quiver marred her voice now. "You will make up the numbers, of course. You can make your offer and bring him around. I have no doubt. Now, explain to me in detail just what it is you want from young Mr. Mallet."

The force of the old woman's support carried Georgiana with it. An ally gave her strength. War demanded allies, and Georgiana had no doubt this was war. Her hope that Andrew would willingly help her died the day she visited his house. If he refused to help her, she would coerce him. Warfare it would be.

Damn, damn, damn. The old woman neatly maneuvered him, and Georgiana threw the shreds of his peace into chaos.

Andrew looked back down the lane. Georgiana's ancient coachman had hopped forward right enough, but the old man was no help. *What maggot ate into her brain to stand there and confront those two dregs of Cambridge alone? She needs a keeper.*

He suspected Mrs. Potter, who looked not a day older than when he was a boy, knew he was on his way to a meeting with Geoff Dunning and perhaps even why. Georgiana must have her in thrall. He had no doubt which lady would make up the numbers at Mrs. Potter's little supper.

Visions of Georgiana followed him everywhere. The line of her neck bent under her bonnet and the curves of her attractive derriere caught his eye as soon as he turned the corner. Lust, always his first reaction to Georgiana, struck him with the force of a battering ram.

He had leered at her so intently that he didn't see her situation at first. When he realized that two of the University's more unsavory bastards were assaulting her, rage almost upended him. He'd acted without thinking. He decided she probably wasn't even grateful. She couldn't have known Murchison's awkward threat hit its mark, and it wasn't her business anyway.

Andrew needed work, not money: work to occupy his mind, work to keep the demons at bay, work to make his father proud. The need to make his father proud gnawed at him. It would require the kind of work Cambridge's scholars guarded possessively. Murchison's gossip could scuttle his plans.

Fellows like Dunning, those stalwart professors of the great University, lived in bachelor's quarters in keeping with medieval edicts that made celibacy a requirement of their position and made their society quick to cut and slow to accept outsiders. His father had carefully trod a narrow path, earning respect for his tutoring and translation but never penetrating the heights. He had chosen a wife and son over University, and the son had failed him.

Andrew scowled at the sudden memory of his father beaming at him over a successful translation of a particularly thorny passage from Plato. He'd given the old man little enough to be proud of despite Edwina Potter's sentimental twaddle. The old man valued learning, not battlefield heroics. Andrew owed him something better, something cleaner.

Murchison's threat sent a shudder through him. *Damn Georgiana Hayden! Is there no end to the trouble she will cause me?*

The bells of Great Saint Mary's rang the noon hour when Andrew ducked into the dim confines of Sam Dawe's coffeehouse. The old establishment, tucked away on Green Street, was a short walk from Trinity, but it made a long road for Andrew's halting gait. He regretted this outing.

Dawe's place filled rapidly. Andrew searched for a seat from which he could easily stretch out his legs without tripping the shop's patrons but found none. He hobbled to a seat by the door and leaned on an uneven table.

"Good day to you, Mallet. Good to see you out and about." Dunning, prompt and cheerful, took a seat. He always struck Andrew as a decent enough sort. His narrow ideas made him no different than most of the clerical citizens of this town of prigs and scholars. Kindness made him approachable. Andrew hoped their fathers' friendship and childhood connection would lead to work.

"Enjoyed our little dinner last month and your most excellent port. Good to sit in your father's study again. Reminded me of what an excellent raconteur Mr. Mallet was. He wouldn't want to see his son become a hermit."

Friendship with a veteran of Waterloo was a coup of sorts. It probably added some cachet to the acquaintance for Dunning. Andrew had to give him one thing: he never flinched from Andrew's pitifully lacerated face.

"I'm hardly a hermit," Andrew murmured. "We've dined together three or four times now."

Dunning gave him a wry face but said nothing.

"I saw your grandmother this morning," Andrew interjected to change the subject.

"Gran? Wherever did you—"

"In front of her house. She was leaving when I passed." Andrew hated the lie and his reluctance to describe his encounter with Lady Georgiana as soon as the words left his mouth.

Dunning didn't notice. Polite conversation flowed smoothly between them. Dunning inquired about his health; Mallet lied that he felt better. University gossip filled several minutes.

"Tell me, Dunning, are you acquainted with Lady Georgiana Hayden?" The abrupt change of subject startled Andrew's companion. *Stupid! I should be more subtle.*

"The Duke of Sudbury's daughter?" Dunning sounded cautious. "Why do you ask?"

"It came to my attention that she lives nearby. The family seat is in Sussex, isn't it?"

"Well, yes, of course. But you would know, wouldn't you, Mallet? Did your time in London, didn't you? You must have encountered them at some function or another. Sudbury's family lives in rarefied air. They aren't likely to frequent the haunts of Cambridge, I can tell you. Outside my scope, old boy."

"But the daughter?" Andrew pressed. He just couldn't drop the subject. He damned himself for a fool.

Dunning nodded. "She is reputed to live nearby. Helsington Cottage, out past Grantchester. Odd for a single woman to have her own establishment, particularly near the University."

"It isn't generally done," Andrew agreed. "One wouldn't expect Sudbury to allow it." That was the truth with no bark on it.

Dunning shrugged. "The house must be a family holding, of course. Gran would know. She knows everyone."

Andrew felt Dunning studying him and forced a blank expression onto his face.

"Perhaps the lady is an admirer of scholarship," Dunning said.

Perhaps? Unless she has changed greatly, scholarship is the air she breathes.

Andrew took a sip of scalding coffee and looked expectantly at Dunning.

"As to the lady's fancies, I can't say." Dunning went on, "I did hear a wild tale that she sought admission to the Wren Library, but didn't put much stock in it. The lady can't be that big a fool, no matter what—" Dunning colored slightly. Andrew waited for him to go on. "The thing is, Mallet, Lawrence Watterson spread a tale that she sought tutelage. He claimed she showed him some crudely translated poetry."

"Poetry?"

"Obscure minor works, unimportant. Watterson claimed the translation was accurate to a point but overly literal. What one might expect of the uneducated." Dunning shook his head and drank deep. "Don't like gossip myself, so I can't say in any detail. Distasteful, isn't it?" His keen eyes scanned Andrew's face.

Andrew shrugged indifferently. "It is hard to say what flights of fancy the very wealthy get up to."

Dunning waited a moment more, as if he debated whether to say something. The moment passed.

"Tell me, Geoff, how is your work on Horace coming?" Andrew distracted the gentleman easily and freed his mind to wonder. *Good God, Georgiana. What are you trying to do?*

Andrew listened to Horace just long enough to be sure the subject of their earlier conversation disappeared from Dunning's mind.

"Perhaps we can do this again, Geoff. Do you think Wallace Selby would join us?"

Dunning started as if remembering something. "Meant to tell you earlier." He reached into his jacket and removed a sheaf of papers. "Selby said he enjoyed our dinner. He was pleased to see your father's study, glad you're taking up his work, and all that. Sent a passage for you to look over. It's a bit by Proclus."

Andrew took the papers with a surge of pleasure. Selby's work on the Neoplatonist philosophers was causing a stir among Greek scholars. Andrew needed exactly this sort of contact. It would open doors.

"Excellent." He grinned at Dunning and opened the papers. "Excellent!" The fragment wasn't a major work, but Selby wouldn't entrust it to just anyone. Andrew relished the opportunity to prove his skill.

Dunning smiled. "Meant to tell you earlier. Got Distracted. Lunch again next week then?"

"That would be excellent, Geoff, but I will see you again Sunday, I believe."

"How so?"

"I am to dine with your grandmother."

Dunning grinned in wide amusement. "She attacks quickly!"

They shared a chuckle and left with an appearance of ease that lasted as far as Trinity Lane where they parted company. Andrew labored past the somber facade of Senate House, its Portland stone and classical lines gleaming white in the sun. The pain worsened. He grimaced; he would pay for this walk when he got home. He thought of Mrs. Potter's little supper. He would pay for that, too.

Chapter Five

"It isn't at all uncommon you know, and nothing to cause shame."

Georgiana sobbed quietly in Edwina Potter's tiny parlor. Her fears for her health were far from "nothing," but the sympathetic words warmed her as much as the fire and the excellent China tea. They beat down the flood gates behind which she hid her fears—fear of death, fear of life, fear of nothingness.

It took all her courage to describe her body's betrayal–the heavy bleeding and infernal weakness—to the older woman. Her failures as a woman shamed her; belief that her deepening weakness presaged her own death terrified her. Here in this parlor, for the first time, she felt less alone in her fear.

"How can it be common? Womankind would all die out."

"No one would live to my ancient age?" The old woman twinkled up at her and reached out to hold her hand.

"Yes, precisely. I won't live long. I know it! I don't shrink from it. I only want to finish my work." The words rang sour in her ears.

"Nonsense! You'll live long enough to finish your work and beyond. You are a vital young woman, with much to give."

Georgiana doubted that. "How can one get past it?"

"Some don't." The old woman shrunk a little under the weight of memory. "My own sister died when a bit older than you."

"There! You see?"

"But she also wore herself out with childbearing."

"Different then. I have no children and no hope of any." Her childlessness weighed on her, more so lately than ever before. After she died, she thought, there would be nothing unless she finished her work, and even then, who would care?

"Not so different. We all have our monthly trials, but some women, for whatever reason, bleed almost to death, children or no. Hannah did that even when she wasn't with child. Doctors in Yorkshire could do nothing."

"The old fool my father sent out from London wants to bleed me —again!"

"Any woman would see that for the stupidity it is."

"Mrs. Potter, do you know anything about a Dr. Peabody? He is a surgeon—and a physician, too, I believe—who has premises here in Cambridge."

"Edwin Peabody? Excellent man. He is the rarest of all beasts, a medical man who understands women's complaints. I planned to recommend him myself. How did you hear of him?"

"My brother recommended him. Richard's research is always thorough. The rest he recommended are all in Edinburgh of all places."

Mrs. Potter chuckled. "Indeed. I believe Edwin studied there. Has no truck with the philosophical approach. He tells me they take a more scientific way at the University there. Proud of it, and Cambridge be damned. I think you would like him."

Georgiana dried her face. "If you vouch for him, I will see him."

They sipped in companionable silence for some moments.

"Tell me about this grandson of yours, Mrs. Potter. How is his Greek?"

"I'm no one to judge, but adequate, I think. It isn't his specialty. That would be Latin. Horace. Not only that..." Mrs. Potter lowered her voice to a whisper. "He's a Fellow of the University—a celibate old bachelor. You did say the works are by women, didn't you?"

Mrs. Potter straightened awkwardly before going on. "Not the man you need. Banish the thought. Now, what shall we do about this little supper on Sunday?"

Andrew's progress along King's Parade slowed with every step. He stayed on the main roads; he avoided Peas Hill this time.

"Harley's right, damn his hide. Something isn't healing." He leaned on his silver-tipped walking stick, head into the wind.

The splendid medieval buildings of the colleges didn't interest him. His mind, to his own great consternation, was filled only with Lady Georgiana Hayden.

Andrew knew what lay behind her visit and the completely unnecessary sympathy note. Dunning's stories made it clear that she needed help with her work. She wanted to be rescued again.

"Damnable woman. Ever the wallflower and still not able to dance with the ones she chooses."

Heads turned at the low growl that came from his hunched frame. This time the suitors were the Fellows of Cambridge, and once again not one would have her. This time she would manage without his rescue. He had sacrificed his father's esteem to rescue her once before. He wouldn't do it again.

By the time he reached Trumpington Road and turned into his own lane, every step increased his agony. Nausea gnawed at him, and he clamped his teeth hard against the pain.

The wretched neighbors are about to be entertained by my undignified collapse, he thought. The mere idea propelled him forward with as much speed as he could muster.

His door stood ajar and saved Andrew the effort of knocking or wrenching it open. He pushed with his good shoulder and stumbled into the front hall. "Harley, blast you! Come here at once!"

Charles Harley stood a few feet beyond the door, taking a gentleman's hat. Two faces looked at him with alarm.

"Damnation," Andrew spat. "Jamie Heyworth. Richard sent a nursemaid again! I don't need any bloody Hayden interference, damn it anyway."

Jamie ignored the obvious lie. Andrew sank unceremoniously toward the floor and into Jamie's arms.

After two hours and much rough ministration at Harley's hands, Andrew felt no better. He glared at his very irritated friend.

"I'm not your bloody nursemaid," Jamie insisted. "Can't an old friend pop in without you acting like a bear with a thorn in its paw?"

Jamie, who picked Andrew up off the floor and helped Harley haul him up the stairs to his bed, was certainly not as gentle or patient as a nursemaid.

Sometime later, the vial of laudanum Jamie had generously offered lay splintered on the bedroom floor, its contents staining the offerer's waistcoat.

"Ruined my best waistcoat!" Jamie complained. "There's gratitude for you."

"A nursemaid would at least be nice to look at." Andrew managed a defiant growl.

Heyworth's face split with a cheeky grin. "Still the old Andrew inside, I see.

"Tell Richard he owes you a new suit. Something better than that one, I trust. And Jamie, go away."

"Not yet, old boy." Major Lord James Heyworth, late of His Majesty's First Dragoon Guards, remained unflappable. He effortlessly raised Andrew while Harley slid warm stones under his hip.

"Good gad, Andrew, you're as white as these sheets."

Andrew didn't answer.

"So, no to the laudanum?" Jamie asked.

Andrew replied with a very soft growl that Jamie ignored.

"Can't say your physician had aught else to offer. If you won't take it, no point in calling him next time. Richard is probably right. You need a surgeon, not a physician. Physics won't fix this."

A quiet mumble from the bed sounded like a strong wish regarding where the devil might put Richard Hayden.

Heyworth chuckled. "Wished him there many times myself, old

boy, but he's right this time. You are worse than three months ago, almost as bad as on the ship after Waterloo."

"Is that why Richard sent you?"

Heyworth hesitated but didn't deny it. They both knew he couldn't afford to turn down any little commission Glenaire might give him, even one involving an old friend, one he would have willingly done for free.

"He sent you to care for me on that bloody ship, didn't he?"

Jamie's temper rose. "I chose to do it, and you damn well know it. Richard didn't pay me to care for you, you blasted fool. I'd have done this, too, even if he hadn't asked. There's the name of a good surgeon in Harley's care and orders to see you use it."

"You don't order my household, and I'll thank you and Richard not to interfere with my servant. What else did our erstwhile friend send you to do? Come, come, Jamie. I can't talk much longer. I'm getting ready to faint."

Heyworth leaned forward, alarm on his expressive face, but the patient snarled at him. "Just finish it."

"How do—" Heyworth sighed. "Never mind. I gave up trying to follow your mind or Richard's years ago. It's trivial anyway. I am to ask you if you've seen his sister. Said to ask casually, blast him. Don't know why. Lady Georgie's too high in the instep for soldiers like us."

"He should choose his messengers more carefully. There's a reason you were never a diplomat or a spy."

"So, have you? Seen her, I mean."

"Tell Richard I have no idea what he's talking about. No. Tell him that Cambridge is none of his damn business."

Chapter Six

Damn Glenaire. Damn his devious eyes."

A great bear of a man paced and gesticulated his way across Georgiana's drawing room. She stood in the doorway for a full moment before he noticed and she came forward to accept his bow.

"Jamie, Major Heyworth! This is a surprise." The understatement she injected into her voice pleased her. Georgiana knew her brother well enough not to take offense when someone complained about his deviousness—even in colorful language—but wondered what one of his closest friends was doing there. She knew her brother wanted something. "What brings you to my little cottage?"

Jamie raked a hand through his scruffy hair and looked around the opulent drawing room as if to ask, "What cottage?"

"Call me Jamie, please, Lady Georgie," he said with a boyish grin. "We're old friends, aren't we?" He had sketched a bow haphazard enough to say, "We're among friends," but correct enough not to offend.

A smile, as warm and genuine as it was practiced, spread over his face and easily melted her reserve. This one would charm her senseless unless she kept her wits about her. If memory served, Jamie Heyworth lived on charm, but he had been a harmless young man for all that. Noticing that he had aged, she wondered if he had matured as well.

"Do sit down, Jamie," she said and tamped down a grin. She asked after his family and listened to vague replies until Eunice

Williams arrived with the tea cart and disappeared with her needlework into her chair in the far corner.

Etiquette neatly outlined behavior for an afternoon call. It gave Georgiana's brain room for more important matters, like asking why one of her brother's friends found it necessary to seek out a spinster he hadn't seen in several years.

"I am surprised you could be pried from London," she said innocently. "What brings you to Cambridgeshire?" She watched under lowered lashes for any sign of dissemblance.

"Business," he pronounced. "Business takes me to Newmarket. Stopped by to pay my respects on the way home."

"I hope your business won." She couldn't stop her smile.

He looked mournful. "Ran dead last."

Georgiana chuckled and earned an appreciative grin. "You always were a good 'un," he said with a smile that warmed her insides. "Never one to cut up at a fellow for his fun."

"Your way home took you nearby, and you decided to visit." It wasn't a question; it was a lure.

"Yes, that's it precisely." Jamie couldn't detect a trap when one opened in front of him. "Knew you'd welcome an old friend. Stands to reason." His face was a player's mask of innocence. He took a third cake.

"Please say you will stay for dinner. My household is small, but I pride myself that I have the best cook in Cambridgeshire." She didn't lie. Her French chef was her great affectation.

Jamie's eyes danced. "Oh, Lady Georgie, I don't doubt you set a fine table. These cakes tell a man that there are good eats to be had." He took another. "Good friends, good food, hospitality! Nothing better in this life," he sighed.

Perhaps promise of a good meal drew him here and nothing else. Perhaps pigs would fly by Michaelmas.

"How is my brother Richard?"

"Fine, that is—" He stopped, caught in his own words. Calculation worked in his face while he framed an answer. "Haven't seen 'im in some time of course. Business. In Newmarket." She had been right the first time. Richard sent him here.

"Don't you see Richard when you're in town?"

"Certainly, certainly. Best friend a man could want, the Marquess. Sets a fine table as well." The cheeky grin widened.

"A Hayden family weakness, I confess," she replied dryly. "When did you last dine with Richard?" She pressed her advantage.

"Goodness, Lady Georgie, I'm sure I can't recall. Weeks ago. It was a fine quail and an excellent fish course. Best thing was the pudding though. Always cakes and sweets with the Marquess."

He didn't recall when, but he could describe the meal. He was here at Richard's bidding; she was sure of that, but she needed information. It might take heavier weaponry to break down his defenses. Georgiana hoped to show off her cellar more than her chef. She carefully selected cognac for before dinner, two dinner wines, and a strong after-dinner port.

The first sortie was successful. He poured a second glass of the cognac before she filled her own glass with sherry.

"When did I see you last, Jamie? It was London, wasn't it?" She sipped slowly, determined to stay sharp. "You danced your way through the city and rushed back to your regiment in the Peninsula as I recall." *He drank his way, more like it.*

"Five years ago, that was. Did I see you then? Didn't have much to do with balls and things, that is—"

"Places ladies frequent? You were too busy with the, ah, pursuits of a gentleman about town, I think."

Jamie colored. Ladies weren't supposed to acknowledge gentlemen's pursuits, at least not the kind Jamie indulged in while on leave from his regiment.

Georgiana regretted making him uncomfortable. He was two years younger than Richard and Andrew. When they were boys, Georgiana felt protective of Richard's friends. Still, if she weakened now, she wouldn't be able to find out what her devious brother was up to. Jamie was no longer a boy; he was thirty-one.

She pressed on. "You had other friends to see I imagine, the inseparable four from Harrow—Richard, Jamie, Will Landrum, and Andrew." Her voice trailed off suggestively. "What did you call yourselves? The Cohort, wasn't it?"

Jamie grinned. "That was it. Andrew wanted 'The Phalanx of Thermopylae,' but Richard told him it was too damned obscure for the teachers to understand." He colored at his own language. "Sorry, Lady Georgie." He quickly went on.

"Andrew didn't come home from the Peninsula that year. Too busy. Will was there though. His father was ill. Went home and came back sorry. Knew he was going to have to sell out. Never saw him as drunk as he was when—"

"Will Landrum? Never say it." Georgiana's brows rose.

"Ok. I won't say it." Mischief in his face hinted at the old Jamie. "Not always a saint, our Will. Ask Glenaire."

"Tell me again, Jamie. How did you find my home?"

"Glenaire gave me your direction. Told him I'd pop round to visit." Jamie delivered lies and half-truths as well as any man, but this one made him squirm. Richard sent him.

Georgiana's gray-blue eyes crinkled at the corners. "He didn't mention it to my parents, I'll warrant. They think Helsington is locked up like a convent."

He flashed a relieved smile at her humor. "Goes to prove they don't know you. Never did."

She attempted to look reproachful, but her mouth quirked into a smile.

"It isn't at all the thing to say, Lady Georgie, but you look peaky. Are you well?" His statement took her off guard.

That's it then? He's inquiring after my health? Richard already knew about her health. She waved her hand in the air vaguely. "It is just an ill humor. I'm not as robust as I used to be." She sipped her sherry.

No more opportunities to probe arose over dinner, but she continued to tease his palate with first one wine and then another.

He took the bait willingly enough when she invited him to take port in her sitting room.

It took only one glass to give her the opening she needed.

"Your sitting room is full of paper, Lady Georgie. Not what a man expects in a lady's parlor. What is it for?"

"You are looking at my work."

"Work? I thought you ladies did embroidery or painted or some such things. Never say you write."

"Not write. Translate, or try to. The works I find are in ancient Greek."

"Translate? That's what Andr—another friend of mine wishes to do. Can't see it myself. Don't tell me a lady can translate also." Jamie's forehead wrinkled as though he tried to remember something. She hoped his brain, fogged with drink, refused to cooperate.

"I am afraid I lack your superior education, but I try," Georgiana said with a carefully controlled self-deprecating smile.

"If you think my education is superior, you must have been sadly neglected." He shook his head and held his glass for a refill.

"Actually, Jamie, I want to employ a tutor or an assistant. You did your time at Cambridge. Would you know anyone who might accept a woman for a student?" She didn't sound as neutral as she planned. She was sure her anxiety about the answer must have been obvious, even to Jamie.

"I am long and happily gone from this place, Lady Georgie, and wouldn't know. Not much of a scholar." Jamie looked like a man who realized he had backed into a trap. His voice suddenly sounded more sober than she thought possible. "Can't help you there," he said.

She forced a laugh. "What a joy you are, Jamie! Don't worry. I won't make you state the obvious. No Fellow would dare endanger his reputation on a female dilettante."

"Didn't mean an insult, Lady Georgie. No offense intended at all," he said, flustered.

"No offense taken." She sipped her port, encouraging him to drink more deeply before she pounced. "Jamie, Andrew Mallet excelled at Greek, didn't he?" She kept her tone casual, but it put Jamie on alert. She swore his ears twitched. "Have you seen him recently? Is he well?"

"Not, not recently...that is, no. If you're asking if he is a scholar" —Jamie swallowed convulsively— "he, well, of course, he was the best. He is long from his studies, though. He doesn't need to take up a profession."

He rattled on to cover the obvious lie. "Was wounded badly at Waterloo. Mad saber-waving charge. Took out four blasted frog cannoneers at their gun. Explosion, shrapnel hit, horse fell on him. Terrible thing. Shouldn't have been with the Dragoons."

Georgiana felt the blood drain from her face. She heard a muttered, "Damn," and Jamie took her glass from her trembling hand.

"More'n a lady wants to know. Sorry. Ugly thing, war." He drained his glass and poured another. "But, it happened months ago."

Jamie's tale stopped too soon and explained too little. She may not know weaponry, but she would bet her quarterly allowance that the line across Andrew's face didn't come from cannon shrapnel. She no longer cared for subtlety.

"You have seen him then?" She pleaded with her eyes.

Her good port must have breached his defenses. He sat back with a sigh, elbows on his knees. He held the wineglass loosely in both hands between them and hung his head. "Yes. I saw him yesterday. Getting good care. He'll be fine." His head snapped up as if at a sudden memory. "Doesn't need work though. Lives alone. Likes it that way." His face looked stern.

Georgiana, beyond caring, dropped pretense. "Why did Andrew Mallet join the army? Didn't his father intend him for teaching?" Jamie choked on his port.

"Don't know, Lady Georgie. Never asked." Jamie mopped drink from his shirtfront. "Joined quite suddenly. I had my orders with the First Dragoons to follow Wellesley in India. Strutted around in my regimentals bragging to them all. Next thing I knew Andrew bought colors in the Fighting Fifth, and we were both off to war. Dashed glad for the company at the time."

"You have no idea why?"

The baron's son shrugged and grinned. "Liked to pretend my sterling example won him." He lowered his glass and began to swirl the dregs in the bottom.

"Did it?"

He shook his head mournfully. "Andrew didn't follow. He led. Always assumed a woman caused it, though I never saw him chase one. Not even sure why he hung around London that last Season after University." His face pinched inward, as if the effort of thought pained him. The glass in his hand stilled. "The upper ten thousand wanted more than a schoolmaster's son for their daughters, though, and especially one more or less penniless."

"You think he joined the army to impress people?" she asked.

"Maybe, or at least so fathers thought he was up to snuff. It was the same for me. Thought the army would help. Maybe he thought the army would make his fortune. In his case it worked out." He ran his finger around the rim of the glass and stared at it with unfocused eyes.

"He didn't care about money," Georgiana said.

"No," Jamie agreed with reluctance. "I didn't expect him to choose the army. I figured him for a university fellow. He wasn't really the celibate type, though. Can't say why he bought colors."

"Where did Andrew get the funds to buy an officer's place? Isn't the Fifth a prestigious regiment? You said he was penniless."

"Don't know. Never thought of it before."

"His father perhaps?" The thought chafed her; it didn't fit what she remembered.

"Old Mr. Mallet couldn't find that kind of money, now that I think about it. Wouldn't have wanted to. Andrew must have found a sponsor." The glass stilled in his hands. "A wealthy one," he said. "Not a small expense, an officer's commission in the Fighting Fifth."

Georgiana remembered that Jamie's maternal grandfather bought his own commission. Richard once said it was the only thing the old man ever did for him and that Jamie had refused Richard's help. She looked up with pity and found Jamie examining her with calculation and a bit of devilment in his eyes.

"What is it?" she asked.

"The more I think about it the surer I am that a woman drove him into the army." He watched her closely. An unasked question hovered in the air between them.

"How can you know that? You said he never talked about it." Heat burned up her neck, but pride kept her from breaking eye contact.

"Broken heart would explain it." He cocked his head to one side, but he held her gaze.

"Perhaps he made a lucky escape from an unwanted entanglement." She looked away, dropping her eyes to her lap.

"Perhaps." He downed his wine, made a face, and went on. When she looked up she found him watching her speculatively. "And perhaps a proud papa wanted him well out of the way of temptation."

Hours after she saw Jamie on his drunken way, Georgiana's heart drummed in her throat, just like it had pounded while Andrew kissed a blazing trail down her neck eleven years before. She had always been certain that no one saw what passed between them in Pembrook's garden that year, but now she wondered. Her response to Andrew's kisses had been passionate and enthusiastic, and she had left Pembrook's certain that he felt the same way she did, certain he would call on her the next morning as he had promised. He did not.

She heard later—a full month later—that he left for India with his regiment. Her father would have acted if he had found out what had happened or if he had feared worse. Her father would buy what he wanted. It fit.

She wondered if Andrew might have accepted bribery, but that didn't fit. All these years she assumed he simply didn't care or that he fled an unpleasant and unwanted entanglement. The army wouldn't have been his choice, however. He wouldn't have enlisted on his own.

Suspicion, once admitted, grows quickly. Hunger to know the truth about that night and the day after took hold deep in her gut. The past stood in the way of Andrew's cooperation with her translations, and she wanted his help, wanted it badly. She needed him.

She stopped pacing and forced herself to be at ease. He would come to Mrs. Potter's on Sunday. Then she would see him.

Chapter Seven

"See, Geoff, one of our guests has arrived," Mrs. Potter chirped when Georgiana presented herself for dinner.

One? Georgiana raised an eyebrow in question. Mrs. Potter gave a slight shake of her head in answer. Andrew hadn't come.

"This is my grandson, Geoffrey Dunning," the old woman went on.

A large man, tall and broad shouldered, stood to greet Georgiana. He wore a modest gray suit, a simply knotted neck cloth, and a stern expression. Mrs. Potter's grandson looked very ill at ease, but he bowed over her hand. "Honored to make your acquaintance, my lady."

His formality felt oddly out of place in his grandmother's parlor. Any other time Georgiana might have sought to put him at ease, but preoccupation with Andrew absorbed her.

No one mentioned him. Georgiana looked around the tiny parlor as if by doing so she could conjure him up, flesh and blood, sipping sherry on Mrs. Potter's pink flowered settee, but he wasn't there.

"Shall we sit for a while?" Mrs. Potter said. "Geoff is a Fellow, you know." The forced sound of her cheer began to grate on Georgiana's nerves.

Georgiana's eyes strayed to the door. *It would be better,* she thought, *if he didn't come.* She forced a stiff smile and made a stiffer reply. "Have you been at the University long, Mr. Dunning?"

There would be no confrontation with Andrew tonight. Even if he came, she couldn't ask the man about something so personal in front of an audience.

Dunning's answer was monosyllabic. Georgiana wondered if he knew of her unfortunate encounter with Watterson and disapproved. Georgiana tried to dismiss the thought that Dunning might be as big a fool as Watterson because it seemed unworthy in her hostess's sitting room, especially since Dunning was Mrs. Potter's grandson. She tried frantically to find polite conversation.

Mrs. Potter leapt into the breach. "Geoff has lived in or near Cambridge his entire life. Do you remember, my dear, that my darling Henry was a canon at Great Saint Mary's?"

"Yes, yes, of course!" Georgiana grabbed on to the gambit. "What was it like, as a boy, in this wonderful town?"

The opening was broad enough. Dunning and his grandmother began to toss humorous anecdotes at one another while Georgiana stared into her teacup. Her thoughts strayed back to Andrew. Ideas planted by her visit with Jamie had fermented for three days. They created a heady brew of self-doubt and anger. She wanted nothing so much as to confront Andrew and demand the facts.

What could I say if Andrew did come? Pardon me, Mrs. Potter, while Mr. Mallet and I reminisce about an intimate moment?

Mrs. Potter asked Georgiana to pass her the decanter. Georgiana stretched her lips in an attempt at a smile and held it out to the old woman. Her eyes continued to move to the door, which remained firmly closed.

Georgiana envisioned Andrew in that door, black cape billowing and dark eyes. *Perhaps I would simply confront him with, "Tell, me, Andrew, did you care at all, or did lust and moonlight intoxicate you?"* That, she knew, wouldn't do at all.

Georgiana regretted coming. She knew she couldn't ask the question that preyed on her mind, not in company anyway. *Who sent you away Andrew? I demand to know.*

They passed an hour in awkward conversation, guided by the old woman, until Georgiana and Dunning found common ground in conversation about Socrates. Dunning, she suspected, hid surprise at her knowledge behind well-developed manners.

The knock came while they finished a final glass of sherry, one more than was customary. Mrs. Potter scurried to the door with speed and agility that belied her pose of frailty. Georgiana's pounding heart prevented her from rising. She forgot to breathe.

He had come.

"I beg your forgiveness, Mrs. P."

Andrew leaned against the doorway, smiling down at the old woman who greeted him. The tender affection for Mrs. Potter in his smile seeped like liquid fire into Georgiana; something deep in her heart melted. "I'm not moving very fast tonight," he said.

Blue shadows under his eyes accented the purple scar snaking across his ashen face and answered her questions about his health. He was still unwell. She thought perhaps he made the effort so that he wouldn't disappoint an old woman. She expected such courtesy of him, or at least she would have expected it once. A limp more pronounced than the one she saw the week before impeded his steps.

"I apologize for the delay," he whispered.

"It isn't a problem at all. Dinner is late. We were just sitting down, weren't we, my dear?" Mrs. Potter turned to Georgiana. A slight smile failed to mask her concern.

Andrew gripped his staff and shrugged off his coat. Georgiana hated the clumsiness. She fought an urge to push forward and help him, knowing he wouldn't welcome it.

Dunning helped him to a chair with great tact and as little ostentation as possible. Georgiana gained a measure of respect for Dunning because of it. "I, for one, am hungry," Dunning said with false joviality.

"It is good to have you back, my boy," Mrs. Potter said to Andrew.

"It is good to be in England, Mrs. Potter. I see I'm not the only guest." A look passed between Andrew and Dunning.

"The lady and I were discussing the classics." Dunning said gruffly as they all sat down.

Andrew accepted some soup. "This looks delightful. Thank you." He smiled at the cook who beamed at the approval.

He always graced her father's house with courtesy to the highborn and the low. She watched him stir the soup but noticed that he wasn't eating it.

"We were deep into Socrates before you arrived." Dunning motioned toward Georgiana with a smile that was rather like the approval the owner of a particularly talented spaniel might give his pet. "Did you know Lady Georgiana has actually read a little in Greek?"

Dunning's comment coaxed a smile from Andrew who looked at her, shrewd amusement lurking under hooded lids. "I heard something of the sort." His lips actually twitched. Georgiana covered her own amusement with a napkin.

Andrew himself had given her a copy of Plato's *Dialogues* and coached her through her struggles to read it. He aided and abetted her in her secret pleasure, hid it from her friends and family, and slipped her texts and textbooks during her first three Seasons. He treated it as a game—a defiant schoolboy game—his way of tweaking her father's nose.

"I think that you read the *Dialogues of Socrates* many years ago. Do I remember correctly, Lady Georgiana?" His eyes bored into her, amusement gone.

"It began then. I haven't changed." *Not as you have changed.* She held his gaze, watching the lines deep in the corners of his black eyes and the pain in their dark depths. She wondered now if she had ever understood him or his motivation.

He looked away first and pretended to eat his soup.

Opportunity to mention her work lay open before her, but she couldn't force the words out. She wished instead to ask, *Is that all you wanted to do—thwart my father?* She stared at the table, struck dumb, while the cook cleared away the soup course.

"Georgiana translates poetry, also, don't you, my dear." Georgiana blinked at the sudden return to reality. Mrs. Potter's puzzled expression urged her on.

"Yes, I—"

"Andrew translates also." Dunning interrupted suddenly, his voice tight. She couldn't tell if concern for Andrew caused it or discomfort with discussion of her work. "I brought him work from Wallace Selby the other day. Are you making a start at it, Mallet?"

"No energy for it, Dunning. Not yet." She could see that he played with his food. *Merciful heavens! His hands are shaking. Why on earth did he come if he is ill?*

Andrew looked up and caught her gaze. "What conclusions did you come to regarding Socrates?"

Socrates got them through the fish course, and *Emma*, the most recent work by the anonymous author of *Pride and Prejudice* got them through the cheese. Dunning's opinions regarding the lady author surprised Georgiana. He didn't dismiss her. He thought the bite of her satire quite sharp.

"I agree, Mr. Dunning, but the conclusions are a bit too tidy, don't you agree?" Georgiana found that the happy conclusions of each of the woman's books left her disappointed with her own fate. They depressed her.

"Lady Georgiana, never say you are unromantic!"

"One might wish for such a conclusion, Mr. Dunning, but in real life it is rarely so, don't you agree?" Her words were for Dunning, but her eyes were on Andrew.

He didn't look back. He responded directly to Dunning in his deep, rich voice. "Lady Georgiana is correct to a point, Geoff. One rarely gets what one wants in life. Duty, honor, responsibility to one's parents, one's station in life all stand in the way."

Georgiana wished he hadn't been so quick to agree.

"Quite the point of the lady's works, I think. Passion leads her lesser characters astray, but the admirable ones, motivated by logic and duty, win happiness in the end. It is often their reward. She is an admirable author," Dunning insisted.

"As I said, Mr. Dunning, life isn't that tidy."

"Utter poppycock!" Mrs. Potter drew all eyes with her vehement outburst. "I enjoyed fifty-six happy years with my Jonah in spite of family displeasure at the beginning. We found a way."

Andrew smiled, sad-eyed. "Life isn't always that simple."

"Who said my life was simple, young man?" The old woman waved a hand, and a light pudding appeared on the table.

"Georgiana, about your work—" the old woman began. Mrs. Potter's determination to recruit Andrew in Georgiana's service pushed ahead of Georgiana's own.

"What of it, Mrs. Potter?"

"Can you describe it for these gentlemen?"

Georgiana felt shy in Dunning's presence. She couldn't afford to let the opportunity pass, however. The work was what mattered.

"It is a work of translation." Dunning looked uncomfortable and distant; Andrew concentrated on his pudding. She wished he would eat it rather than stir it. He needed to eat. "I have collected fragments of poetry, written in Greek, from the classical era."

"Which poems, Lady Georgiana?" Dunning's well-mannered question was forced. Any polite interest would evaporate when dinner was done.

"Those by women."

"Really? There can't be very many." The idea genuinely stunned Dunning.

"You would be surprised, sir." Her words were for her hostess's grandson, but she continued to watch Andrew, who had given up pretense of eating. He held his hands flat on the table as if to still them.

"But where are they, I mean to say, how do you find and collect them?" Dunning's bafflement irritated her.

"They hide in plain sight. They can be found in anthologies. They are quoted in larger works by men. Most are fragmentary, but they are very much there. I believe their contemporaries, or more likely men who came after, didn't treat their work well."

A frown creased Dunning's forehead. "But they can't be of great importance if they haven't been studied."

"That is exactly why I wish to do so!" Georgiana's temper rose.

The sound of cutlery hitting the floor interrupted them. Andrew lurched forward and knocked his spoon and knife off the table.

Mrs. Potter leapt into action, cleared space, and located a coverlet to put over him. She brought water for him to drink and urged him to keep his head down until the weakness passed.

Andrew refused to allow them to call in a physician. Dunning, to his credit, summoned a chaise, assisted him into his coat, and insisted that he accompany Andrew home.

Georgiana did not help; she could think of none to offer that he would accept. A soft rustle alerted her that Mrs. Potter had come up behind her. The two women watched them leave.

"He will never help me, will he?"

"Oh, my dear, don't give up hope. He needs you as much as you need him. Our job is to make him understand that."

Georgiana turned a puzzled gaze on the old woman.

"The work," Mrs. Potter said. "He needs the work."

"Your grandson doesn't see the value. Andrew has Selby, and—"

Mrs. Potter waved the thought away. "Your unique talent is outside Geoff's experience. Given time, he would come to see the value. But it is young Mr. Mallet you need, not my crusty Latin-scholar grandson."

Georgiana nodded. She fervently hoped the old woman was right. She swallowed back tears and turned to hide them. She looked back in the direction of the chaise. It was gone.

"He will heal," said the voice behind her, gruff with age but underpinned with steel.

"Some things will." She choked. Grief for the young man who would never come back from war washed over her, and she began to shake uncontrollably.

~

"PLEASE, I am *Mister* Peabody. Leave "Doctor" to the University men."

Richard's Mr. Peabody claimed greater pride in his training as a surgeon than his status as a physician. Georgiana found that refreshing after the insufferable London physicians who fawned on her mother's patronage over the years, pushing powders and flattery down patients' throats. A few years younger than Georgiana and a foot shorter, Peabody managed to command respect through common sense and robust good humor.

He examined her person with rigorous thoroughness, more than she dreamed possible. He went about a process she expected to find mortifying with a complete lack of self-consciousness that somehow conveyed itself to her. She was at ease with his physical examination, but not with his probing questions. Questions about what he called her "history" didn't sit as well. She made jumbled replies.

Undeterred, Peabody began to tell stories about his practice. He stood with his back to her and kept up a stream of steady conversation while she righted her clothing. She knew he was deliberately trying to set her at ease. Buttoning her bodice, she realized it was working.

"You have a clinic for poor women?" she asked in astonishment. "Whatever brought you to that work? When I think of it, isn't your focus on women and their unique complaints unusual?" The failure of her body and the weakness that continually threatened to keep her from life devastated her. She knew that other women must feel the same. She had never met a man who understood.

"Sisters." He peeked around and smiled benignly. "Six of them, all older. I watched them grow up, marry, have babies. They always forgot about me when they talked. Female complaints were familiar to me before my teens."

"Is that why you became a physician?" Georgiana had never heard anything like it.

"Quite! Pleased my father to no end when I became a physician. I would probably still be dispensing physics in Bath to the rich old ladies as my father wished but for some chance events."

"Would that have been terrible?"

Peabody's cheerful countenance dimmed. "Perhaps not, but I came to see it wasn't enough. My oldest sister never recovered from the birth of her fifth child. She wasted away, but they went on having them."

Others waste away, she thought, *but at least Peabody's sisters had children to show for their womanhood.* Georgiana had only her work.

"She and the seventh died the same day," he continued sadly.

"How horrible!"

"Angered me, I can tell you that. Hated feeling helpless. Soon after, fortune led me to Mr. Forester and the work he does in Edinburgh."

Georgiana could respect a man possessed by his work; she knew that feeling well. Her work gave her the courage to come here.

Peabody knew his business. He interjected questions into his chatter, and she answered them.

"Are your courses regular?" he asked. "How much bleeding precisely? How long does it last?" She told him with little fuss.

"Have you ever born a child or had relations with a man?" Those questions silenced her. And yet there was no judgment in his voice, only concern.

A voice deep inside her wanted to wail, "No, and I never will!" She looked at him in distress and saw nothing but compassion. Humiliation passed.

"No." The whisper came from deep inside her. "No husband, no lover, no children." There never would be. Her failure was complete.

Peabody ignored the dejected droop of her shoulders. He outlined a course of treatment with brisk common sense and warm encouragement. She could improve. She certainly would. He insisted upon it. He buoyed Georgiana along on the waves of his certitude.

Morose thoughts walked with her down the ugly stone stairway, where the smells of dirt, damp, and camphor emanated from the walls. Her face burned hot at the memory of the things she told him, things she had told no one else. No one. Not even Andrew.

She knew it was ridiculous to think of him now. His earnest young face, the face that didn't come back from Waterloo, danced in her mind. She might have confided in that person, but she could never confide in the man he was now.

She stepped gracefully around one more landing and forgot to breathe. As if conjured by her thoughts, he stood silhouetted against the sunny entry arch, one foot poised indecisively on the bottom step, an ebony cape across his shoulders. Beneath disheveled hair, black as the clothes he wore, Mallet stared back through golden rims.

In the depths of her despair, his sudden appearance horrified her. She wailed inwardly. *Why does the blasted man have to plague me now?*

Four days of pain laid Andrew in his bed, unable to walk or even stand, after his foolish walk to Green Street and even more idiotic attempt to stand by his promise to Mrs. Potter. *Damn Georgiana Hayden anyway.*

The pain—and Harley's impudent badgering—finally forced him to surrender. He ruffled through the references that Glenaire sent to him via the ever-helpful Jamie Heyworth until he found the only one in Cambridge. Two days later he waited to be carried to an appointment with Edwin Peabody. He waited with little patience and less cheer.

"Where is the damn chair?" Andrew disliked the old fashioned display of a sedan chair, but that mode of conveyance damaged his pride less than being lifted into a carriage.

"The damn chair is waiting at the corner." Harley handed him his staff and hat. Four doors to the corner was agony enough. He faced the sedan with loathing.

"Mind the step," Harley warned.

"I see the bloody step. I don't need help."

Andrew pulled his hand free with a violent yank and half fell into the sedan. He swallowed pain-induced nausea, sank against the unyielding seat, and grimaced as the chair was lifted unevenly by its four corners. Travel proceeded slowly but smoothly enough; a carriage from the public livery would have been worse. After a half hour of teeth-gritting pain, the bearers lowered the chair to the ground with a bump.

"None of yer nonsense. Take my hand." Harley reached in and pulled him to his feet. He was too weak to object.

"Enough," he said, leaning on his staff. He closed his eyes and fought back dizziness for several long breaths.

Harley's hand darted out when he took one step forward, but Andrew shook it off. "Enough," he repeated.

He mustered his dignity and entered the building under his own steam, determined to walk in upright only to let loose a string of curses. Everywhere he looked there was a barrier, from the raised threshold to the uneven flagstone floor. He took two steps before letting loose another colorful string of curses at the realization that Mr. Peabody's premises were above stairs. He was faced with the choice between a painful climb and the humiliation of being carried.

Harley's obvious intention to carry him goaded him forward, and he lifted one foot to the step only to recoil before an even greater problem staring down at him from the landing and smelling of lilacs and honey.

"Damn it to hell." Georgiana's eyes burned so intensely he expected them to bore holes in his face. He squeezed his eyes to shut the pity he saw there. It was more than a man should have to bear.

The scent of lilac moved closer on the rustle of soft muslin and a deep, sensual voice said, "You may well wish me to perdition, sir, but surely our relationship hasn't come to such a pass that you condemn me to that place without some greeting."

He opened his eyes and blinked twice. Fate played foul jokes with his life and left him helpless.

"I see there is no pretense of not knowing me this time," she went on without waiting. "We have become dinner companions, if not yet friends." She held her mouth at a wry angle, her chin high. She expected a response. *God, but she is beautiful.* His body responded, whether he willed it or not.

Andrew dipped his head in the shadow of a bow. "Lady Georgiana, no." His voice dropped to a hoarse whisper, "No pretense at all." He spat the last four words in a staccato rhythm and watched her expression soften. She looked at him as if she cared. He hated that more than her pestering ways.

"As much as I might wish to tarry, I am afraid I have business to conduct just now." He gestured up the stairs with his eyes and cane.

"Ah, business." Sadness and amusement moved across her expressive face and fit comfortably together. "I won't keep you from it. However—" She paused and looked in his eyes, demanding his full attention. He had no choice but to give it. "Given your admitted lapse of manners in the past and the abrupt end to Mrs. Potter's dinner, I think perhaps you owe me some compensation."

He could think of no possible response to that.

"Dinner, Mr. Mallet. You appear to be out and about again. You will have dinner with me tomorrow night. The Rose Arbor at the foot of Regent Street isn't exactly up to the standards of London, but they serve a pleasant dinner. It sits near Parker's Piece. Shall we say six o'clock?" The imperious words came out in a rush.

A slight, but clearly visible, flush that rose from her neck to touch her cheeks belied her confidence. No lady ordered a gentleman to sup with her, not even a Hayden. When he hesitated, she snapped, "It is perfectly respectable, and I will be chaperoned. You needn't fear that you will be compromised for goodness sake!"

He shook his head to stop a laugh and nodded in surrender. He would dine with her—if he could. He knew that she would try to solicit his help over dinner. He would refuse, and that would be the end of it.

"I will dine with you, Lady Georgiana."

"Tomorrow night?"

If she believes that to be possible, I must have masked my condi-

tion better than I thought. "Certainly." He nodded. *Move on before I collapse, Georgiana. I will deal with you later.*

She smiled tightly. "Until then, Mr. Mallet."

Andrew labored up the first step while she passed. She looked for a moment as if she wanted to assist him, but he glared, without yielding, into her troubled blue eyes. He could see her accept just how unwelcome it would be and pull back.

A moment later she was gone, and his shoulders sagged. "Harley," he whispered.

"I know. I've got ye."

Chapter Eight

Once again he didn't come. Only a fool would have expected him to.

John, the footman, arrived with the news just as her maid, frustrated by her mistress's uncharacteristic indecision about what dress to wear for a simple dinner, dissolved into tears. Georgiana waved the maid away, snatched the note, and stalked about the small chamber in her dressing gown. This time he wouldn't come.

"He regrets? What does that mean? Who brought this? Does he wait for a reply?"

"His man, my lady. The man seemed somewhat anxious to return. I might catch him below stairs if—"

"Hurry! Stop him. I wish to speak with him. Go, man. Hurry!"

Georgiana tossed her dressing gown aside.

"Mary, dry your tears. It wasn't your fault." She grabbed the nearest dress as she spoke and pulled it over her head. "Do me up quickly. Truly, it wasn't your fault. There's a good girl."

Five minutes later she opened the door to the public salon and found Charles Harley, impatient to be gone.

"I understand that you need to return to your master, but I wish you to clarify."

"It ain't my place to clarify," the sullen little man snarled.

"What nonsense is this?" She waved the note in the air. "What does he mean by 'I regret that I am unable to keep our engagement'?"

Harley clamped his jaws shut.

"He prays his 'change of circumstances' doesn't cause me hardship. What circumstances? What is the nature of these circumstances, Mr.—Harley, is it?"

Harley's sullen face and his determined answer, "Not for me to say," revealed nothing.

Georgiana stood very still. The authority she mustered would have made her mother proud. "Of course not," Georgiana said, "and it is to your credit that you know it. I last saw Mr. Mallet on his way to a surgeon's premises. He is an old family friend about whom I am understandably concerned."

Stony silence.

"Come, come, man. Sooner told, sooner over. If you wish to get back to Mr. Mallet soon I suggest you answer my questions." She raised her Hayden shoulders and glared down her aristocratic nose.

He shook his head wryly. He was laughing. *Cheeky creature!*

"He isn't well. Told you before. Leg bothers him awful most of the time. That surgeon may do him good in time, but yesterday he just wore him out. Had to be carried back in the sedan chair, and he hates it."

The man looked her in the eyes while he spoke. *What kind of servant makes eye contact? Not a well-trained one.* Georgiana could see truth in Harley's eyes, though, and loyalty to Andrew. She could also see the moment he came to a decision.

"The surgeon thinks he can fix the problem somewhat. He may never walk without th' limp, but he can get some of the pressure off 'the nerves' as he calls it. There's still metal shot in the hip he says, and it has to come out. Won't be pretty, but if he can survive the surgery..."

He said those last words deliberately, eyes locked on hers. Georgiana paled but held her ground.

"If he survives, he'll be able to walk about without coming to grief every time. He's to stay off it until day after tomorrow."

"Mr. Peabody is the surgeon?"

Harley nodded.

That much relieved her. "He will do surgery in two days?"

Another nod.

Georgiana caught her lip between her teeth. Peabody's presence reassured her, but Harley's words didn't. *If he survives the surgery—*

"Won't take help," Harley broke in. "Likely to shy if you try it. Won't take help from his friends in London."

"No, I don't expect he would." She realized that Richard knew but chose not to tell her. Her thoughts raced.

"You may tell Mr. Mallet that I accept his gracious apology and will expect him to keep his word at a later date."

Harley took a half step. Her hand darted out to keep him from leaving. "He doesn't need to know he's being helped," she said. "You will tell me when he needs something—anything at all." Empresses gave orders with less command.

Harley's impudence didn't hide his shrewdness. He weighed her words. "Oh, yes, Milady, that I will." By the time he left, Lady Georgiana knew every detail of the proposed operation.

"You will most certainly keep me informed, Mr. Harley, whether you wish to or not," she said to the empty room. "We will make sure Mr. Mallet gets the best of care and then, Mr. Mallet, oh yes, then you and I will do business."

"CHEEKY BASTARD," Andrew grumbled under his breath. He glared at Harley.

He kept one servant and that one reluctantly. Andrew knew Harley to be strong, capable, and loyal, but the man didn't know his place. Harley did what he pleased. In the three weeks since the hellish procedure in Peabody's surgery, Harley became a miracle worker as well. "Cheeky bastard," Andrew repeated.

Peabody deemed Andrew's own house, with its bedroom above stairs, inadequate for recuperation, so Harley found rented space on the first level of a private home very close to Magdalene College and, more importantly, Peabody's premises.

Peabody ordered round-the-clock care for several days, so Harley found two excellent women and a kindly lad to help him.

Since boredom threatened to make Mallet unbearable, Harley brought reading matter but was unable to explain how he found books and journals so well suited to Mallet's interests.

When he was not eating well, improved food and tempting dishes appeared. When he wished for fruit, there were oranges in winter from someone's succession houses.

Andrew confronted him only once. "You can't expect me to believe that you've done all this yourself, and in our budget."

Harley did his best to look affronted.

"You were given explicit orders not to accept help from the Marquess of Glenaire."

Harley swore convincingly. "Never spoke to the Marquess. I know my orders."

Andrew could think of no other explanation. *Damn Richard for corrupting my servant.* Powerless in his weakness, he let it drop.

Andrew endured the regime for two weeks before he exploded during Mr. Peabody's daily visit. "You can't expect me to get better here. Let me at least take to my own bed."

It took another week and Andrew's promise to stay in bed to convince Mr. Peabody to move him.

"You don't need me every day. Healing nicely. Stay down until I tell you and you can go."

Harley arrived with a well-sprung carriage, its plush interior converted to an ingeniously constructed bed. Andrew sunk into the mattress without questioning the source of his miraculous conveyance.

He endured a blessedly brief, if not pain-free, journey home. The carriage bounced down the cobbles of Little Saint Mary's Lane and rattled to a welcome stop.

"You may tell Glenaire that we used his damned help well at least," Andrew spat at Harley when he yanked open the door.

"Told you, I never took help from the Marquess, just like you ordered." Harley spoke while he unbuckled the pallet, avoiding his master's eyes.

Questions that sprang to Andrew's lips died in discomfort and confusion when two young men reached in to lift his pallet out. They handed him down, turned, and carried him head first through the narrow door to his house.

A bustle of activity greeted him. Strange servants carried linen and porcelain jars up the stairs. Noises and the delicious smell of food baking emanated from his kitchen. "Harley, he growled, "Who —" A woman walked toward him from the kitchen.

"Bloody hell," he swore.

"Quite," the woman said. Lady Georgiana stared back at him, assessing his condition.

Her eyes slid over his face and down his chest. They rendered him incapable of breath or speech. He could only gape at her eyes, her stunning body, and the expression on her strong, intelligent face.

She leaned over to examine the dressings on his leg.

"Damn!" He pulled at the sheet and belatedly covered his lower body. He felt pale, weak, and disheveled with travel. He hated being seen like that.

Her eyes returned to his, but she didn't speak. He spared her the trouble. "Have you applied some new cosmetic to your nose, my lady? White powder covers it."

She put her hand to her face without breaking eye contact, puzzlement in her expressive eyes.

He began to laugh. "Now you've done it. Your cheeks are covered." She looked down at her hands and smiled.

"Flour. I didn't know flour was so difficult to manage."

"What is Lady Georgiana Hayden doing with flour in my kitchen?"

"Tarts. Raspberry. I couldn't risk losing the best French chef in Cambridgeshire by ordering him to your little kitchen. I came myself."

He could only laugh.

"Do you think I'm not capable?" She stretched her shoulders upward in outrage.

"Oh, I believe you're capable of a great many things." Pain returned and fogged his sight. He shut his eyes in resignation. "Now remove yourself and your little army from my house."

A sharp command sounded, and he felt himself lifted to the stairs. A voice at his side broke through his discomfort.

"Told you I weren't taking help from the Marquess."

Andrew never looked so vulnerable or so pale. He had never looked lovelier to her. When he laughed at her, the sound of it resonated inside her; the sensation created a flicker of warmth.

When he looked at her, she melted inside and the warmth began to spread throughout her body. His eyes said more than most men's words, at least they did to her. He was tired. He hated being carried. He didn't want to see her, and he particularly hated having her see him as an invalid.

Georgiana took a moment to realize their conversation exhausted the last of his energy. She vented her frustration with herself on the servants, barking orders to get Mr. Mallet above stairs to his rest.

Before she could move, his long-fingered hand gripped hers and brought her to a sudden, silent stop. She couldn't have spoken to save her life. His melodic baritone voice, whispered through cracked lips, broke into her hypnotic state. "Go home, Georgiana. Leave me."

Deflated, she stood back and watched her servants lift and carry him, grim-faced, step by step. Harley spoke to him, something impudent no doubt, but Andrew made no reply.

Chapter Nine

Mallet woke in the grip of erotic dreams. A lush, ripe body entwined with his. A sensual voice begged him not to stop while his own voice murmured over and over, "Mine! You are mine!" The woman smelled of raspberry and lilacs.

He wanted this dream lover. He wanted her honorably; he wanted her completely; he wanted her any way he could get her. He came fully awake with a jolt of shock. *Fool.* Georgiana had never been his by any means, and he knew she never would be.

He squeezed his eyes shut, but he didn't see the face of a pretty young woman. A more mature face, illuminated by intelligence and masterfully resolute, haunted his nights.

The same face haunted his days as well. *Lord, but she would make a good general.* He half expected to find her at his bedside.

"Vexatious woman would try to feed me broth and chaff my hands."

"You should be so blessed." Harley's voice, hoarse with sleep, responded. "Do y'need a bit of water? Perhaps some of the powders?"

"None of Peabody's powders. I haven't needed them in a week. Let me recover from the journey home. I'll take some water though."

"It don't matter to me none unless you plan to stay up and keep an honest man from his bed."

He took the water, watched Harley situate himself on a makeshift pallet near the fire in the outer room, and closed his own eyes. Sleep escaped him. Long after Harley, honest man or not, found his sleep, Mallet lay awake consumed by thoughts of raspberry tarts.

Fool. He wanted her still. *Fool.* The word echoed in his head deep into the night while he listened to his servant snore and the fire crackle.

~

Lady Georgiana called at noon the next day. She had Chef Henri's beef broth in her hands and tired, anxious lines around her eyes.

"Very good, Mr. Harley. Eunice Williams and I shall be but a moment in the kitchen."

"No need for that—" Harley began.

"Nonsense. Your time is needed above stairs. My cooking may not be up to London standards, but I warrant I can keep your master fed."

She swept into the kitchen, looked at the panic on her companion's face, and felt confidence drain from her as rapidly as water from a broken cup.

"Calm yourself, Eunice. I am merely taking stock." She set the crock of broth down on a plain but finely oiled table and tried to settle her racing thoughts.

The Duchess always insisted that the key to maintaining one's station lay in always looking like you knew what you were doing—underlings must never see hesitation. The Duchess, of course, viewed all of England, except perhaps the royal princes, as underlings to the Haydens. Her daughter may lack real competence below stairs, but she could make a good show of it.

"I will manage," she insisted. "You may take your needlework to the parlor."

With Eunice gone, panic returned. The cold reality was that she had no idea what to do. She really wanted to see Andrew and nothing else. Her attempt at baking the day before had resulted in misshapen, barely edible tarts and a disordered, flour-covered kitchen, the remnants of which were still visible.

Baking wouldn't work. Georgiana spent several previous days devouring what information she could find about convalescing patients. She looked in books and listened to wisdom from Mrs. Potter. She had concluded that a weak patient required broth. She herself sipped beef broth daily at Mr. Peabody's advice, and she was determined it would strengthen Andrew. She certainly felt stronger.

She examined the crock she had carried from Helsington warily. Henri made even beef broth sound like an engineering marvel, but now that it was here, it didn't look threatening. She believed even she could manage to transfer the broth from crock to kettle and heat it. When it began to bubble, she felt the thrill of triumph.

Just as quickly her spirits sank. She didn't know what to do next. She opened cupboards and crocks, bustled about, wrote notes on foolscap, and made a great show of business whenever Harley entered the kitchen, until she finally located a few slices of onion and some garlic from the larder. She added them to the broth, soon filling the house with savory smells. Henri would faint.

Georgiana could think of nothing else to do. She glanced up at the ceiling and wondered what new excuse she could find to stay in his house.

"Won't wake 'im up that way. Likely to sleep all day."

She jumped at Harley's voice and whirled around. He stood two feet behind her, in the doorway. "Good," she said inadequately. "Sleep heals."

"I'm an honest enough man to admit your cooking is better than mine. Are you going to make bread? Could use some warm bread." Harley stomped up the stairs—where she longed to be.

No need to be a fool. She sent Eunice Williams to the baker and added a short list for the green grocer as well. Mr. Mallet's cupboards were bare.

"Tell them to put it all on Mr. Mallet's account," she said. *One mustn't bruise pride more than we need to.* "Wait!" *On second thought, it might be useful to have him in my debt.* "Put them on my account."

In an hour Georgiana had run out of work and excuses to stay in Little Saint Mary's Lane. A sense of uselessness weighed her down. *Would I be of more use at Andrew's bedside?* She longed to find out, and her insides grew disturbingly warm at the thought. She knew she couldn't go there; she knew it wouldn't do.

Eunice would faint, she thought wryly. *Harley would—What would_Harley do? Come to think, what is he doing now, while his master sleeps and I commandeer his kitchen? The old fraud is hiding above stairs.*

She searched for a bell pull until the ludicrous picture of a Duchess signaling from the kitchen to one above stairs made her laugh out loud.

"John Footman, summon Mr. Harley. I have instructions for him."

John returned quickly, and alone. "Mr. Harley says he is," the boy hesitated, "too busy, my lady."

"Too busy?" *Ridiculous.* Good sense and a flash of insight lit the fuse of her temper. *Why didn't I see it before? Andrew is awake. Of course Harley is needed.* Color filled her cheeks.

She strode to the stairway and startled the footman who leapt out of her way. She reached the top of the stairs in moments. A closed door greeted and momentarily flustered her. *One doesn't enter a gentleman's bedchamber unannounced. How ludicrous! One doesn't enter a gentleman's bedchamber at all.*

She wondered how one did enter. No ladylike tap would work in this situation. *How do men bang upon doors which such an air of command?* She raised a graceful fist to try.

"Oh do come in." Andrew's irritable voice interrupted her. "We aren't likely to prevent you in any case."

The door gave way to her touch easily and opened into a room that wasn't, after all, a bed chamber. This small room, redolent with beeswax and lemon oil in testimony to loving care, guarded a treasury greater than any in her father's house.

Books lined every wall from floor to ceiling, end to end, over doorways, and around diamond-paned windows. Books overshadowed the sturdy wooden furniture and the thick Moorish carpet. Books lined both sides of a remarkable fireplace to her immediate right, dramatically carved with vines and honeybees in dark walnut.

Across from the fireplace another door stood open. She could see that it led to a small sleeping chamber. Andrew leaned on the doorjamb. His elbow caught the sleeve of his silk robe on the frame and pulled the fabric, royal blue and shimmering in the light from the fire, across his strong, disturbingly muscular chest. The fabric flowed in gentle folds until it hung unevenly at his knees. They were a soldier's legs, strong and beautifully formed. The vision stunned her. Years in the army transformed the gentle scholar. *How could a man who appeared fragile and walked haltingly stand on legs so well-muscled?* she wondered. Even the jagged scar that snaked from under the robe above the left knee and around the calf added to an impression of power.

"Well, my lady?" The deep, rich voice was amused. "Did you wish to speak to me or simply to ogle?"

Her eyes shot upward and were caught and held by a pair of mocking black eyes. The sound of her heart pounding in her chest almost deafened her. His ravaged face, strong and less pale beneath its scars, relieved her, but the deep lines around his eyes still worried her.

She snapped her jaw shut and lifted her chin into an aristocratic pose perfected over centuries of breeding. "You, sir, shouldn't be standing up."

"I quite agree. Harley and I were just working on that. Excuse us so we can get on with it," he said. "Unless, of course, you would like to assist me in using the chamber pot."

Blood drained from her face and then rushed back. She could feel her cheeks burn. *He lies. He is goading me to leave.*

He almost succeeded, but Georgiana wouldn't allow it. She called his bluff in a swish of skirts and presented her back to him.

"Don't let me keep you from your comfort, Mr. Mallet. I can wait, but I do need to talk with you."

"Oh give it up." She could hear his uneven steps moving toward the chair and the fire. *Chamber pot, indeed!*

A pink-cheeked, out-of-breath Eunice appeared at the door where Georgiana stood a moment before, her eyes fixed firmly down at her feet. John Footman knew his duty. He sent her companion to lend countenance as soon as she arrived back from the bakery.

Georgiana chanced a backward glance. Andrew sat in a high-backed chair while Harley tucked a coverlet around him and pulled the ends of his robe together under his chin. Mallet batted the man's hands away. She turned to face him.

"This isn't a good day to conduct business, my lady. I know Harley is grateful for your assistance, but I'm not in a position to reciprocate."

He gave her the perfect lever, the very tool she needed to compel cooperation with her work. She watched him shrewdly for a moment and savored the thought.

Questions about their past sprung to her lips, but she bit them back. *Not now,* she thought. That particular business would have to wait until they took time to get reacquainted.

The work mattered more.

"As a matter of fact, Mr. Mallet, there is a way you can help me. I have a proposition for you."

A "SIMPLE BUSINESS MATTER" she called it. Andrew thought the woman should be in the Exchequer if this "simple matter" demonstrated her negotiating skills.

"First of all, Mr. Mallet, you are aware that I have been able to provide you with some assistance. There were the premises near

Magdalene College, the nursing staff,"—he glared at Harley but didn't interrupt— "some other minor details that don't require enumeration, and, of course, the redesign of one of my better traveling carriages for your transportation."

Harley avoided his glare by making himself busy in the sleeping chamber. Eunice pretended to be deaf and dumb.

"Since you returned home, I have been able, as you yourself pointed out, to be of assistance to your staff."

My staff? Harley? he thought. *Doing it up a bit too fancy there.*

"You can't help but be aware that your diet has improved considerably due to my involvement." She went on without waiting for a reply. "I am prepared to ensure that you continue to enjoy the services of a decent cook and household help. Mr. Harley will, of course, see to your personal needs."

He could do all that for himself; he could certainly afford it. She failed to mention that, but since she well knew that he hadn't, in fact, actually done any of those things, he conceded the point.

"Do you wish payment, my lady?"

"I most certainly do not!"

He expected her indignation. He shouldn't goad her, but she looked magnificent when riled. He watched her pace his study and wring her hands as she often did when deep in thought or caught up in uncomfortable emotion. He wondered how she would feel if she became aware that he recognized such a revealing little trait.

"What I require in return, Mr. Mallet, is the assistance of a respected scholar."

"If I knew any, I would refer you. As it is, I don't."

"Don't be obtuse!" She resumed pacing and went on. "I have been engaged for some years, as you know, in a work of locating and translating works from the Greek that haven't been readily accessible in English."

"The works of women."

She looked at him without flinching in that frank and open manner of hers. If she waited for him to say more, in protest or derision, she wouldn't hear it. She resumed pacing. "The poets, as you pointed out, are all women. None has the respect and few have received the attention of scholars."

She meant to say that none have the respect of male academics. Watterson, for example. Or Dunning. Obviously there was another sort of scholar. He listened while she went on.

"I have made it my life's work to ensure that their voices are heard."

Life's work! How lucky she is to have one. He didn't try to interrupt her. On the contrary, the movements of her body while she described the breadth and scope of her project fascinated him. Her enthusiasm, as powerful as a force of nature, enraptured him. She gestured with graceful hands, and an inner glow transformed her animated face while she described research that was thorough and comprehensive, far beyond what he had guessed.

Distracted by the sway of her hips, Andrew caught few of the names she mentioned. He knew most of the ones he heard but not all of them. The number far exceeded his expectations. He could hear pride rise in her deep, throaty voice and became fascinated with the pulse that beat in the curve of her neck.

Passion for her work threatened to break out in an emotional outpouring; he watched her struggle to hold it in check. He felt as if she stripped herself naked before him, and his mind filled with images of other passions, other nakedness—Georgie there before his fire, her hair down on her shoulders, her skin warm and rosy, asking him for a very different sort of help. His body responded, and he allowed a moment of full rein to the fantasy of her naked before him.

"Andrew? Did you hear me? My translations!"

Abrupt descent to reality and the direction of his mind and body shamed him. She didn't notice the desire he thought must be obvious. *Look at me, Georgie. Take a good look,* he thought, but she went on without seeing him.

"The translations are serviceable. I know that my work is accurate and precise, but it is not..." Her even white teeth caught her lower lip. She sought the right word. "It isn't subtle or stylistically sophisticated enough to give the writers their due."

She looked at him finally. "What I need, Mr. Mallet, is a mentor or, barring that, a tutor. Your assistance would be of great value to me."

She held her breath. The same Georgie he found behind the palms in her father's orangery, who struggled alone through her brother's schoolboy Plato, stared out at him and defied him to criticize or laugh.

Humiliation made him mute. Caught up in her own objectives and how he might suit her purpose, she didn't see him. His feelings, his desires meant nothing. His instincts longed to refuse her, shut her out, and remove her from his house.

He opened his mouth to do so, but he watched her stand her ground while every nuance of her fear and uncertainty radiated from her posture and face. He could no more resist her courage now than he could when they were young. He drew a slow, deep breath.

"Let me recapitulate," he said. "You, for your part, are prepared to feed me, assist with the housekeeping, and relieve my man of his nursing duties—things which, you must be aware, I am perfectly capable of providing for myself. Is there anything else you can offer me?"

She looked dumbfounded. She opened her mouth as if to speak and shut it again.

"No?" He leaned back. "Then I, for my part, am to give you the benefit of my training, share the subtlety of my mind, and jeopardize my respect in the classics community of Cambridge, for your sake. Does that summarize your proposal?" *All benefit to you at great cost to me.*

He watched her chin rise in the characteristic Hayden gesture of superiority. In Georgiana the expression represented her armor, her shield against hurt. He had loved her for it. She didn't speak. Neither did she back down.

"Well, then, your proposal seems fair enough," he said with

obvious sarcasm. "I am afraid, however, that I'm not up to the labor today."

"Of course not, I—" Her words came in a rush but not fast enough.

"I shall have to sink deeper into your debt, my lady," he said with finality. "Shall we begin at the beginning of next week? Some rest and I believe I will be ready."

"As you wish, Mr. Mallet. Do we have a contract?" He could tell she didn't know whether to believe him. Hope lurked in her eyes.

"Yes, my lady, I believe we do."

"Shall I take my leave for today?"

"Please." No demurring. "I will come to you when I am able."

"No."

"I beg your pardon?"

"No. No, you will not come to Helsington. It will be a long time before you can come with some frequency, and make no doubt, Mr. Mallet, I will require your assistance with frequency. I'll arrange for my work to be transported here. Shall we say one week?"

The condition worried him, but he rapidly lost strength to protest. He would figure a way out when he recovered.

"Very well," he said. "One week. But there is one more thing."

He had her attention.

"Hire whomever you will, but under no circumstances do I wish to eat your cooking. It will increase my debt to you if you wouldn't force me to do so."

The raised chin appeared again. She was fierce, his Georgie.

"Very well, Mr. Mallet. Very well. I agree to your terms."

Chapter Ten

Every jolt of the carriage over Little Saint Mary's cobbles sent a spasm of anxiety through Georgiana. Transporting her life's work terrified her. *Why did I refuse Andrew's insistence that he come to Helsington?*

The carriage lurched to a stop and swayed for several moments under its burden. Georgiana leapt down, waved off her footman's helping hand, and ran to peer around the back. The precious cargo was in place. Relief flooded her. Her babies had arrived safely.

She turned to discover the avid faces of her servants studying her. With a snap to her skirts and tug to her sleeve, she summoned her dignity and said, "You may announce me to the household."

She caught sight of a woman peering through curtains across the street. Two more paused down the lane and openly stared at her. She wondered if they recognized her and saw that an unmarried lady visited the scholar's house.

She suspected the nosey neighbors puzzled over the mountain of boxes delivered with her and hoped that, at least, gave value to the commotion she caused. She remembered what Mrs. Potter had told her? "Give them something to chew on, Georgiana, and they'll ignore the rest."

"I see the contents of the great library at Alexandria have been located. And to think that for centuries we thought they were lost in the fire."

Georgiana spun on her heels. Andrew stood in his doorway.

Quick assessment showed excellent color, confident posture, and no sign of his staff. Relief trumped his irony. She followed him in.

"It is quite a lot," she admitted.

John Footman, she saw, had begun to neatly stack the first few boxes in Andrew's little sitting room just to the right of the front door.

"I suggest we place my boxes upstairs in your study," she said.

She suspected her boxes would fill the little sitting room on the ground floor, and she longed to work in his book-lined study. She gestured toward John Footman who hesitated in the doorway, another box in his hands, silently commanding him to go up the stairs.

Andrew blocked his way.

"I work upstairs," Andrew said with authority that brooked no contradiction.

"Yes. The work belongs in the study, and—"

"If I turn my study into a warehouse, I won't be able to work. If I am unable to work, I won't be able to provide you the tutoring you require. Your papers will be safe and dry in my sitting room, my lady, or I wouldn't have ordered it. You can trust me with them."

She hoped that her doubt was evident on her face. She bit her tongue and glared until she saw fires ignite in his eyes. "Very well." She squeezed her lips tightly and spat. "The boxes can be brought above stairs one at a time."

"Perhaps you could describe the general contents, and *I* will decide what to do."

Stubborn man. She forgot that about him. No one bullied Andrew Mallet. He knew his own mind and did as he chose. *Could anyone bully such a man into joining the army?* He had said, "I will call on you tomorrow," and he meant it. Then he disappeared from her life for eleven years. That wasn't like him. This vexatious stubbornness was.

Georgiana opened her mouth to ask him why he joined the army so abruptly all those years ago. She shut it again.

"Whatever you are going to say, don't. I know what I am doing.

Can we get on with the work?" He looked thoroughly annoyed. She found it oddly endearing. "The work, my lady?"

"The work, yes." She had won one battle. For now, it was enough.

ANDREW IMMEDIATELY REGRETTED DEMANDING an overview of her boxes, but he let her continue with the description. *How can a few fragmental poems take up so many boxes?*

"Let me begin with the individual boxes. There is one for each author. You will note that some boxes are fuller than others. Some have only a few scraps." She hefted one to show him how light it was. "Those are cases in which I have been unable to find much for the poet other than a name and a line or two."

Andrew noticed the carefully lettered name of a poet on each box. Only her organization kept his sensation of drowning at bay. *At least the fool woman injected some method into her madness.*

"Within each there are papers, folders, and parcels. On top of each is the original in Greek." She opened one to demonstrate. A neatly transcribed text on one sheet of paper rested on top of other sheets and scraps of notes.

"Under that is my current translation, such as it may be. On the bottom is my research—sometimes extensive, sometimes sparse—into the poet, what I know of the period, the location, and so on. That, by the way, is the hardest part, and I—"

"We will talk about the specific work later. What is your global view of this body of work?"

She blinked, visibly confused.

"What holds the individual works together? How do you envision the final product?"

"I, that is, I don't know. I think of each one as its own self."

"What is your vision for them?"

"I have none. They just need to be heard."

"Voices that need to be heard. Fair enough." He had no doubt whose voice needed to be heard.

Georgiana fussed about on one side of the worktable in his study, reviewing the contents of just one box; two others identified by their labels as related notes rested nearby. He kept the well-worn table between them and tried to concentrate on the work.

Georgiana reached for the papers he perused and smiled. "Korinna. She gives me great difficulties but also great rewards."

He deliberately set his face into its best schoolmaster mask.

"This body of work is much more extensive than I realized, my lady. I will require time to review the whole before I can begin to address your questions and the individual translations."

Her protests were loud and immediate. "I wish to begin work today."

"If you want my tutelage, you will permit me to become acquainted with the whole first."

"But you will need my explanation and—"

"I asked for your brief description of the treasures you've scattered over half of my sitting room so that I would know what is in each. Finish, please, and then I will need silence." He nearly growled that last.

"Mr. Mallet, I—"

"Lady Georgiana, which of us is the tutor? Do you want my help or not?" She agreed in the end to a week.

She described each box and its contents for another hour, giving him a clear commentary on the general state of each part of the work. She managed to communicate most of her questions at the same time.

He resorted to a firm hand on her elbow and steered her to the door.

"I do have a question, Lady Georgiana." Her eyes, instantly alert, met his. He hesitated. One question had plagued him since he encountered her leaving Mr. Peabody's premises, a personal question that he hesitated to ask.

"What is it?" she rasped.

"Your own health. I believe...that is, it seems as if there may be concerns. Forgive me if I intrude, but will your health interfere with this work?"

An alarming shade of red flooded up her neck and exploded onto her cheeks. He couldn't decide whether she felt anger, embarrassment, or both.

"I apologize," he murmured, "if I overstepped."

"My health, Mr. Mallet, isn't your concern except for this—I will finish this work!" She swallowed, shook off his hand, and steadied herself. "There may be times, periodically, you understand, when weakness prevents me from being as industrious as I wish, but those are becoming fewer. It won't be a problem."

She looked back at the boxes with a wistful expression, stricken like a mother who was leaving her only child.

"Georgiana, I will care for them as though they were my own. Your work is safe with me." Her given name came naturally to his lips. She didn't seem to notice. He longed to comfort her and take her in his arms, but he didn't.

Three weeks later Andrew watched Georgiana frown glumly at an open book and scribble notes in furious bursts of activity. She had visited him every day for two weeks, save Sunday.

He thought that he should interrupt and help her with the passage she was struggling with, but he couldn't bring himself to do it. For one thing, the sight of her at work in his study gave him more pleasure than he ought to allow, so much pleasure that he tried again today to insist that he should come to Helsington.

"Don't be absurd, Mr. Mallet," she had declared. "However much good Mr. Peabody has done you—and I beg to reserve judgment about that matter for some weeks longer—you aren't ready for a daily carriage ride."

"Daily is perhaps excessive, my lady."

"Daily, weekly, however long it takes. It won't do for you to travel to me. If your reputation cannot sustain visits from a lady and her companion, I can arrange to—"

"I shudder to think what you might arrange. I have no desire to go from pan to fire."

Andrew had given in, but concern for her reputation vexed him. He knew Mrs. Potter gleefully put it about that he had taken a student. She gave Georgiana the cover of her sterling reputation in Cambridge. He ought to be grateful, but he didn't like it. Still, he knew that whatever maggot Georgiana got into her brain next might be worse. Her obsession with the work outran her common sense.

The second reason he chose not to interrupt soon proved fruitful. His father taught him that a student learns best when he reaches conclusions on his own. The teacher merely provides the opportunity.

"This is no use." Georgiana tossed down her pen and glared at him. "How can it be translated any differently? The words mean what they mean. Too literal they may be, but they are what they are."

"Think for a moment Geo—uh, my lady. In English you might describe an incident thusly, 'the Countess, who wore white, overturned the cup and expressed herself in high-pitched tones.' It would be accurate, but not the entire truth."

"How so?"

"Compare that to 'The white clad countess shrieked when she spilled the wineglass.'"

"They are the same," she considered, "but the second one provides more of a picture."

"What else?"

"Emotion. The Countess is furious," she grinned, "and afraid she has ruined her court dress in front of the upper ten thousand."

"It doesn't say that," he pointed out.

"It does when you word it right."

"Exactly."

"But I know that because I know the Countess–or ladies very like her–and I know court dress and the world in which she moves. How can I possibly know those things for Korinna?" Georgiana wrinkled up her brow.

"You can't, at least not as precisely anyway. You can, however, read about her world, compare her words to the words of other authors, and make a shrewd guess at what nuance and emotion lay beneath the words. You are able to be shrewd, are you not?" The quirk to his crooked lips belied seriousness.

"Not today. I confess I am weary."

Her pallor worried him. He wanted to know how much of her desperation about her translations—and he saw the desperation daily—came from fear about her health. She wouldn't talk about it, and he wouldn't make the mistake of asking again.

Andrew leaned back, and they passed a long moment in comfortable silence, black eyes on blue, each one lost in thought. She reached up at last and brushed back the coarse black hair from the rim of his spectacles.

"Andrew, how did you get this terrible scar?" Her graceful fingers traced the puckered line across his face. An electric shock trailed behind her finger. He took her wrist firmly and replaced her hand gently on the table. "A French saber," he said without breaking eye contact.

Questions formed and reformed on her expressive face. "Waterloo? That is to say, I know there were other battles, but it is fully healed. Was it long ago?"

She would flay him alive yet. "Yes."

"Which?"

"Yes, long ago. No, not Waterloo." No amount of pushing would get her more. He wouldn't describe the horrors of a French prison to this lady, and by God, he didn't plan to relive it himself.

He rose and gestured toward the door. She held her seat, with avid interest on her face.

"Give it up, my lady." He emphasized those last two words. He fought to keep formality between them. "Some things are not fit for polite company."

He regretted that approach immediately when she pounced on his words. "Nonsense! I am no frail flower."

"That may be true, but my face isn't a topic for discussion."

Outrage exploded across her face. He suspected that she thought he accused her of attempting to criticize his looks. He let her believe it.

"I'm sorry, Mr. Mallet. It is of course your private business." She sputtered and began to pack her work slowly.

"The other scars—" she began, coloring deeply. He remembered her face when she saw him in his dressing gown, her eyes on the long red line that snaked up his leg and around his knee.

"—are none of your business, my lady, but yes, some are from Waterloo and some from the good Mr. Peabody's attentions." He took her firmly but gently by the elbow and guided her to the stairs.

"I think we can dispense with tomorrow. One day's rest will clear your mind." He put a finger to her mouth to silence her when she would have protested. "No," he whispered, fascinated by the sensual spot where his finger lingered. "Enough Georgiana."

He felt a slow smile curl under his finger when she heard the sound of her name.

"Very well, Andrew" she whispered back.

His boundaries had already slipped. He had agreed that she could come to him just for the pleasure of seeing her seated at his writing table, surrounded by his books, warmed by the sun through his diamond-paned windows. Now she called him Andrew. He would regret it. This road led to nothing but trouble.

Georgiana skipped lightly toward her waiting conveyance. Even Eunice, silent as always, couldn't lower her mood. Joy bubbled up. Not tomorrow, but soon they would talk about the past.

Abigail Clarke stepped from her door directly across from Andrew's and cast a shadow like a great black bird across Georgiana's path. Georgiana met her once or twice when Mrs. Potter or Molly

Harding had invited her to tea with Cambridge wives. She didn't care for her.

"Good day, Lady Georgiana. Visiting our Mr. Mallet, I see." The woman's eyes were avid but not kind. Unmarried women didn't visit men's homes. They both knew it, no matter how Mrs. Potter tried to wrap it up in fine linen.

"Certainly, Mrs. Clarke. We study together. He is one of the best tutors in Cambridge, aside from the Fellows themselves, of course."

"Study. Of course. I heard something of your interest in his scholarship." She dragged out the last word suggestively while she looked Eunice over as if to evaluate her worth as a chaperone. Poor Eunice shrunk even more.

Georgiana lost patience with her. She drew herself up, chin high, for a set down. *You don't question a Duke's daughter, Madame.* "Good day, Mrs. Clarke. I must be on my way." She left, but she would be back. The neighbors could make of it what they would.

Andrew's "one day's rest" turned to four, however, when Georgiana's own weakness overcame her on schedule. She sent a message round and told Andrew she would be delayed until Monday. To her delight, she felt much like her own self by Sunday. Mr. Peabody's regime of beef broth, large helpings of dark green vegetables, and water from a particular iron-rich spring ordered down from Yorkshire appeared to be working.

A missive delivered on Sunday afternoon crushed her buoyant mood.

Lady Georgiana,

I regret I will be unable to keep our appointment tomorrow or for some days to come. I am indisposed.

I understand we have an agreement and will keep the bargain when circumstances permit.

Yours respectfully,

A. Mallet

. . .

Shaky writing snaked across the paper in uneven lines. She reread them. The fear that he might relapse, which had lapped over her the entire previous week, struck her like a tidal wave. Immediate disappointment turned quickly to alarm.

She wrote two messages in rapid fire succession. The first, to Mr. Peabody, described his patient's failure to heal. It offered him three times his normal fee to attend Mr. Mallet at his own house as quickly as may be possible. She hesitated over the signature. Finally, she scribbled, "Lady Georgiana Hayden, Mr. Mallet's neighbor." Close enough.

The second message, to Harley, proved to be more difficult. She stopped mid-sentence, reread her words, and crumpled it. With the message to Mr. Peabody in her reticule, she called for her carriage and set out for Little Saint Mary's Lane.

Chapter Eleven

Harley preferred to carry out the wishes of his master, except of course when they were just plain wrong. Today the man was mad as a hatter.

He couldn't drag the man to Peabody if he wouldn't go. The lady could, but Mallet threatened to flay him alive if he so much as peeped to her. Harley knew that Mallet would never have done it. He also knew that his employer would drop of the fever unless someone did something.

The loud rap of the knocker below stairs saved Harley from coming to any conclusion. When no barrage of colorful cursing greeted the sound of the knocker on a Sabbath afternoon, Harley thought, "The man be ill all right."

Lady Georgiana didn't stop to sit or pause to greet him. Like a ship at full sail, she swept into the sitting room crowded with her boxes and bins and demanded, "Have you sent word to the surgeon?"

"Someone has to, but he won't let me," Harley answered.

Georgiana handed John Footman a sealed packet of vellum without responding. "This is to be given directly to Mr. Peabody himself, do you understand? Tonight. His premises are on the second floor of the same building we visited near Magdalene College. If you don't find him there, search. Take the carriage."

"But, my lady, if I take the carriage, how will you—"

"If you value your position, don't hesitate another moment." How she would travel back to Helsington, if she went back, was not his concern.

Harley watched John Footman leap to the carriage and licked his mouth in satisfaction. He did like the lady's way of getting done what needed doing.

"Now, show me upstairs."

"Gladly, my lady. Needs someone to take charge, he does."

"You won't take my leg." Andrew felt Georgiana grip his hand and hold it firmly. He wanted to bat it away, but he found himself holding on for dear life.

"The wound has festered." Peabody, to his credit, didn't try to coddle him. "We discussed the possibility. Another surgeon would take the leg. I'm surprised they didn't do it in Belgium." Andrew heard Harley, who fought the surgeons off when they tried, snort rudely.

Peabody attempted to cover concern with a jovial tone, and Harley fretted. Georgiana stood steadfast and earned Andrew's gratitude.

"You won't take my leg."

"No, I won't." The young surgeon paused and appeared to choose words carefully. "All I can do is drain the poison and cauterize it. The process may be even more painful than actually removing it, but it should do the trick." *If I survive the process*, Andrew thought.

Andrew held Georgiana's hand more tightly. She should leave. "Georgiana, you—"

"No. I will stay." There was steel in her voice.

Peabody protested. "My lady, I really must insist that you leave."

"Do you wish it?" Georgiana's eyes searched his.

No, I don't wish it. "You ought to go," he said aloud.

She shook her head.

"My lady, this is no place for a woman." Peabody's compassionate voice was firm.

"I will stay."

"Give it up, Peabody." Andrew clung to her hand. "No one moves Lady Georgiana Hayden when her mind is made up." That was his last coherent speech for several days.

~

"Georgiana?" Andrew heard his own voice as a distant and unfamiliar rasp, but he was sure of Georgiana.

"Andrew," she said on a breathy whisper, "all will be well." When she said it, he believed it. He wondered if even God could bring Himself to gainsay Lady Georgiana Hayden.

"Are you feverish? Has it returned?" She took his hand in one of hers, deftly checking for fever with the other. Relief registered on her face when there was none.

"No. No fever," she said. "It abated even more quickly than Mr. Peabody predicted. You are healing for good this time, I think."

She had overridden Peabody's protests and stayed with him through the procedure. While she allowed Harley and her footman to hold him down, she murmured reassuring nonsense in his ear and kept a firm grip on his hand until the surgeon finished the nasty business.

"What is it, Andrew? What do you need?" In the cool dark, her words were balm.

I need your touch, to hear your voice. The timbre of her voice soothed his soul, and the sweet scent of lilacs filled his senses. They had become the rhythm of his life. "I need some water." She had anticipated him. The cool drink was almost as welcome as her care.

"Hush now. Sleep." He did.

A week passed before Peabody decided Andrew needed to get out of bed for a short time every day. Andrew attempted a few tentative steps.

"The pain is lessening." That surprised him. The searing burn of the cauterization remained uncomfortable, and weakness threatened to overset him; but the deep pain that cut into his hip and back no longer cut through him.

"And not soon enough! You had more than your share," Georgiana said.

She watched his halting steps with fear-filled eyes. He hated the anxiety he saw in her expression. A primal need to protect her and to prove her wrong propelled him the final two steps. He sank into his deep wing-back chair. After a moment to rest his eyes, he gave her a reassuring look. Her relief made him proud.

He closed his eyes for a moment's rest and then drank in his study, letting his books soothe his soul. His eyes found something out of place. A pallet, coverlets neatly arranged on it, rested in the fireside corner.

"What is this?" Harley had never folded coverlets so neatly. Andrew realized that it wasn't Harley who had come to him in the night. He called himself every kind of fool. *She comes to me in the night, every night. Georgiana must be sleeping on the floor of my study!* It outraged his sensibility. He knew that he should send her away.

"Don't say it." She stood over him like a general.

He bit back a retort and mumbled, "It can't be comfortable."

"I am comfortable, and I am where I want to be. I am needed, and that, I tell you, is a novel feeling." She smoothed a blanket over him and reached up to bring him a warm cup of tea.

Well enough to realize what she had done and gentleman enough to know how great a scandal it created, he still felt too sick to care. *One more night. I will send her away tomorrow. For now, I will rest.*

"Georgiana?"

"What is it Andrew? Another nightmare?" Her hair stood in disarray; a dressing gown covered her nightclothes. He was too desperately ill all those previous nights to notice her nightclothes.

"Nightmares? I don't remember," he lied, hoping against hope that he hadn't called out in his sleep. It sickened him to think she might know the nature of those nightmares. "Did I speak?"

"Yes. No. Nothing I could understand. You seemed disturbed." Deep green velvet wrapped her from head to toe, but tantalizing snatches of white ruffle peeped out at her wrists and neck. "What do you need?"

Relief seeped into him. She hadn't heard his nightmares, but her nearness disordered his thoughts. "It is nothing. I just..." *You, Georgiana, I needed you.* "I awoke confused. I shouldn't have disturbed you." The white eyelet around her neck fascinated him. Honey gold hair lay next to it. He reached up and took a lock of hair to give it a gentle tug. "You shouldn't be here."

"I no longer care. I am where I am needed. It's too late to change, in any case." Her face looked less confident than her voice sounded.

"I'm grateful for it." To say anything else would be churlish. "I meant to ask yesterday, how did you get Peabody here so quickly that night?"

"Foolish question. Money and title, of course–and a well-sprung carriage. He came without complaining. After his error, I'd have brought another surgeon, if I knew of one."

Andrew smiled wanly. *Lioness!* "I think he's done it this time. He did know his work. He had an ugly wound, badly healed, to work with."

She looked doubtful. "He better be right. I need my tutor back."

"Ah. Your tutor." He felt her body lean over him where she sat on the side of his bed. Her thigh pressed against his uninjured hip. Her hand caressed his. Her breath, warm on his face, overwhelmed his will. His body responded to her nearness of its own volition, and he thought ruefully that his strength appeared to be returning more rapidly than he expected. He groped for words to send her away but could find none. He could only whisper her name.

"Georgie," he began uncertainly.

"Georgie." The sound of her old pet name in his deep voice caused heat to pool deep inside her. She cupped his cheek and rubbed a thumb across his lips to silence him.

"Hush. Go back to sleep. You need to rest. I want my tutor back." His face took on an odd look when she said "tutor." It seemed to her that he had forgotten the nature of their relationship. "While you've been ill I've been making free with your library. I read the entire list of works you suggested to understand the lives of women in ancient Greece. Shall I tell you what I found?"

His face looked pained, but he nodded. He didn't let go of her hand.

"Not much." She laughed. "I did learn a little." She began to talk about the lives of women then and now. The words meant nothing. She intended only to quiet and soothe him. He listened only briefly before his eyes drifted shut and she felt his grip on her hand loosen.

Drowsy and ill at ease, she rose, but the sound of his rhythmic breathing held her fast. It sounded endearingly different from the sound he made when feverish and ill. In the gloom she could make out the line of his arm, elbow bent so that his hand pillowed his head. She followed the line of it up to his strong shoulder and continued up his neck to the sight of black lashes against his cheek. Since his color had improved the now familiar scar looked less stark. Her eyes drifted down to watch the rise and fall of his chest. She could see the covers bunched down around his waist. His shirt opened at the neck.

Propriety demanded that she cover him, that she go, that she shouldn't even be there. Even Mrs. Potter fretted, and the normally impassive Eunice looked ready to faint when she arrived only to be sent home. The damage was done.

She told only a partial truth earlier when she insisted she wished to be in his house. The place she longed to be above all others was in his bed. She wanted to feel his warmth; she needed his closeness, if only for tonight. She couldn't bear to be alone. Need overwhelmed reason.

She removed her robe and slipped onto the narrow edge of the bed. She slid beneath the coverlet, taking care to stay well away from the sleeping man. He would sleep deeply now. She knew that from experience the past several nights. He was unlikely to be disturbed. She would slip away unnoticed before he woke.

Very little light penetrated Andrew Mallet's windowless sleeping chamber. The occupants of his narrow bed slept long past sunrise, late into the morning.

Georgiana opened one blue eye and then the other. The bed felt heavenly, more comfortable than the pallet. In fact, she felt warmer and more content than she had felt any morning of the past eleven years. She breathed deeply, stretched to greet the morning, and froze in panic. A man's strong arm surrounded her, and memory flooded back. Andrew had rolled onto his good side. The warmth she felt was his body, wrapped along her entire length. The realization rocked her to her core.

She blinked to clear her head. She couldn't remember what madness led her to crawl into his bed. Among the dozens of reasons it was wrong, the worst was that she invaded his bed without his permission. A sleeping man couldn't refuse her.

In the night she had assured herself that he was too sick to disturb. She believed she would be safe. She was certain that an aging spinster dressed in her old night rail and dressing gown, with her hair tumbled everywhere, would arouse no passion in a man, particularly one so recently ill.

In the cold light of morning, she suspected she had been wrong. The body curled around her own was fully male and fully aroused, though her inexperience made her less than certain. *Can they do that when they are sound asleep?* Apparently they could. Georgiana allowed herself a small smile. She had learned something very interesting already this morning.

She had planned to slip quietly out before he woke. She miscalculated about that also. When she attempted to gingerly remove his arm, she found it heavy with sleep. She raised the arm just enough to move her body forward. The second she escaped his protective embrace she fell with a thump onto the floor, and the bed shook forcefully.

For a fleeting moment, she anticipated scooting out the open door while he slept. His voice showed her how futile that was.

"Georgie? Georgie, what happened? I heard a sound." His voice, hoarse with sleep, repeated, "Georgie?"

She briefly considered crawling out the door, but she was too late. Black eyes looked down at her over the edge of the bed.

She rose up on one elbow with a sigh of resignation and pushed herself up until she rested her chin on the side of the bed. No words came to her.

Andrew propped himself on both his elbows. "What are you doing on my floor?" he asked reasonably.

Georgiana continued to stare at him, devouring the sight of sleep tousled hair, morning beard dark on his face, and his muscled chest crossed with now familiar scars visible through his gaping nightshirt. She couldn't help herself. His eyes, sleepy and unfocused without his spectacles, looked puzzled. He was adorable.

"What happened to your robe?"

She almost choked on her gasp, ducked below the bed, and groped about for the robe. She found it and stuffed one arm in a sleeve. She was convinced the morning couldn't get any worse.

"I see everyone is awake at last. Thought I heard a bump. Coffee is ready." She grasped the side of her robe to her chest and looked up, mortified, into the laughing eyes of Charles Harley. It just got worse.

Chapter Twelve

Why? You have to ask why?"

Andrew ran an agitated hand through his hair. The stubborn woman would be his demise. "Don't be absurd, Georgiana. You know as well as I do that this will not do."

He had blurted out a marriage proposal while he still lay on the bed, with Georgiana on his floor looking like a frightened rabbit and Harley laughing in the doorway. It had all the earmarks of pure farce. Her haughty refusal, however, struck him as having no humor whatsoever.

It took him two painful hours to dress respectably and all his control to ignore Harley's knowing looks while he did. The time allowed him to nurse his anger. *What possessed that woman to get into my bed? Has she no sense?*

Her refusal of his proposal made more sense. The woman wouldn't lower herself, even to avoid ruin. She had spouted some pompous nonsense about the honor he did her and the demands of her own honor that forced her to refuse. He may have imagined the bitter edge to her voice. She had run from the room before he could pursue it.

Now he stood with bare feet planted on his study floor, hands fisted behind his back, and temper precariously controlled.

Georgiana, primly dressed with a book in front of her, sat at his worktable. Her self-possession inflamed his already hot anger. *She may be made of ice, but I certainly am not.* The memory of her peeping over the edge of his bed in her ridiculously innocent night rail made him want to haul her back to bed right in front of Harley. *This has to stop.*

"If it is my thoughtless behavior in the night—"

"Thoughtless? Insane! Your presence here was improper when I was incapacitated—which I wish to make clear I no longer am—and it can't go on."

"Andrew, it is too late for those considerations. What difference will a few more days make?"

"Your assistance, *my lady,* was unsought and unneeded. It is certainly no longer required." His voice dripped acid as he emphasized her formal title.

Harley's impertinent amusement began to break into chuckles, exacerbating Andrew's determination. Black eyes met blue implacably. It took all his will power not to look away from the hurt in her eyes. Long moments passed before he spoke again. The catch in his throat when he did annoyed him.

"If you wish to resume our work, I will thank you to leave me to my peace for one week. Then, if you still want it, we can take it up again."

Another long moment passed.

"I'm not accustomed to being dismissed." Her voice had a wispy air as if it came from far away.

A raw sound burst from deep inside him. "You are not being dismissed! Who would dare dismiss the Lady Georgiana Hayden?"

"Who indeed? One person would, and I would like to know why."

Why again. Why what? She can't seriously believe this morning's actions were acceptable.

"That is my condition, Mr. Mallet. If you wish me to go, I will go. Before I leave, however, you must tell me why you left me. Don't pretend confusion. You know very well I mean before."

Before? His throat went dry. *She can't mean what happened years ago.* He could hardly cope with this morning.

"Spare us both any foolishness, Andrew. Why did you leave me after that night in the Pembrook's garden? You told me you would call on me the next day. You didn't. A month, a full month later Richard told me you had sailed to India to join Wellesley. Why, Andrew?"

He stood in mute dismay; silence, thick in the air, weighed down his heart and trapped the breath in his lungs. Her eyes drilled into him; he didn't speak.

"I thought—never mind what I thought. You said you would call, and you did not." She paused and waited for an answer. He couldn't give her one.

"Was I so repulsive that you had to bolt the country?" Her cry of the heart split the air.

He still couldn't answer. The vivid memory of her face–young, joyful, and eager in the dim light of the garden and of the warm spring air, scented with the lilacs, tore at his heart. The hurt in her face lacerated his soul. He swallowed painfully and directed his gaze downward.

Georgiana noticed Harley's presence too late in Andrew's opinion. "Mr. Harley, would you please remove my trunk? It is clear I will be leaving today." Harley looked like he wanted to refuse, but she stared him down. The man lifted the trunk, shaking his head the whole time, while they waited in silence. When he went through the door and down the stairs, she didn't follow.

"I will leave when you give me the respect of an honest answer. What happened that night? Was it my father? Spare me the tale of your longing for adventure and the sword, your great ambition for glory. I may have believed it then, but I don't believe it now. What happened?"

He wavered at last. "No." His eyes met hers. She looked infinitely sad, gripped by a deep and unfathomable grief. "The army wasn't my life's ambition." He didn't recognize the sound of his own voice, harsh and far away. He turned his head, unable to bear the sight of her sorrow.

"It wouldn't do," he began. "You must have realized that. A

schoolmaster's son. Four years your junior. In every way your inferior. No prospects. No funds. I planned to offer." He was pleading now, looking at her, willing her to understand. "I planned to abase myself before the great Duke of Sudbury."

She went still. He thought her heart stared out at him through those stormy blue eyes, but she didn't interrupt.

He swallowed the bitter taste of shame. "God forgive me, I even thought to take advantage of your misfortune. I was actually glad there were no other offers, happy for your great difficulties. God forgive me. No one in your own social class wanted you, and that made me glad. It tempted me to dream that perhaps my suit might be accepted. I sat for hours planning various approaches to convince him."

"What happened?" she asked in a choked whisper.

"Glenaire knew what had passed between us. I don't know how. His eyes missed little, even then. He came to my quarters deep into the night, certain he would find me awake. He was reasonable. He was sympathetic—as much sympathy as Richard is capable of—but he was implacable. It would not do."

He emphasized each of those last four words one by one but didn't stop. The words poured out of him now. He wanted her understanding, needed it desperately.

"We downed several bottles of brandy while I ran through every argument, and he, well, he answered every one with the same immoveable fact. His father would never permit it. He would hound us to the edge of the world. He would make your life hell. By the time the sun came up, I had agreed to accept Richard's help—long since repaid, I assure you—and obtain a commission. You know the rest."

"Richard? I had thought, that is, I assumed it had to be His Grace."

He could see into her soul; her brother's betrayal lay embedded there like a knife.

"Perhaps your brother did your father's bidding. Perhaps he acted alone." He took a firm grip on his own emotions and tried to ease hers. "I don't know. But I know he was right. Your father would have caused you great misery."

She looked rebellious but didn't speak.

"He was right, Georgiana. He wished to spare you further humiliation, and he was right. Don't blame him. I never have. Damn it, Georgiana, he was right!"

Georgiana's face twisted in anguish. He thought she might break, but she didn't. She squared her shoulders instead.

"Very well, Mr. Mallet. I asked for an honest answer and, at long last, I have one. Thank you for giving me that much respect." The air crackled with a slight, very electric pause before she continued. "He was wrong, though. The two of you very neatly decided my life for me that night, and you were wrong. You were both very, very wrong."

He had no answer to that. "Goodbye, Lady Georgiana."

"For now, Mr. Mallet." Her words were clipped. "We have a bargain to keep, and I expect you to fulfill your part of it. One week, sir. I will see you then."

He should have let her go at that. An old agony worked to the surface and forced its way out. Something ate at him, something he had to know.

"Georgiana?" he whispered.

She looked back at him, a pained furrow between her eyes.

"I thought they would have arranged a suitable marriage."

Her throat moved as if she tried to swallow rocks or combat tears.

"They did. They offered me to Viscount Pfeil."

"He was my grandfather's age!" It was a roar of rage. "Your father is a bigger fool than I thought."

"Pfeil had neither teeth nor manners. The Duchess deemed his title adequate." She met his eyes and bit out, "No one else cared to offer. I refused, as you can see. I discovered that I value my independence more than any dubious honor marriage or the machinations of men might confer."

~

Georgiana returned to the watchful eyes of her servants, the comforts of her well-run establishment, and the sterile silence of her life. No one questioned her absence. No one at Helsington Cottage ever contradicted her. No one ever shared her thoughts. No one spoke to her at all beyond "Yes, my lady," not even Eunice. The week became an eternity.

Her time came again and passed after four mildly uncomfortable days; her energy returned immediately. Mr. Peabody's regime continued to improve her condition, but to what purpose she couldn't say. Attempts to work were desultory; walks in the garden were frequent but inevitably brief.

On the fifth day, a missive arrived from Little Saint Mary's Lane. It relieved her fear that he would find an excuse to abandon their bargain. He would come.

Lady Georgiana,

As we agreed, I will take up our work in three days hence. I will call upon you at Helsington Cottage at one o'clock that day. I will bring the material of our current project. The rest of your materials will be returned to you as soon as may be possible.

Yours Respectfully,

A. Mallet.

She wasn't to be seen in town again. She doubted that a change in their work habits would quiet gossip. She didn't care; he might. She placed the missive on the mantel in her sitting room.

At least the work was to continue. The thought no longer filled her with contentment, and she couldn't say why. *Work, Georgiana. It is about the work.*

She called for Chambers, her capable butler, and gave him instructions to sort out space for their work in her home. Her dainty upstairs sitting room wouldn't do. They would find a place on the ground floor.

On the sixth day, an unexpected visitor broke the silence of Helsington Cottage. Jamie Heyworth might be shallow and drink too much, but his charm and thorough knowledge of everyone in the upper ten thousand never failed to amuse. Once she would have welcomed him gladly.

Now, however, she glowered at him over her tea and his sherry. He came as Richard's emissary. She couldn't forget that Jamie served as Richard's eyes and ears in Cambridgeshire.

The charming wastrel pretended not to notice her mood. He managed a smooth flow of conversation in spite of her monosyllabic answers. "On m'way to Newmarket," he said. "Hoping to make a few quid on a sweet goer I saw run in a challenge race a while ago. The race is in three days, so I thought I would pop in and see how you go on."

Georgiana's thoughts were as sour as the lemon with which she flavored her tea. She wouldn't have believed such a clunker even before Andrew's revelations about her brother. No man about town, least of all the utterly poverty stricken, Jamie Heyworth, Baron Ross, would admit he had nothing else to do but "pop in" on the spinster sister of a friend in her maiden household.

"I take it my brother is still too busy at Whitehall to come himself." Her sharp eyes dared him to contradict her.

Jamie colored but didn't deny it. "He worries about you, Lady Georgie, alone here. Says you never have visitors. I know Her Grace doesn't like to leave London, especially during the Season."

"And you know perfectly well she prefers her embarrassingly gauche and sharp-tongued elder daughter stay buried in Cambridgeshire. Let us spare ourselves some effort and take care of business. What exactly are you here to find out?"

He looked away first.

"Are you well, Lady Georgiana? He wishes to know if you are well, and I do too. The last time I came here and the last time

Glenaire visited himself, you were pale and ill. It worries him. It—it worried me too." His handsome countenance, no longer youthful and untouched, looked sincere enough. "You look better, I must say. Color in your cheeks, all that, but looks deceive."

"Not this time. Your observations are correct. I am somewhat better. You may thank my brother for his kind referral. His Mr. Peabody treated me every bit as well as Richard expected him to. I told him that myself when I wrote." She paused and sipped her tea. "What else, Jamie?"

"I beg your pardon, my lady?"

"What else does Richard want to know, Jamie? Come, come, let us come to the end of this farce."

"He asked after your work. Have you been able to find assistance?" Heyworth schooled his features in a look of innocence.

"Richard never asks about my work and has no interest in what sort of help I might need. What did he tell you to find out, Jamie?" She stared him down again, but this time he didn't speak. "It isn't your fault, you know. I am aware you have to do his bidding." She went on relentlessly, no longer attempting to spare his feelings. "Obviously the Hayden family honor holds his great interest. What is it you are required to find out? I would much prefer that you do not question my servants."

He couldn't stand against the force of her determined assault. "Andrew," he said at last. "Have you seen him?"

"Yes."

He waited for more. She allowed the silence to stretch.

"I'll thank you to leave now," she said as she rang for the footman. She turned. "Jamie, there is one more thing."

"For you, Lady Georgie, anything." His practiced smile melted away under the determined glare of her direct gaze.

"Andrew's face. What happened to it?"

All pretenses fled. His eyes flew open. "He prefers not to talk about it."

"I know that. And now I know that you know the answer. What happened?"

Heyworth colored. "I may dance to the Hayden family tune, but this time you have to ask the man himself if you want an answer." He blustered, but she didn't back away. "I will tell you this much. The French held Andrew prisoner for months after Salamanca. Richard got him out on a sliver of luck. He never talks about it to any of us, at least not when he's awake."

I have nightmares? Did I speak? She remembered the fear in his voice when he said it.

Jamie shook his head when she continued to watch him, and her mind raced to form questions. "No, you don't. No more questions. Isn't mine to tell."

"Just one. When the French captured him, was he doing Richard's bidding?" Her brother's work at Whitehall had tentacles even then.

"Not mine to tell." He repeated, determined not to speak this time. She couldn't tell if he shook his head in denial or disgust.

She remained seated when he left the room.

"Damn you, Richard!"

Chapter Thirteen

Andrew Mallet, man of his word, appeared at exactly one o'clock at the formal entrance to Helsington Cottage in spite of his conviction that he would soon regret doing so.

Chambers took his hat and showed him into the sunny breakfast parlor at the back of the first floor with a minimum of respect and no comment. Furniture had been removed and extra tables and bookshelves brought in. From the looks of them, they were from the Helsington attics.

Andrew had eyes only for Georgiana. She sat at a worktable next to wide windows overlooking a garden and lawn that rolled downward toward the River Cam. The light, perfect for an afternoon's work, glowed around her like a halo. She took his breath away. All thoughts of work fled. He could cross the room in two steps and have her in his arms. He could kiss her senseless. He did neither.

"Good day to you, Mr. Mallet." She tilted her head and looked past him. "I see my material has returned with you."

Harley, his habitually inappropriate expression distorted in irritation, brought boxes into the workroom assisted by two of Helsington's sturdier footmen.

"I reviewed our progress to date with Korinna," she said, ignoring the bustle. "I attempted, as you encouraged, a less formal translation of the Asopos fragment. I should like your judgment of it." She waited, chin high, all business.

Her armor was on. *Good, Georgiana. Keep it there. You need it. I need it.* He reached for the book containing the Korinna original and for her translation and began to review them without speaking.

Many of the poem's images had multiple meanings, and many of those meanings were subtly erotic or, at the very least, improper. He wondered if she had known that. Andrew groaned inwardly. There were others in her collection likely to prove worse. *Dangerous works indeed. How did I let myself get drawn into this? I am mad to continue.*

He extended his hand with a sigh of resignation. "Do you have your first version at hand?" She rose and went to a box labeled with the poet's name. "Your first version was correct to a great extent. I want to compare your choice of words in that one with this one."

The teacher read, compared, and reviewed in silence. The student sat in stiff attention. She wouldn't be amused if she knew how obvious the high cost of her restraint was to him. Awareness of every fleeting expression, every breath she took, made reading difficult. He read the pieces over and over, as slowly as he could, put the paper down even more slowly, removed his spectacles, and rubbed the space between his eyes.

When he looked up, he saw trepidation in her transparent eyes and color rising up her neck. The fragment she had translated described the fruitful results of the nine daughters of Asopos who had been carried off and "taken" by various gods and heroes, often two or three to a hero. The better she understood the implications, the less confident he expected her to be about the English translation. He found it easier to obfuscate, glossing over the action in the poem, rather than to find words to describe what Georgiana may not be able to imagine.

"Better," he said at last.

"Better. Is that all?" She was outraged.

"Better. 'Better' indicates progress since last we met. Isn't progress the nature of education? Lay this aside for a day and move on to the second fragment, the mountain lyric. Have you reviewed your earlier work?"

"Must we?"

"We must." He needed time to give his peace of mind an opportunity to reassert itself.

Georgiana continued long after he left, until a light scratch at the door interrupted her.

"Come in, come in. Stop that infernal scratching."

Chambers gestured two footmen into the room. They lit candles rapidly and silently. Georgiana paid them no attention.

"Will my lady wish for dinner?"

"No, I—" she began. Several hours had passed since Andrew left. She realized it had gotten dark when she saw the footmen waiting for her nod before closing the window covers. "Yes, Chambers, I think I will have dinner. Apologize to Henri for the delay." *It is the people above stairs who are at the mercy of the staff, not the other way around. Chambers expects dinner to be on time, and so it is.*

"Very good, my lady. At half past the hour then."

Her work had already claimed her attention. The page baffled her. Her meager knowledge of mythology enabled her to recognize the story of Kronos's attempts to kill the infant Zeus, which seemed to be the gist of the story, but the rest of the poem confused her. It talked about "Cithaeron" and "Helicon."

The names weren't familiar to her in the slightest, nor were they included in any of her books of mythology. Georgiana had no idea where to find the information. She wondered whether her brother or any man with a decent education would know. She couldn't translate the fragment if she didn't identify Cithaeron and Helicon. Frustration boiled up inside her.

"What are you saying to me?" Korinna, dead these thousands of years, didn't answer. No one did. She suspected Andrew didn't recognize the names either. He left her to struggle in silence most of the afternoon.

Drat the man, he acts like a teacher. Andrew had shed the forced intimacy of his illness and put on a manner even more formal than before. He refused further discussion about their past. Their confrontation over it had, at least, overshadowed his pitiable proposal. He made no attempt to repeat that bit of nonsense. She didn't need his pity.

Since then, he had firmly enforced a tutor-pupil relationship. He set a new, very strict schedule for their studies. They would meet every other day for two hours at Helsington Cottage. On the off days, Georgiana would read material related to the particular elegies, fragments, or verses they were studying in order to further expand her knowledge and the depth of her translations and interpretations.

All his conversation centered on the work. She reminded herself that the work alone mattered, nothing else. She quashed all other thoughts.

Today he had explained that the fragment in her hand was most likely a choral work between two competing voices, a device used for public performances. Georgiana hadn't known about public choral recitals, and that knowledge expanded her understanding considerably. But she wanted to know who Cithaeron and Helicon were and why they were competing.

She dropped the paper in irritation. Chambers wouldn't be happy if she failed to dress for dinner. Like most of her dinners, it would be eaten in splendid solitude. Chambers never forgot what was due a Duke's household, however remote from the seat of power it might be. His mistress cared less every year.

A footman approached her on her way to the stairs, bowed, and handed her a parcel wrapped in brown paper secured with twine. It resembled a book.

"This came to the tradesman's door, my lady."

"Thank you, William." She opened it to find a note.

Lady Georgiana,

Please review this work before our next session two days hence.
Yours respectfully,
A. Mallet

She turned the book over in her hands to discover a contemporary travel book. That seemed odd to her. Puzzled, she read and reread the title, *The Geography of Greece and Its Islands for Those Who Explore by Foot.* A slow smile came over her face; at least she wouldn't be bored tonight.

"Mountains? The voices belong to mountains?" Laughter bubbled up in Georgiana's incredulous face, spilled over, and engulfed Andrew. Laughter of his own drummed in his chest.

"Mountains don't have voices!" Incredulity contended with her laughter.

"Are you sure?"

Rising eyebrows gave her the expression of a very wise owl. She didn't speak.

"Yes. Mountains," he said. "I recognized the choral form Monday, but the identity of the competing voices eluded me as much as it did you. It took me two hours in the Wren Library to find the information after I left you."

"Only two?"

He ignored her sarcasm. "I thought I recognized Helicon, but the other was new to me. Look here." He unrolled a map of Greece and the Eastern Mediterranean onto the table.

"See here, above the Gulf of Corinth? Helicon is in the center and Cithaeron to the East below Thebes."

"Personification of mountains isn't a device I would have expected, but yes, it makes some sense." She didn't sound convinced.

"Remember this is choral poetry, meant for public performances. Let's try reading it that way."

Georgiana looked dubious. He tried for his best commanding officer voice. It worked with soldiers. "Read it. I will read the competing voice."

She picked up her copy. They spent a few moments expounding in Greek. Andrew tried for dramatic effect. Georgiana didn't.

"Lines are missing in this fragment. It doesn't all scan," she suggested after she read a particularly bland sounding passage.

He suggested they try it in English. "This first part would be a narrator's voice, perhaps the main chorus. It tells us that the baby is in danger. Remember, Kronos wishes to kill his own son, the infant Zeus." He cleared his throat and read, "'The Korybantes hid the infant.' Do you remember who they were?"

"Dancers. Male. In armor."

Most likely naked. Their "armor" would be a shield. *Damn but there were traps on every side.* He would fall into one yet. He didn't think she needed to know about the armor.

He recited again, "'The Korybantes hid the infant.'" He strode across the room while he recited and spread his arm toward Georgiana at the end of the line.

"Took? Is that the best we can do? She seized, grabbed, snatched, or wrenched him."

"'When Rhea took the b.aby and took great honor.'" Her voice hesitated.

"She uses that same word a number of times in the Greek."

"That doesn't mean you have to, and it doesn't mean you have to choose the weakest English word. I can't believe Korinna meant for it to be dull."

She raised her chin and tried again. "'When Rhea seized the—the divine baby and grabbed honor.'"

"Better. I'm not so sure about grabbing honor."

"Back to 'took'?"

"Perhaps. You can decide at the end."

"'Gained,' perhaps?"

"Better."

Georgiana began to get into the spirit. "So. They decide to hide it in a cave. Ah! But what cave? The gods are ordered to vote." She glanced up at him for approval. He nodded, not wanting to tamp down her enthusiasm. He loved watching her face light up with new knowledge. "It appears Cithaeron won the election. He took it by force," she went on without noticing.

"What makes you say that?"

"Her choice of words."

"So, how would you translate it?"

"'Great Cithaeron shouted that he had captured the beautiful victory.' Maybe not by force. It isn't explicit."

"Good. 'Captured' is good, or 'taken' perhaps." He intoned the line again in deep voice, "'Great Cithaeron shouted that he had captured the glorious victory.'" He gestured to her to continue.

"'Helicon was taken with a dreadful pain.'" She moaned dramatically. "It is certainly passive voice in the original. Something mighty seized him. No, wait, 'Helicon was grabbed by a dreadful pain.'"

Andrew watched her with delight. He gripped his chest melodramatically and took his turn, "'The victor received the crown, his heart overflowed with happiness.'"

Georgiana leapt in without hesitation. "'Helicon groaned and tore a large rock from his own side, hurling it down.'" She demonstrated the poor loser's angry response and peeped up at him. "No wonder he groaned. He tore out a piece of himself. That must have hurt."

Andrew felt a wide grin split his face. Georgiana laughed out loud.

"It begins to make sense when you put it like that!" she said. "Of course! The infant Zeus, father of us all—we being the pagan Greeks, of course—is to be hidden in a cave on a mountain, rescued from foul infanticide. The mountains compete for the privilege, campaigning loudly. The winner crows with delight. The loser is a very poor loser indeed. Oh Andrew, you are a miracle worker. I would never have understood the very point of the fragment without your help."

The gray of her eyes shifted to brilliant blue in her excitement. The color grabbed him by the throat and held him prisoner, helpless to let go. To give her this thing—the sense of her own ability, the ecstasy of sudden understanding where there had been merely puzzlement before—filled him with joy. Her face, flushed with laughter, held him; the intensity of her triumph crushed his very bones.

He wanted to seize her like Rhea seized the infant Zeus. He ought to leave and never return. He should go far, far away from Georgiana and her blasted family. His good sense told him to break off this sham of tutor and student, but he couldn't.

"Very good, my lady," he rasped. "Very well done. You have this passage exactly. Shall we go over it line by line?"

"I think I would like to try that tomorrow by myself. Can we go back to Asopos's daughters?"

Why not? It was mostly about capture and offspring. Some of the elegies of the other poets would be worse, much worse.

Andrew behaves like a pompous— She groped for a conclusion—*male.* At least he agreed to finish the poem about Asopos and the mothers of the heroes. She tried to be patient.

"I'm not a girl right out of the school room, you know. I do know the basics of reproduction. If the ancients didn't worry about the niceties of marriage...well, they were the pagans, weren't they?"

"They certainly were. Your mother would be shocked," he insisted.

"Don't mention her." She glared at him. "Don't ever mention her in this place!"

When they read the mountain chorus, the very air had vibrated with his laughter, as rich and warm as it was unexpected. It caused reverberations in her chest that emptied her lungs of air, but when his laughter stopped and he withdrew behind those spectacles of his, the sun fled. The teacher returned.

"Very well, Lady Georgiana, let us begin with a review of the Olympian family tree."

That family tree twisted and turned in knots, fraught with infighting, violence, and incest. Andrew didn't shrink from the facts of the stories. He made sure she understood which mother bore which hero and the circumstances (usually violent) of his conception. Unlike his explanation about the singing mountains, however, he didn't seem eager to volunteer information or to speculate beyond the obvious.

"How can I do this if I don't understand what is actually going on? What are they feeling? What is it they want?"

"That knowledge, my lady, won't come from a book." He wouldn't look her in the eye. "Some knowledge comes from life." He began to rearrange his notes.

What would Lawrence Watterson make of my questions? She understood, with sudden clarity, those pompous fools who found Greek translation dangerous to a well-bred woman. Those same folks would be apoplectic over the direction her work took today.

"You're leaving?" She watched his graceful hands straighten the papers.

"We've done enough for one day," he said without meeting her eyes. "You did well. Rewrite the mountain lyric. I will look forward to your final word choices. Perhaps the heroes fragment doesn't give us enough to go on. Some poetry is simply dry."

She doubted it but didn't say.

"The day after tomorrow then?" He didn't wait for an answer. He left her alone with her poems and her thoughts.

Chapter Fourteen

It sang. One of Georgiana's translations seemed to sing to her when she read it out loud. She rewrote the lines of the mountain lyric one final time early the following day. The musical flow of the lyric delighted her.

Her best work lay on the paper; she could do no more. She should be satisfied. She wasn't. Odd restlessness, the unexpected agitation she had begun to feel in Andrew's absence, overcame her.

She put the poem away and began reorganizing some of her older work boxes. When she repacked the same one twice, she put a fluttering hand to her hair and bit her lip. Not one box needed her attention. The steady tick of the ormolu clock sounded louder in her silent house than it deserved. She couldn't concentrate a moment longer.

Georgiana wandered to the window and looked out at the wide expanse of lawn as if she might find purpose in the green fields and the gold reflections of the sun.

It was early afternoon of a day too fine for the dark thoughts that crowded in on her. Andrew hadn't fled from her eleven years ago after all. That knowledge had proven to be cold comfort. He hadn't stayed either. Now he came, but only for brief interludes, and then he left her to work alone.

Georgiana sympathized with the boy Andrew had been. Only a heartless woman could blame him for running from her family's long reach and iron grip. She could find no sympathy, however, for the way he and Richard had neatly arranged her life without her consent. They gave her no choice. That, in the end, she couldn't forget.

He proposed marriage when he found her tumbling from his bed; she ought to have accepted. Her behavior had been unforgivable, but she would be damned before she let him think she trapped him into marriage. After his revelations about Richard, she'd be damned before she would let a man order her life for her again.

Georgiana shook her head against the gathering shadows in her mind and focused on the sun. A walk might settle her nerves, or at least shed light on the dark recesses of her thoughts.

An hour later, a deep blue cloak billowed behind Georgiana's long figure while she strode along the Cam. She found it oddly pleasurable to walk thus along the river without conveyance; she couldn't have done it a year ago. Mr. Peabody's odd regime worked. She had more energy every week. She would live to finish her work at least. That gave her some comfort.

John Footman, who followed at a discrete distance, struggled to keep up. She hiked almost as far as Cambridge, on the river path, detouring occasionally over fences and through fields.

The sight of the spires of Cambridge sobered her, however, and she turned back. No welcome waited for her there. Briefly, Andrew had welcomed her into his home, but now that door had closed. She wondered if other doors were closed. Edwina Potter continued to visit, but she was the only one.

"My goodness, Lady Georgiana. I am surprised to see you, dear!" Molly Harding, one of the few Cambridge wives that had once welcomed Georgiana's futile attempts to join their circle, came puffing toward her. "I thought to walk as far as the bend in the river. The harebells are still so colorful there this time of year. Isn't it glorious?" She bobbed a belated acknowledgment of the younger woman's rank.

"Good day to you, Mrs. Harding. It is a most excellent day, and you are quite correct about the bend in the river. The banks there are lush with foliage. I had to skirt the undergrowth."

Georgiana tried to leave, but the older woman moved to keep step with her.

"May I say you look well, dear. I haven't seen you in three months, and you have positively bloomed in the meantime."

"Ah, well, you can attribute that to modern science, Mrs. Harding. Mr. Peabody, the physician who keeps premises over by Magdalene, prescribed a regime to strengthen my blood, to enormously beneficial effect." She increased her speed as if to demonstrate how robust she had become.

Molly Harding breathed heavily, but she kept pace.

"I've missed you at the Cambridge Wives' Tea. Mrs. Potter expressed great disappointment when you didn't return."

"You are very kind. I believe Mrs. Clarke and her ilk made it quite clear my presence was unnecessary."

"Abigail Clark? She can be, well, that is, perhaps it is for the best with what has happened and all."

"And what would that be, Mrs. Harding?" Georgiana asked.

"Mr. Mallet has been quite ill. I understand that, dear. Mrs. Potter, who knew him as a boy, has been quite adamant that we are to be grateful for your assistance. One can understand he might be grateful. It is just that—"

"Abigail Clarke and the others disagree?"

The older woman's discomfort showed on her face, but she blundered on. "It *wasn't* proper, you must know. People do talk. Even someone of elevated rank as yourself can–"

"Make herself untouchable?"

"You needn't assume everyone thinks that way. Oh my. I am an old lady, am I not?" Molly's face turned a vivid shade of red. "How does your work go on, dear? I know when last we spoke you were seeking a man—a sponsor, I believe—to vet your work.

How is it possible she keeps getting redder?

"Tutor, Mrs. Harding. Someone to assist with my research and to help me flesh out the work."

"And so it appears you have. How does Mr. Mallet get on, dear? Old Mr. Mallet was such a good man. Well-loved in Cambridge. I understand the son is—"

"Better." No point in pretending she didn't know. "He sought treatment from a surgeon for his wounds, and he is better. He is able to walk without pain."

Mrs. Harding's eyes were avidly attentive now. She didn't interrupt.

"Let me put you at ease," Georgiana went on, "so you don't need to follow me home. Mr. Mallet has agreed to serve as my tutor. As you so obviously know, I sought training at his home while he was ill. Now that his health has improved, he attends me at Helsington. Is that what you wished to know?"

Georgiana swelled to her full height, chin up and eyes blazing. A more intelligent woman might have cowered; Molly Harding did not.

"Oh my, dear, I didn't need to know anything. There are those, well, that intrude and gossip, but I always say what a man does in his home is his own business. Unless, of course, he wishes to be... But it doesn't matter. No offense intended."

"No offense taken, Mrs. Harding. I'll be on my way now. Enjoy the harebells. Good day to you."

There was always talk, and it shouldn't have surprised her. She could simply ignore it. The implication for Andrew, however, distressed her. What men did in their own homes was, as Molly said, their own business. *"Unless,_of course, he wishes to be.." What? Respected as a scholar?*

When Andrew so sarcastically implied that his reputation would suffer when she demanded his help, she hadn't paid attention. She never considered that he might have meant his standing in the scholarly community. Dunning said he had work from Selby. Now she wondered what had become of that?

Georgiana stopped abruptly, struck dumb. In truth, she hadn't considered the cost to him at all. When they made their bargain, her only concern had been her own need. She felt like an idiot.

She brushed aside low hanging branches and ducked under them when the path took her closer to the river. Would the wagging tongues of Cambridge find her presence in his house to be the biggest scandal, or, if they knew about it, the nature of the work? Before she began to study with Andrew, her work garnered mostly derision, not outrage. If he wished the respect of the University community, he had good reason to avoid involvement with her. That derision would make any pretense of scholarship impossible.

She walked faster now. John footman ran to keep up. *Why should my work, my private business, outrage anyone?* Georgiana gave a rock on the path a very unladylike kick. It flew into the river with a satisfying splash. She picked up another and threw it. It felt good to make an impact on the river.

John footman stood an appropriate distance away and tried to seem invisible. It would, of course, be reported in the servant's quarters that Lady Georgiana acted peculiar.

My life is exactly like that, she thought. *When it is invisible, it is greeted with silence and quietly ignored. When I make an impact on the river of life, it is greeted with shock, horror, and outrage.* She picked up a larger rock and flung it as hard as she could. The splash was truly splendid.

"See me? I am here. I am alive!" She shouted into the wind. That would most definitely be talked about below stairs.

Determination gave force to her steps. *I will do this work,* she thought, turning back across the fields toward home. Determination also gave vitality to her thoughts. *There is no one else who cares to draw together the women of ancient Greece. I care, and I will do it.* She kicked at a tall clump of grass. "I will do it!" she shouted.

Deep inside, a quieter voice warned, "With Andrew's help."

Georgiana tripped and almost tumbled; a hand immediately appeared at her elbow. The ever-present servant.

She felt like she could do anything with Andrew's help, but she didn't know how long he would continue. Fear that he might quit became a canker inside her; she needed him. She needed his access to the libraries and resources of Cambridge. She needed the workings of his mind. She needed his confidence in her in order to do her work.

Georgiana's face turned upward, struck with the realization that she needed him like she needed sun and air. The realization buffeted her like the winds. She thought perhaps her questions should be "How long will he continue to help? How long before he disappears from my life again?" When he left, and he would leave eventually, she would sink back into the half-life she had before he returned to Cambridge.

Helsington lay ahead of her, burnished yellow by the sun that dropped low in the sky, flashing light off the empty windows. Without Andrew, it would gape like an open tomb. Today she had work, and in the work, there was life. Tomorrow he would come. She wouldn't look beyond that.

ANDREW ENJOYED neither sunshine nor visitors that day. He responded to a command of a different sort. He had work to do.

Andrew had at long last translated a slight passage from Proclus, the obscure Neoplatonist philosopher whose work Geoff Dunning brought him weeks before on behalf of Wallace Selby. He worked on it at odd moments during the previous week. It had been trivial, two evenings' work at best, but he sent it off with an apology for lateness to Selby.

The great man himself had been too busy to join Andrew and Dunning for coffee or, more likely, too self-important. Selby had come to dinner only once, and Andrew suspected the opportunity to inspect his father's exquisite library had been the primary attraction that night. When Andrew became ill, invitations ceased.

Selby's response to Andrew's work on Proclus, as welcome as it was poorly timed, came while Andrew introduced Georgiana to Great Helicon and choral poetry. It sat unopened by his door. Grateful for whatever wisdom led him to cut his hours at Helsington short, Andrew replied immediately.

Selby approved of the work he sent. There would be more work to fill his evenings, work his father would have admired. Proclus loomed ahead of him, a portent of future success. He wished that he looked forward to Proclus and the Neoplatonists with as much joy as he did Korinna and her sisters.

~

"The Korinna translations are complete, or as much so as we can make them. Is it your intention to publish merely the poems and poem fragments or a commentary as well?"

Georgiana froze; terror forestalled coherent thought. Publishing had never entered her mind. It seemed far beyond the realm of possibility.

"Lady Georgiana, did you hear me?" The gentle voice came from far away. His dark eyes, when she finally looked at them, were wrinkled with concern, the tiny lines in the corners of his eyes deep.

"Yes, yes, of course. I just don't know the answer. I hadn't thought of it."

"You hadn't considered commentary? Who better to do so? It is customary to explain your word choices and your interpretation of a classical work. Your notes are extensive, and it would be short work to reformat them into commentary. The additions and expansions you've made—"

"We've made. The newer additions were your doing. Commentary is the least of it. I hadn't considered publishing."

"Why ever not? What on earth did you plan to do? Pack it away and take it out once a year to read in splendid solitude? You have an obligation as a scholar, my lady, to expand knowledge."

Her brows rose in amused skepticism. "I suppose you would like me to commandeer a lecture hall at Trinity to present my findings?"

"Yes. No." He laughed. "I suppose not. But they should be published. The Grande Dames may not let their daughters read them, but their sons would benefit from seeing what women can do and have done. If you hide them away again, you would be condoning the sin of neglect. Your work–"

"*Our* work," she said.

"*Your* work," he insisted.

"I couldn't have gotten this far without help," she returned. "Each fragment of text came into sharp focus when you added the background and setting. Until then, they lay slack. Any commentary would be as much yours as mine."

Fire lit his eyes, but she didn't flinch. "Stubborn woman," he said. "Do you suggest that I publish a commentary without you? That is absurd."

"No, I think not." *He is the stubborn one.* "It took ten years of research to find the works we have, and to do the preliminary translations. I won't give that up."

She saw approval in his eyes and felt her confidence build, but niggling fears ate at her. Anxieties crowded up inside. "Publish? Where? How? Who would read it?"

"It could be done anonymously. Your family doesn't have to associate you with it."

He had read her thoughts correctly. It always came back to her family. A sudden vision of the Duke and Duchess of Sudbury's reaction to such a book shook her, and she shuddered. It might be possible, however. Publishers often attributed popular works to "A Lady" who remained nameless.

"Critics will savage it." She harbored no doubt on that point.

"Perhaps," he admitted. "Will it surprise you to find that some elements of the scholarly community are fools?"

"No." She smiled. "Your education gives you insights I will never have, and you have access to libraries locked to me. Even if I decide to publish, I couldn't do it without you. It's dishonest to pretend our relationship is one of tutor and student. It would be as much your work as mine."

He looked dubious, but she thought he looked pleased—and perhaps even touched. "They are your ideas and your insights. It is your work, Georgiana. Yours! You don't need to share it."

"I already have." She spoke around a lump in her throat when he used her given name. "And it has brought me great joy. It might be possible to prepare a manuscript for publication if I had a collaborator. As to whether a publisher can be found, I remain doubtful." Her eyes sought affirmation.

He stood silently. Lending his name to this work might not enhance his own reputation. *Surely he is trying to find the words to let me down gently.* "You needn't lend your name if you do not wish," she said. "Or you too could be anonymous."

"Collaborator." He said firmly. "I like the ring of that."

Georgiana's heart caught in her throat. She opened her mouth, but no words came out.

He didn't appear to notice; his carefully schooled voice remained proper. "Are we to consider all debts paid and begin a new relationship, my lady?" His emphasis on *my lady* was firm, and his meaning clear.

Oh Andrew, very well. I will keep my distance.

"Yes, collaborators," she agreed and extended her hand to shake his. "Do we need a written contract?"

"I don't think so." He held her hand in his firm grip. "Partners it is."

She left her hand in the warmth of his grasp and her gaze in the warmer grip of his dark eyes. "So, tell me, Mr. Mallet, how does one prepare a manuscript for publication?"

Andrew's hand, poised over a sheet of clean vellum, shook. Insanity drove him to agree to any working relationship with Georgie. Madness was the only explanation. He wasn't sure how he would manage this partnership when he could no longer hide behind the safety of a teacher's authority and the ground rules he had set. Once again, Lady Georgiana Hayden, haughty, self-centered daughter of nobility, had looked at him with vulnerable eyes, and all his resistance fled.

His voice shook also, and that worried him. His new business partner needed a confident businessman, not a randy schoolboy. "How did you plan to organize the work?" He could see from her face, knotted in dismay, that she hadn't considered it at all. She never planned to make her work public. *How could she be so foolish about something she held so dear?*

"Take a step back, my lady. Think of the entire body of your work. How do you organize it in your mind? How did you organize it in your boxes?"

"Each writer has her own voice." She paced behind his chair. "Each has her own things to say, would we but listen."

That sentence expressed her passion in a nutshell, the attraction to women no one really listened to, women with voices and ideas. "Excellent! Each chapter can be one individual."

"Some of them will be pathetically small."

"That can have a meaning also. There are some about whom we know almost nothing. We can let each section seek its own size." He turned to find her standing over him; his heart beat erratically at her impish expression. "What? Why are you smiling so?"

"We. You said 'we.'" Her generosity struck him like a cannon shot. Rush of desire at the sight of her radiant face would have buckled his knees had he been standing. He was grateful he wasn't.

He reached up to draw her closer, unable to stop himself, and she bent her head to his hand. Lilac scent flooded over his defenses when she lowered her joyous face to his. He brushed her lips with his once and then again with feathery touch.

She drew away slightly. Her eyes, wary but welcoming, never left his. He watched for the slightest sign of rejection or denial while he rose from the chair and moved his head with exquisite slowness to touch her mouth again. She closed the distance and brushed his lips with hers. Her innocent response was all the permission he needed.

He slid one hand up her neck to cup her chin, tipping it toward himself. His thumb brushed her cheek, and his long fingers feathered the edges of her hair. He used the other hand to pull her close until their entire bodies touched, until he could feel her breasts pressed against him and the curve of her hip under his hand. It was as he remembered it, as he longed for it. His mouth moved over hers softly at first and then became more demanding. Her immediate surrender held no reservation. He deepened the kiss; she opened to him completely.

It rapidly became impossible to stand. With one hand behind him to find the chair, he guided them, still embracing, down to it. He pulled her into his lap and leaned her soft curves into the crook of one arm so that he could bring his mouth down on hers. At the same time, he caressed her with hands no longer tentative or gentle but questing and demanding.

Her hand, warm on his neck, pulled him closer and sent shivers through him. The small, cautious voice floating inside him drowned in a sea of sensation. He trailed kisses down her face to the base of her neck. Soft noises from her throat assured him that he gave her pleasure, and the power of it inflamed him even further. He could feel her kisses on his hair and forehead when his searching hand found her breast and she moaned deeply.

"Georgie," he whispered against her mouth, kissing her again, "Georgie."

He knew, of course, where this would lead, but in that moment he didn't care. He could take her there in the workroom, and neither of them would be able or willing to call a halt. The scent of her, the feel, and the soft moaning noises drove him on.

A muffled voice penetrated the fog of desire. Andrew raised his head and gulped for air. Chambers announced tea, scratching on the closed door as servants were expected to do. Andrew stilled his trembling hands. He set Georgiana upright and saw her blink in confusion. He began to set her clothing right, all the while watching her deep uneven breaths and her struggle for control.

The scratching sound was repeated.

"Tea is served, Your Ladyship." Georgiana heard it that time. She pushed Andrew's hands away and summoned the voice of command enough to say, "One moment, Chambers. Let us set our work aside."

Her swift kiss stunned Andrew. She pulled back mere inches and shut her lips tightly to suppress a laugh. He couldn't pull his eyes away from those luscious lips. He watched in fascination as she rose and floated across to the worktable. Her aristocratic instincts reasserted perfect control. She left him to correct his own appearance as best he could and intoned with authority, "You may enter."

She amazed, bedazzled, and confused him. One moment she was panting in his lap; the next she was the picture of aristocratic self-possession. He envied her. He possessed neither self nor control. The feel of her warm and responsive body against his intoxicated him and put rational behavior out of reach.

Andrew did the only thing he remained capable of. He departed as quickly as decently possible. He wondered how long the redoubtable Chambers, who was used to Andrew leaving before tea, listened at the door before he spoke up. *Idiot! Georgiana deserves better than that.*

A twinge of discomfort twisted through Andrew's hip when he climbed the steps to his chaise. Months before it would have been blinding agony. Now, absorbed in what had happened in Georgiana's workroom, he barely noticed it.

What in God's name have I done? A bitter laugh escaped him. What happened was obvious to him. He had allowed erotic longing to overwhelm good sense. Unfortunately, it was obvious to the servants too.

Andrew urged his team to pick up speed and whipped them around Helsington's lane out onto the highway in a shower of pebbles and dirt. *Damned fool. You're going to destroy the work.*

The thought struck like a fist in his gut. He realized with a shock that he had come to treasure the work as much as she did. Their sparring and the bursts of creativity that exploded from it gave joy to his days. It gave him a reason to live. Now, he was letting schoolboy lust threaten that very partnership.

Lust outweighs the work by far, he thought. *It gets worse every day.* No good would come of it, he was certain, and yet another thought, one buried deep behind the black cloud of his confusion and frustration, danced into the light: *Georgiana struggles with the same problem.*

He couldn't stop the smile that began with a slow twitch in the corner of his mouth and spread until it transformed his mangled face. The coming weeks may be riddled with traps, but they would be interesting. She asked for knowledge, and knowledge she would get.

Chapter Fifteen

B*ufflehead! What do you think happened?*

Georgiana cringed at the mockery of the voices in her head. She needed time to sort out what had happened the day before. *Andrew kissed me–or perhaps I kissed him. No! We collaborated.* It had been an impossibly pleasurable collaboration. *There was nothing to it, really,* she tried to tell herself, but the mere recollection flooded her with liquid heat.

This wouldn't do. She needed time–time for perspective and time for control. She didn't have it. A message, one she neither hoped for nor anticipated, lay on her worktable.

My Dear Georgiana,

I wish to inform you that I will attend you in person five days hence. I look forward to seeing you again. Jamie Heyworth informs me that you look well, and I wish to see this for myself.

Your brother,

Richard

Lord Richard Hayden, Marquess Glenaire

Drat the man! A day to prepare the message and another for it to travel left her with just three days. She felt certain he must not have liked the information that Jamie took back to him.

She adored Richard in spite of his pomposity. She loved him still, in spite of his betrayal eleven years ago. Of all her family, only Richard accorded her any respect or kindness. Normally, she looked forward to his visits. They provided, until recently, the only light in her existence. Not this time.

His complicity in her separation from Andrew years ago left a raw wound. She needed time to heal and still more time to sort out what had happened with Andrew the previous day.

She could still feel his kiss. Nothing would ever be the same for her again. She let her mind run through the catalog of sensations. It would take years to sort out each one. Much about yesterday was less obvious. She experienced a profound shift, a life-altering event. She understood now with acute perception that pain and pleasure were remarkably close sensations. Both were life. Their opposite was nothing, the black expanse of nothingness.

Never again could she fall back on her rank or seriously entertain Andrew Mallet as a teaching authority. She knew she had heard the last of "my lady" from him, but she didn't know what they were now. They had agreed to be partners, but she was unsure of the nature of their partnership.

She set aside Richard's message in an effort to set his interference aside with it. Work was her salvation. She bent once again over the Nossis of Locri texts. Andrew would come tomorrow. They had one more day to work before she had to deal with Richard.

She attempted to make her work, as always, her sturdy bulwark against the blows of life. This time, the work only added to her emotional vortex. She read the epigrams with new eyes, and what she found there disturbed her. "Erotos" she knew meant love, certainly, and romantic love at that. *How should I translate this line?* she wondered.

"'Nothing is sweeter than love.'"

"'Nothing is sweeter than Eros.'" In English the meaning tilted slightly with the change of wording. The next phrase appeared to be about delight or pleasure.

"Definitely Eros," she said to the empty room. Whatever it is,

Nossis prefers it to honey. Yesterday, Georgiana wouldn't have understood. Love has a taste; she knew that now. She recalled the feel of Andrew's mouth on hers, and the taste when he opened and let her explore. The taste was sweeter than honey, indeed. She felt warmth rise again deep within her. Heat colored her neck and pooled deep in her belly.

The words of Nossis hadn't changed since yesterday, but Georgiana had. Andrew had kissed her when she was a girl, sweet innocent kisses, not like he had kissed her the day before. The raw pleasure of it opened her eyes to Nossis. She understood nuance and meaning she didn't see before. *What other secrets do they hold? With these distractions, how will I ever finish the translations?*

"'Nothing is sweeter than desire.'"

"'Desire,' Georgiana?" They had moved on to the poet Nossis of Locri, and, Andrew knew, to more treacherous ground.

"'Erotos' is very specific," she said with more confidence than she would have a month ago. "I could translate it as 'love,' but each of the five or more Greek words that could be translated as love has a slightly different meaning. I could translate it as 'eros,' using the actual word, but in English that is pretentious. 'Nothing is sweeter than Eros' doesn't ring true."

"Perhaps not," he said but withheld comment, allowing her to consider her choices.

"Isn't Eros also another name for Cupid?" she asked. At his nod she continued. "That left desire. I think eros or erotos refers to physical love. Am I correct?"

She had been pale, his Georgie, when he first encountered her weeks ago. Lately she had a sweet rosy glow, but today a bright pink colored her neck and face.

"Plato understood eros as the deep longing of one soul for union with another," he explained. "Could 'longing' be your word choice?"

"'Nothing is sweeter than longing.' Interesting. I'm not sure that conveys the author's intent in this case."

"Perhaps not. 'Desire' does come closer," he said and continued reading her translation, "'All other delights are lesser.' Clumsy that. You might invert it, move the negative, and it becomes 'No other delights come as high' or 'are as great.'"

"That isn't quite right either." Her willingness to contradict his suggestions delighted him. He watched her worry her lower lip with her teeth in the adorable way he had come to expect before she went on. "'All other pleasure takes second place,' perhaps?"

It was an excellent suggestion. The teacher in him kept his tone even or he would have overwhelmed her with delight. "Your variation works very well. It will do nicely. 'Pleasure' or 'delight'? Your initial translation was 'delight.' Did you consider 'joy'?"

"'Pleasure.'" Her voice was firm, but the delightful rosy color rising up her neck deepened. *Knowledge doesn't always come from books.*

She looked at him without shying away. "'Pleasure.' 'Joy' can convey a world of meaning, depending on the ear of the listener. I think 'pleasure' is more precise and closer to the author's intent."

"'Pleasure' it is then. That leaves us with 'Nothing is sweeter than desire. All other pleasure is second to it.'"

The air crackled between them. Her feminine scent filled the air and awoke his senses. Lilacs and springtime. Andrew felt his breathing slow until it became labored. He felt rather than heard a catch in his voice. Hoarseness undermined his effort to retain the tones of a teacher.

"The next line looks the same as before."

"There isn't much you can do with spitting out honey," Georgiana said. "She just spits it out of her mouth. She says, 'Even honey I spit from my mouth.'"

So much for poetic rapture. He couldn't imagine what else to do with spitting; honey clearly didn't match up to other delights. He laughed. It was the only possible response.

"Oh, do be serious. The honey is what it is. We have

NOTHING IS SWEETER than desire
All other pleasure is second to it.
Even honey I spit from my mouth.

SHE PACED WHILE SHE TALKED, as she always did when agitated, gesticulating broadly. "The part that comes next–Andrew, do pay attention. The next part, about what or who 'Kypris' did or didn't love confuses me. Nossis makes some sort of declaration. She says it outright. 'Nossis declares...' or 'So says Nossis...' or even just 'Nossis says...' Do you see?"

Andrew struggled to focus on Georgiana's words and not on the sight of her morning gown stretched across her breast when she moved her arms, but he lost the struggle. He nodded without hearing her. "Go on."

"I can't. I have no idea what to do with Kypris. I thought at first Kypris was a man's name, but I have never seen it used thus. Does she refer to the Island of Cyprus?"

"I'm sorry, Georgiana. Cyprus?" He pulled his wandering thoughts back to the words.

"Kypris. Who is it? Do we have geographical features speaking again? Romance with an island seems unlikely, but Nossis says 'She whom Kypris hasn't loved.'"

Andrew realized her expressive face had altered. She went pale and then flushed. He knew the many uses of the verb "to love." He wondered if those meanings brought the blush to her face. He wouldn't sort it out for her. She would have to work it out herself. He wondered what she knew about Greek culture to reconsider whether the person in question was a man.

The identity of Kypris presented an easier topic.

"It isn't a man's name, Georgiana. You correctly identified it as

Cyprus. However, in this case, I don't believe the island itself is what is meant. Cyprus was the birthplace of Aphrodite and her son Eros. She refers, I think, to Aphrodite herself. It is a common enough poetic image."

"So, it is whomever 'Aphrodite hasn't loved' or 'doesn't love' perhaps?" She considered the matter; she worried her lower lip again while she worked out the author's meaning. He couldn't look away. He watched a question form in her mind, watched her hesitate, and watched her square her shoulders when she determined to ask it.

"Could it mean 'the person who has not been made love to by Aphrodite'? That wording is clumsy, but could that be the sense of it?"

Too amused to hide it, he spoke quickly before she could get her back up at his laughter. "I think that interpretation is possible, but it stretches the meaning of the text. The poet describes someone who isn't the beloved of Aphrodite, but not necessarily someone who hasn't been the lover of Aphrodite. Of course, a person who is the beloved of Aphrodite would be aware of the arts of love and the sensual delights. That would be true, in this context, regardless of whether or not the person learned them from Aphrodite herself."

He wondered if he had gone too far when her blush deepened. They were on dangerous ground. She swallowed, and—God help him—wet her lips with her tongue.

"So 'the one whom Aphrodite does not love' is best." She seemed to seek his approval. "I think I understand the words so far, but the final line confuses me completely. When I look at it, I wonder about the entire poem. She talks about flowers and roses."

"There is no ambiguity about the literal meaning of the words. They—the ones Aphrodite doesn't love— 'can't tell what sort of flowers these roses are.'"

"She doesn't mean it literally, though, does she? She says, 'Nossis declares...' What does she declare? That 'anyone who is not the beloved of Aphrodite'—or isn't Aphrodite's beloved—'can't tell what kind of flowers roses are'? I don't think she means it as a treatise on gardening."

"No, certainly not. Nossis is obviously making a serious declaration about herself."

"Is it about her life or her work?"

"Excellent question, Georgie. What do you think?"

She glared at him. "Teacher's trick–putting it back to me. I take it you don't know either."

"Partner. My partner is as capable of reasoning that out as I am."

She shot him a scathing look of disapproval but continued her analysis. "If she is making a statement about her work, then the 'roses' would be her poems?"

"Brilliant. Yes, they certainly could be. If you read 'roses' as her epigrams, what is she saying?"

"Unless someone is or has been loved by Aphrodite, they cannot understand what sort of poems she has written." She frowned thoughtfully, and suddenly he saw her face light up. Georgiana, excited by new insights, captivated him. Her passion enchanted him.

"The beloved of Aphrodite would understand the arts of love. Unless you–the reader–understand the arts of love, you won't understand my poems. That's what she is saying!" She danced around him.

"Are you sure?" The teacher in him wouldn't let it rest.

"What else can the roses be? If it is about her life, perhaps she means her children. 'You can't appreciate what sort of beauties my children are...' The rest of the poem doesn't follow then." She thought about it silently for a while.

He knew he should offer some ideas, but watching her gave him pleasure; and the direction of his thoughts was extremely improper. His ideas about the epigram and about Georgiana were as erotic as Nossis of Locri probably intended.

"Perhaps she refers to the ladies of Locri."

She shocked him; he couldn't hide it. It amused her to continue; he could see it in her devilish eyes. "If the ladies of Locri are roses, then no one who is without knowledge of the sensual arts—as someone beloved by Aphrodite would be—could appreciate them or know what sort of 'flowers' they are." She peeped at him impishly. "Have I totally given up all hope of propriety?"

"Yes." He schooled his features to disapproval, or at least he tried to.

She laughed at him.

"But it is a pagan poem," he went on. "You wouldn't expect it to be entirely proper for a sheltered English maiden."

"Maiden Aunt, I fear is more accurate," she said in a huff, "and not so sheltered!"

He didn't speak. He thought of all the things she still had to learn and allowed realization to grip her.

"Could Nossis be referring in some fashion to herself?" Her eyes lit up with awareness.

The light in them held him fast. Georgie learned quickly. Monday's lesson in the sensual arts, brief as it was, had already broadened her vision of the poems.

"She could." He swallowed before he continued. "What are you suggesting?" He wondered if she could even imagine the imagery that poets used for a woman's most feminine anatomy. Roses were the least of it.

"Perhaps she is saying that only someone really loved by Aphrodite would appreciate her own..." She groped for a word. He watched in horrified fascination. She was on her own with this one.

"...charms," she said at last. "Her beauty? Her body?" She looked at him, challenge in her eyes and vulnerability in every line of her face and posture.

Andrew found reasons to study his fingers. He spoke very carefully. "Exactly how do you propose to convey that in English?"

"I don't." Her wicked grin was as unexpected as her answer.

She sobered and continued. "It is impossible to tell from the context which interpretation is correct. Nor could we express my suggestion about the ladies of Locri without the risk of communicating ideas that are mine and not hers. It is likely that the roses are poems, but I refuse to say 'poems.' I think in this case we will call a rose a rose and let the reader draw her own conclusions."

"Our readers are to be ladies, are they?" He noticed she no longer doubted there could be readers.

"And why not? Perhaps married ladies will see one meaning and young girls another. Our choice of 'desire' for line one would undoubtedly set up a variety of interpretations."

"Young girls?" He gasped. "Yesterday you didn't believe our work would be printed. Today you think it will invade the school rooms of young girls. How likely is that?"

"Not very. Far more likely this work will never see the light of day in English. The more we go on, the more I wonder if that isn't the safest result."

"Are you losing your nerve?" *Still wavering, Georgiana?*

"Certainly not! Don't look so hopeful. The works are what they are. These voices may not be respectable English voices, but they deserve to be heard as much as Sophocles and Euripides."

"What about the folks who find any translation of the ancients dangerous to women?" He couldn't resist provoking her. Georgiana, ready to do battle, her eyes blazing with determination, stirred him as nothing else ever had.

"Fools, every one of them. Foolish old men afraid of anyone smarter than they, anyone they can't control." She paced, a fury of movement propelling her across the room. Ten years of indignities spilled out of Georgiana in a flood, and desire raged through him like a pillaging horde.

"Men listened to Korinna in her lifetime, but scholars buried her work. Nossis, Anyte, all of them were pushed aside. Buried!" Anger gave way to anguish. Andrew's eyes prickled, and his throat constricted. From the day he left her, Georgiana was pushed aside. "Buried!" she repeated, and he had no doubt that was how she felt. "Buried alive." Her voice faded on a sob.

Rampaging desire laid siege to his common sense and set fire to his heart. He could only reach out, take her hand, and pull her close.

"We will finish it, Georgie. We will give them a voice." He rasped out. He rubbed her palm with his thumb and drank in the blue of her eyes. Dangerous electricity filled the air of the workroom.

"Andrew," she whispered. "I can't bear it alone. I can't bear it any longer."

He froze at the sound of his name in her mouth. Her eyes were on his lips, and her own parted as if in anticipation. She wanted him. He could take one taste, one soft gentle brush of her lips. All other delights would come second to that.

He lowered his head and felt her sweet breath on his face. The lilac scent of her filled him.

She swayed toward him, almost touching. He released her fingers and ran his hand up her arm to cup her cheek.

"Door," she breathed, voice husky.

The unexpected word confused him. "Door?" he repeated without taking his eyes from her mouth.

"It isn't locked." She turned her head to point it out. That small gesture broke the cord holding them. The door stood slightly ajar.

Dear God! A house full of servants loyal to the Duke of Sudbury and Andrew was ready to seduce his daughter on her Axminster carpet. Good sense flooded back into him, and he released her.

"Excellent idea, Lady Georgiana," he said with unnatural force loud enough to be heard beyond the door. "If we're to bring this project into a whole piece," he continued in a voice so gruff it was as if the words were torn from his throat, "we had best continue."

Andrew limped over to the table and put it and distance between them. He looked up to find Georgiana staring back, hurt vivid on her face. He turned away, but he could still feel her eyes on the back of his head.

"Record your proposed translation, my lady, and make notes for the commentary." His words sounded harsher than he intended. He feared what she might say if he gave her the opportunity to speak.

Faint shuffles in the hall told him all he needed to know. This house was not safe, not safe enough for a schoolmaster's son to make love to a Duke's daughter. If he did what his body urged, her reward would be humiliation, harassment, and hurt. He wanted to protect her from it even if she wouldn't protect herself.

Andrew picked up the pen and began to write. His entire body betrayed him. His eyes refused to focus. His hand wrote shaky words on vellum, but his mind gave no meaning to them. The rest of him, body and soul, yearned with an ache that destroyed all rational thought for the woman who stood across the room as still as marble. Her indignation filled the air as thoroughly as her lilac scent.

Chapter Sixteen

Georgiana heard the sound, the scurrying of mice feet, the telltale rustle of an eavesdropper, the traitor, the spy.

Andrew bent over his writing. He picked up a passage in Greek and pretended to study it. She could see the pretense in the quiver of his hand.

He had almost kissed her again. He came so close she felt his breath hot on her mouth. He stopped when she pointed to the door. *He stopped—drat him—and he probably thought it noble.* Nobility was cold comfort, no use to her whatsoever.

Andrew. She spoke, but no sound came out.

"Andrew." She managed a hoarse whisper. He kept his eyes down and pretended not to hear. Resentment began to build in the pit of her stomach. She cleared her throat and attempted hauteur. "Mister Mallet, you—" *You pigheaded beast.*

"You are quite correct, my lady. We have overrun our time."

Hauteur failed; resentment rose, built stone on stone with rising anger. She was beyond speech.

Andrew shuffled papers into a haphazard pile, a sham of order. He still wouldn't look at her. "I'll call for my chaise and—"

The slap startled Georgiana. She felt her hand, hard against his ravaged face, so hard the ridge of his scar left a line across her palm. One moment she stood still, the next her hand stung with the pain of her attack. She remembered no thought, no intention, only violence, and the rage that drove it. The silent echo of the slap resounded in the workroom.

He looked at her now, unable to ignore her, but he didn't speak. His crooked mouth, with its scar-torn corner, pulled tight with emotion, but no reprisal rose in his dark eyes. Deep pools of sadness filled them. She thought she might drown in them. She wished he would answer her anger with anger of his own to feed her hurt, to justify her rage.

Andrew took a step, his uneven gait more pronounced than she had seen it in days. Her heart drummed against her chest until her throat hurt from the pounding. Fear compounded her anger.

"Andrew," she said in a shaky voice when he took one step closer and then two. He looked at her but didn't speak. "Please," she begged.

He slid past her, the rich wool of his jacket brushing the front of her dress, and walked toward the door. She heard him whisper, "Not here. Not now."

The hard pound of his boots echoed in the hall and then she heard no sound at all. She stood for a moment, willing him back, willing him to speak to her, and knowing it was futile.

One explosion of movement, one sweep of her arm, sent papers, books, and other tattered remnants of their shared labor flying across the carpet to lie in ink-splattered disarray. Pens scattered in three directions, and a bottle shattered against the hearth tiles, staining them black. *If not now, Andrew, when? If not here, where?*

There was no one to answer. She heard only the gasping of her breath and the pounding of her heart. In suffocating silence, anger drained from her body. Her hand, fluttering in the aftermath of rage, blindly sought the back of a chair and gripped it for support.

In one long silent minute, the stillness of her perfectly run establishment reasserted itself, wrapped itself around her, and began to squeeze the life from her lungs.

A voice at the door spoke in tones that left no ripple in the still pool of order, "Chef Henri informs me that tea is ready, my lady. Miss Williams regrets that she is indisposed and begs permission to remain in her quarters. Does my lady wish to take tea here or in her sitting room?"

Georgiana heard Chamber's voice as though it came from a great distance. For a moment she couldn't respond.

"What does my lady wish?" Her butler expertly skirted a narrow line between subservience and disapproval. He would brook no disorder in a ducal household.

Georgiana called on seven hundred years of aristocratic breeding, raised her head slowly, and stood erect. If the servants could act as if she had real power, she could maintain that pretense also. She turned with exquisite slowness and stared down her regal nose.

"I will take it in my upstairs sitting room. You may inform Miss Williams her presence is not required."

Chambers gestured to an unseen footman.

"That will be all, Chambers."

Chambers hesitated, eyes scanning the room, and began to bow out. She interrupted him.

"One other thing. There has been an accident here. See that all sign of it is removed."

"Yes, my lady."

Georgiana walked from the room, head high. Her graceful, steady tread would have made her governesses proud if they had witnessed it. Even her mother might have approved. Feet of lead, however, and the weight of silence made her performance miraculous. She managed to sustain the illusion of control during her entire walk across the parquet foyer and up the swath of marble stairs to her sitting room.

Two footmen, alerted by Chamber's gesture, appeared from the servants' stairs, bearing her tea. The Duke of Sudbury's servants were trained to be invisible. Neither man spoke to her; neither looked at her. One held an enormous tray while the other laid the table with fine linen. They worked with economy of movement and were done within moments, leaving her with pastries baked by the finest chef in Cambridgeshire, a tea service worth a small ransom, and solitude.

She took a bite. Chef Henri's masterpiece crumpled on her tongue like sawdust. Thick suffocating silence choked her. She heard only the voice of Nossis of Locri singing in her head.

Nothing is sweeter than desire.
All other pleasure is second to it.
Even honey I spit from my mouth.
The one whom Aphrodite hasn't loved,
So says Nossis,
Cannot know what sort of roses my flowers are.

No comfort there. She put down the tiny silver fork, stared out the window, and waited for darkness. Then at least she could sleep.

Hours passed. Servants moved on quiet feet, cleared her tray, and brought endless tea. They helped her dress for bed and then they left her alone.

The despond that replaced her anger gave way, in turn, to doubt in the still hours of night. His Grace was a generous donor to Trinity and perhaps others of the colleges. She feared that her behavior might have put Andrew in jeopardy. In Cambridge, as everywhere in England, her father's influence loomed. He could make it uncomfortable for Andrew.

She knew that Andrew didn't fear the whispers of her servants. She hoped that he didn't fear the opinions of his neighbors. She suspected he thought his behavior was noble. He was puffed up with honor and some misguided notion of protectiveness.

Botheration but that man is stubborn! When will he ever let me decide for myself. The thought echoed in her mind.

Georgiana snuggled deeper into the luxurious coverings of her lonely bed. Moonlight filtered through her broad windows, casting shadows through her intricate lace hangings. It brought with it the voice of Nossis.

"'The ones Aphrodite has loved,'" she sighed. *That most certainly does not include me, more is the pity.* She wondered if she should feel guilty for associating herself with a pagan goddess. She didn't.

Georgiana attempted prayer, not knowing what else to do, but God felt far away, as far away as Andrew. She couldn't believe that it was truly her fate to be alone her entire life with no one to talk with, laugh with, or work with.

"If You intended eros only for marriage as the clergy preach, didn't You allow something for a freak like me, someone no one—at least no one acceptable—would want, ever? Someone with no hope of marriage at all?"

She waited for an answer. None came. Georgiana sat up.

Can God, who is in his very nature love, be so unfair? Does He mean for me to lead a loveless existence? No answer broke the silence.

She padded to the window on bare feet. The full moon, viewed from her window seat, lit the Cambridgeshire countryside with pale blue light. The world had passed deep into December. It would be cold, but bright enough to walk outside safely. She could be to Andrew in an hour, get her kiss, and be back long before the servants woke.

She had endured thirty-five years without affection, but now she knew better. She refused to go back to her half-life.

She arrived in Cambridge even sooner than she expected to. Less than an hour from the time she hastily dressed and pulled on her half boots, she turned into Little Saint Mary's Lane. Clear of the river and in the gloom of the lane too narrow to be illuminated by moonlight, the exhilaration she felt faded and her courage began to fail. She didn't know if she'd be able to find his door in the dark.

Steady, Georgiana. You've come too far to turn back now.

It wasn't yet midnight. She was sure of it. There were six hours before sunrise–five before the kitchen staff arose–in which to get home and slip back into her room. She had time but none to waste. Her hand slid along the rough bricks of the row houses while her eyes examined the dark façade and she estimated the distance to his door.

Several moments passed in agony before she noticed a light just where she thought his windows must be. It flickered from the upper story behind diamond panes. His study–she was sure of it.

He can't sleep either. Serves him right.

The thought gave her courage to knock at the door. No response came. She reached over to pick up a handful of pebbles, but the door opened before she could toss them at his window.

Harley, disgruntled and disheveled, looked her up and down irreverently. He gave the street an irritable glance as if to look for her servants and turned a thunderous expression to face her again.

"He's up. Honest man can't get a good night's sleep around here."

Harley shut the door behind her and disappeared into the kitchen. She stood alone at the foot of the stairs. in the darkened house. She guessed Harley had gone back to bed as no light appeared in the kitchen.

She removed her half boots and cloak and began to climb the stairs in her stocking feet. Giggles bubbled up at the oddity of it, and a nervous twitch bedeviled her belly. She ignored both.

Dim light shone under the door on the landing; a gentle touch opened it.

"What now Harley? I thought you went to bed." Andrew's deep voice sounded weary.

An oil lamp burned brightly on the worktable to Georgiana's left. She could see Andrew in the shadows to the right. He slumped in a wingback chair, an unopened book in his lap. He stared at the fire. A candle burned low on the table next to him; it illuminated a half-finished glass of brandy. She hoped that that glass was his first. For a moment, doubt paralyzed her, but the sight of him half-dressed drove doubts from her mind. His jacket, waistcoat, boots, and neck cloth were nowhere to be found. He wore a bright white shirt open at the throat with its sleeves rolled above strong forearms. She turned the lock behind her with a firm click. Andrew rose to his feet at the noise. Too late to back out now.

A growl brought her eyes higher to study his face, once gloriously handsome. She found that face ravaged with scars, but no less beloved. She knew him well now and could read emotions he could no longer mask. She saw longing quickly replaced by fear and concern. She assumed it was for her and thought him foolish for it. She saw irritation, too, indecision, determination, and, again, longing. The last gave her courage to walk across the room, to pass the chair, to stand in front of him.

"The door is locked." She handed him the key. "It is locked this time, Andrew."

HONOR BE DAMNED, Andrew thought, staring at the vision that had invaded his sanctuary.

He wanted to take the foolish woman on the floor of his study. He wanted it. She wanted it. He knew he couldn't do it. He had loved her too much eleven years before to offer her a shabby relationship; he couldn't do it now. One night would never be enough. Unless he could have her honorably, he wouldn't do it.

"We can't do this, Georgiana. You shouldn't be here."

She stood close enough for him to feel her heat. He could pull her to himself if he reached out. He wanted her with every part of his body and soul. He mustn't reach out.

She looked adorable in her stockings. She obviously dressed in a hurry, her rumpled clothing testimony to haste. He wondered if she remembered her stays, and he rather hoped she hadn't. If he reached over, one touch would tell him. He ruthlessly suppressed the thought. He would not reach out.

"We can't do this," he repeated.

"Are you saying I shouldn't be here?" she asked.

Of course I am, you dratted woman. He didn't answer her.

"Are you one more person who wants to keep me prisoner at Helsington, Andrew? Am I to be condemned to thirty more years of solitude?"

She was an idiot, an infinitely desirable idiot. She leaned inches closer to him. He need only raise a hand to touch her. Everything in him longed to do just that. He wouldn't.

"Is that what you want, Andrew?" she continued, angrier when he didn't respond. "For what crime should I be so punished?"

She moved abruptly but stopped a foot away. "What is it you want then? Shall I be the marble goddess, cold, hard, and artistically arranged for you and Richard to admire? Is that what you want? How will you label that tableau? 'Propriety?'"

"Merciful heavens, Georgiana, is that how you see your life?" He should comfort her. If he touched her, he could comfort her. If he touched her, he would take her there on his study floor. He groaned in frustration; he held back.

"How else is there to see it, Andrew? I live surrounded by people trained to be invisible when I pass, not one of whom will talk to me. Even my 'companion' is invisible. Cambridge derides me. London despises me. My parents and sisters prefer to forget me. My brother, my most loved brother, the one person who cares for me at all, gives me no voice in what is good for me."

Shame forced him to look toward the fire. Those words–her anger at Richard–were for him also. He didn't want to see the anguish in her eyes. He and Richard had done what was right. He refused to believe otherwise.

"You arranged it between you, didn't you? You condemned me to solitary confinement at Helsington Cottage. Don't even try to deny it! You knew that no one wanted me. Once you left, I was completely alone."

"Don't speak of yourself so, that isn't—"

"True? Isn't it? Please, Andrew, let there be honesty between us."

Her eyes burned blue fire, a cauldron of fury and need. He couldn't hold against it.

"You deserved better," he began, voice thick. "Your father wouldn't have permitted it. We could have run, bolted for Scotland or the Continent, but what then? Poetry in a hovel? That kind of romance dies in a day."

"'Poetry in a hovel,'" she repeated. "If that's what I escaped, what did I get in return? Glorious solitude? No one suitable, no one acceptable to the Duke of Sudbury wanted his eldest daughter, the daughter too tall, too lacking in grace, and too eccentric in her conversation to ornament an aristocrat's home."

"There is nothing wrong with your conversation, Georgiana. Don't deride yourself."

"No? I never learned to find a man's waistcoat more fascinating than his politics. I never learned to pepper my words with on-dits rather than the books I read. No man wanted me, not one. Even Lord Pfeil—old, bald, and smelling of horse—acted as if he had been asked to do a favor for my father, and a distasteful one at that."

Her eyes burned into him. "That is one fear you can lay to rest," she said.

The workings of her mind were complex tonight; she had lost him. "What do you mean 'fear?' What are you talking about?"

"Isn't that what your 'honor' is about? An honorable man, and Andrew Mallet is a very honorable man, does not 'ruin' a woman because no respectable man will want her for a wife. You needn't fear it because it's too late. No man wants me." Her eyes defied him to deny it. "Not even you."

He thought he must not have heard her correctly. He wanted her with an intensity that bordered on lunacy.

"Not true." His voice thickened. "I want you as I want air to breathe, Georgie. I have wanted you since I was seventeen years old, a foolish lovesick boy unable to sleep with the pain of it. I want you so badly that just being with you, working with you, has been a physical ache. You have no idea how badly I want you right at this moment." He watched hope flare in her eyes, and he had to step sideways when she moved toward him. He raised his hands to fend her off.

"It won't do, Georgiana. It's impossible. Your family will never tolerate it."

"My family?! What do they have to say about it? My family doesn't care about me."

"They would care if you attempted to marry someone unsuitable."

"Did I mention marriage? I don't remember discussing marriage."

It appalled him that she valued herself so cheaply. "It's the least you deserve—not some shabby affair."

"Ah, nobility again. The noble man decides what I deserve, what I need. Take a look, please, at how little I actually have. I have wealth, or use of my father's wealth. Since I have none of my own, I have none of the power that makes wealth worth having. I have status..."

The items she ticked off seemed to make a very familiar list. *How long has she brooded like this?*

"But that status serves to isolate me from most of the human race and frighten away any ordinary man who might be interested in me. Shall I go on? I have an elegant home to enjoy in utter solitude."

He couldn't move, and didn't speak, but she drew him like a moth to a flame.

"Touch me, Andrew. Hold me."

He stood, head bowed, groping for strength to send her away. *Show me how to love her as she deserves,* he prayed.

"I can't bear being alone any longer. Not after time with you. Please, Andrew. Hold me." The pleading in her eyes clawed at him.

"I could cause you to be with child, Georgie. Have you considered that?"

He recognized the flicker of surprise before a brief flash of joy took its place. Just as quickly her face folded with a terrible grief. She pressed her lips tightly together and swallowed with difficulty. Her voice filled with tears.

"I have you there, Andrew. I'm afraid I have you there. I can't, you see. There will never be children for me. Mr. Peabody was quite, quite certain about that."

The accumulated losses in her life buried him in shared grief.

The yearning to comfort her shredded the remains of his control. He took one step.

"So you see, there is nothing to ruin, nothing to protect, and no danger of fatherhood. Only me. Here. Now. I need you. Hold me. Please."

He reached out a hand and pulled her into his arms.

In the end, it was simple. She was his beloved Georgie, and she needed him. He couldn't disappoint her.

ONE MOMENT, she stood alone in a vast universe of darkness. The next, she sank into the warmth of his embrace. Strong arms enfolded her while he buried his face in her hair. She breathed in the musky male scent of linen and brandy and felt his mouth move over her ear and down her neck.

"Andrew," she sighed.

He pulled back for a moment as if to search her eyes. She reached a tentative hand to touch his cheek.

"I won't deny you now, you foolish man," she said.

When he smiled, she did what she had longed to do for weeks—she ran her finger over his brow, down the long puckered scar, to rest at the corner of his mouth.

Andrew stood, still as stone, breathing heavily, but he didn't object. Georgiana closed the distance between them and kissed the place her finger touched, the place his scars joined at the edge of his mouth. She felt the rough edges of it with her tongue.

A hoarse moan vibrated in his throat. He took control of the kiss from her, leaned her head back for better access, and covered her lips with exquisite care. His mouth slanted over hers, moved slowly back and forth, and sent ripples of pleasure through her.

When he began to press at the closed line of her lips, she anticipated him. She knew now that he urged her to open for him, and she savored it. His tongue slid slowly into her—exploring, tasting, caressing—and she rejoiced when heat spread up her thighs and into her belly. The weakness of desire no longer frightened her; she sought it.

She slid her hands up his chest and into his thick black hair, savoring the changes in texture of the softness of his linen, the rough skin of his mangled face, and the coarseness of his hair. She needed to touch him, to feel him. She felt him gasp when her hand slid down his neck to explore the front of his shirt.

When he pushed her slightly away, she groaned in protest. One arm held her securely, however, and his face hovered inches from hers. "Open it. Untie it."

She had never unfastened a man's clothes before. She tugged at the shirt with trembling hands and pulled it loose from his waist. She yanked the ties open and ran her hands under the linen and over his chest. Another glorious mix of textures—hard muscles, harder scars, soft hair, tight nipples, and silky skin met her eager hands. Each one fascinated her in its way. She tried to push his shirt up to see what her exploring hands felt, but he was too impatient. He yanked the shirt over his head and tossed it aside to give her better access.

She stood fixated, one hand on each side of his ribs, and traced the path of first one scar and then another with her eyes as though taking stock of the damage. Jamie said shrapnel had hit him. *Was shrapnel the reason for these small uneven gouges?* She found one long ridge. *This must be a saber cut,* she thought, *and not shrapnel.* His body was damaged but beautiful, the lines of muscle and bone even and strong beneath the scars.

A sudden instinct startled her. He might fear her reaction to his body. She looked up at him directly and willed him to see how beautiful he was to her, to know that his scars were precious. The black eyes were unreadable. She struggled for words to express what she meant but found none. She could only bend her head and kiss the damaged places one by one, allowing her mouth to linger on each.

His head dropped to hers, forehead resting on the top of her head. "Georgie. Oh my darling, Georgie, how you humble me."

His hand cupped her chin to raise her face to his. He kissed her deeply again and again, moaning her name against her mouth. His hands restlessly massaged her back before sliding upward to undo the laces of her dress.

She marveled at his concentration, centered on his own hands, while he unlaced her dress and slid it off her shoulders. The fire in his black eyes engulfed her when he finally allowed the dress to drop to the floor. She wore neither petticoats nor corset, just a cotton shift and pantalets trimmed with simple lace put on in haste an hour ago.

Sudden shyness overwhelmed her. Her body had never been tiny, and it was no longer young. Her long frame had begun to thicken with age. A profound longing to be beautiful for him struck her and, yet, with her newly found wisdom, she knew she couldn't shrink from his eyes any more than she allowed him to hide his damaged body from hers. She took a step into the circle of light next to the chair, stood before him, and forced her eyes to his face.

Andrew wasn't looking at her face. The ravenous look of a starving man devoured her from her feet, still clothed in stockings, up her calves and thighs, to her belly. She thought she could feel the hunger in his eyes as they roamed to her breasts. She felt it there, across her shoulders to her neck. She flushed hotly when at last his eyes met hers. He must have seen her uncertainty then because he smiled his crooked smile and said, "You are the most beautiful sight I've ever beheld." Just then, in that moment, she believed him.

He put out his hand. "Come," he said. She did.

Chapter Seventeen

"Come." She took his hand; he hoped she didn't feel how badly his shook. He pulled her toward the bedroom, needing to make her comfortable, hoping he didn't lose control, wanting to love her as she deserved.

"Wait!" She removed her hand from his and darted across the room to retrieve the oil lamp. He watched her approach the table through a fog of desire. Lamplight, reflected through her shift, outlined her lush body. It drove all rational thought from his mind until she turned back to him and the impish expression on her face brought him back to earth. This earth goddess was his Georgie. She deserved his attentive control.

She smiled and followed him into the bedchamber, lamp in hand. He took it from her and placed it on a tall wardrobe where it could illumine the room safely. When he turned, he found her perched on the edge of the bed, watching with anticipation. He smiled down at her ruefully.

"It is a lot of light," he said.

"I want to see and remember." Her throaty voice, huskier than he remembered, drove him. He began to remove the remains of his clothing, achingly aware that she watched him avidly. "There is more to learn than Greek, my love." *Ever curious about life,* he thought, *Georgie's curiosity is insatiable.*

He felt a surge of gratitude for the loose fitting Cossack trousers he had been forced to adopt to accommodate his injuries. He removed them along with his small-clothes in one fluid movement.

When they slipped to the floor, he stood hard, erect, and ready for her. He searched Georgiana for any sign of distress. She didn't shrink away, but she looked dazed by the sight. She stared for a moment and then glanced quickly up at his face and then down again, puzzlement clear on her face.

He let her look her fill until he could stand it no longer, and he knelt to remove her stockings. He tried to remove them with slow, sensuous movements, but amusement overcame him; and he dropped his brow on her knees, shaking with silent laughter.

"What? You are laughing." She sounded outraged.

"The look on your face." He could feel his face expand in a smile of pure joy. "It does seem unlikely, but it works. You will have to trust me."

Georgiana stilled. "I do." Her trust sobered him; he prayed he didn't disappoint.

One tug pulled her shift up over her head. A gentle gesture laid her back onto the pillow. The entire time he held her eyes, watching for distress or denial, hoping there was none. He put his hand under her knees and moved her legs around onto the bed, untied the ribbon fastening her pantalets at the waist, nudged her thighs up, and removed them slowly. He caressed her inner thighs as he did.

She lay completely naked before him. He couldn't help but devour her with his eyes. Desire built in her eyes when he slid his hand up the inside of her thighs, over her pubic mound, over her belly, to caress her breasts before cupping her face in his long fingers and kissing her deeply.

She reached for him to pull him closer, shaking with eagerness.

"Easy, Love, not so fast. Let me love you as you should be." With gentle care, he set out to do just that.

DESIRE WARRED WITH CURIOSITY; desire won. Georgiana swiftly moved beyond analytical thought. Andrew's hands were as nimble as his mind; they explored her relentlessly. They brought her pleasure in places she could scarcely have imagined capable of such sensation.

His mouth, soft but insistent, followed his questing hands until her entire body sang with delight, every nerve end alive and seeking.

She moved beyond action as well. In some distant part of her mind, she wished she could give as much as she received, but she couldn't control her hands. Loss of control left her drifting without direction. Sensation rose, layer upon layer, heat upon heat, until she could no longer move but only whimper foolishly, begging him to stop, begging him not to.

His lips were on her neck then, his breath warm, his voice hoarse in her ear. "Almost, my love, almost."

Her restless hands scraped his back when he moved over her. He paused to push her knees apart and pull them upward. A thought flitted on the edge of her consciousness, something she thought she should remember, but it wouldn't come to her. Her awareness centered now on the hot, moist place between her thighs where he nudged against her gently, entering her slightly, and then withdrawing, once, twice, slowly.

He covered her mouth with his, and she felt one sharp thrust deep within her. A swift tearing pain preceded a sense of immense fullness as her body stretched to accommodate his. Pain, that was what she had forgotten, but it didn't matter. The sense of closeness, of intimacy, overtook all other sensations. She felt her body relax on a sigh and allow him to slip even more deeply inside her.

He lay still, but she felt his entire body vibrate with tension.

"Try to relax, Georgie," he whispered, "Don't think. Let yourself feel it."

He kissed her eyes, her mouth, her ears, and his actions banished all thought, until awareness of discomfort dissolved and only the sense that she was possessed and cherished by another remained. She felt the tension drain away, and he began to move inside her then with a slow rhythm. Her breath quickened with the rhythm, and she held on to him as though her very life depended on it.

A sharp sword of pleasure rose up inside her; his movements brought an unanticipated tension. It quickly became unbearable.

"Andrew, I can't, I..."

His mouth silenced hers. She felt him reach down where their bodies joined and caress her intimately. That touch dissolved all thought. An utterly unexpected explosion of pleasure erupted. The immensity of it disconnected her body from her mind and shattered her consciousness. For a moment, she knew only sensation.

His moans brought her back toward reality, and the spasms of his body above her gave her a profound sense of completion.

He buried his face in her neck when he collapsed against her, fully spent, and kissed her once again. For the first time in her life, Georgiana knew perfect contentment. The experience of his pleasure left her with immeasurable peace. Her eyes drifted shut, and she slept.

Georgiana, burrowed deep in Andrew's bed, slept soundly. Her naked back, curled away from him, held him captive. Her arm caressed the place where he had been lying moments before, and it took all the tattered remnants of his self-control to keep from slipping back into bed to make love to her again.

He had just enough light before the lamp sputtered out completely to dress and grope in a drawer for his timepiece. The night was far gone, but he thought they had enough time to get her back to her own house before her staff stirred—assuming they hadn't already been found her gone and sounded the alarm. It was too late to worry about that in any case. For now, he wanted to get her back where she belonged and quickly.

He caressed her with one last longing stroke and pulled the soft coverlet over her. He knew it would be a shock to her system to wake up naked in a man's bed.

"Georgiana, my love, wake up," he said softly.

"Mmm?"

"The night, I fear, is disappearing. We need to get you home."

Her eyes blinked open, and confusion gradually gave way to awareness. Her lips parted a fraction, and she smiled up at him.

"She whom Aphrodite has loved." She reached her arms up for him. There was no shock.

"Now you know why they are dangerous works," he murmured as he surrendered to her kiss.

"Enough," he said a moment later. He said it several times into her mouth. "Enough. We don't have much time. You are going back where you belong." It almost killed him to rise up, his body fully ready to take her again.

She started to protest, and he silenced her with a tender hand. "We can talk later. I have to hitch up the horse."

"Yourself?"

"Do you think I'm some aristocratic fribble who can't hitch his own chaise? Besides, Harley would be very unhappy if we woke him up."

She looked skeptical but let go of him so he could put on his jacket.

"Quickly now. It will take me but a few minutes."

Andrew walked round to the public mews behind the lane. The cool air made his bones ache; they were too old for sneaking around at night. And yet he felt more alive than he had in months, perhaps years. There was no going back, of course. That much was radiant in its simplicity; a clear path opened up before him. He had no idea how they would manage the thing, but family approval or not, they would marry. He needed her too much to live apart. *Eros—the longing of one soul for union with the other.* Quick sex in the dark would never be enough.

~

"I COULD STAY." She hoped she sounded more confident than she felt. They whispered, heads bent toward one another, while he walked his horse to the public thoroughfare as quietly as he could. He was hatless, his jacket thrown on haphazardly, his shirt fastened crookedly. She thought him altogether adorable.

"I could stay," she repeated, "and—"

"No." Her confidence didn't matter. His "No" was immediate and emphatic.

At the turn, he reached to hand her up.

"I wish to stay with you." This time she said it firmly, and he rewarded her with a smile.

"Good," he said, and he climbed up next to her with some effort. He used strength in his arms to compensate for lack of it in his left hip and leg. She thought about those strong arms around her in the night and felt heat rising. "Good," he repeated, but he didn't look at her. He took up the reins. "I wish you to stay with me also."

"That's settled then."

"I don't think so. There is a good English name for what you want, Georgiana. It is called marriage."

"Don't be ridiculous." Georgiana's heart plunged in horror and began to beat in panic. The word marriage terrified her.

"Is the thought of marriage distasteful to you?" She could feel the tension in his body.

"Marriage is, it is...something arranged."

"Dynastic contracts?"

She nodded so nervously she had to remind herself not to be a ninny.

"The melding of lands? Compact of strangers? Cold conversation for dinner and separate bedrooms?"

"Yes, yes, that's exactly what it is."

"No, it isn't."

"My sisters—"

"Your sisters aren't typical of anything, except perhaps Hayden family misery. Look around you, Love. Much of the population manages quite well with a little warmth and affection."

She supposed he meant that she should look at the common run of man. Haydens never considered what was common when they thought of their own lives. The idea confused her.

"Think, Love," he said. "You say you want to stay with me. I want that too. I want you there more than just this night. I want you there in the morning. I want you to share my house—the one in Little Saint Mary's or another if you prefer. I want you in my bed, not occasionally and furtively, but every night and every morning. I want to belong to you and with you, and I want the world to know it."

His seductive voice tantalized her, but his words made little sense. Her parents rarely spent a night under the same roof, and never in the same bedroom. She suspected they must have gone about the quick begetting of children for the estate before going off on their separate ways, but they were indeed separate. That would be worse, much worse than what she had now. She was sure of it.

He drove the chaise past the outskirts of Cambridge proper. The moon hung low in the sky and would soon be gone, leaving them in darkness.

"I want..." She couldn't complete the sentence.

"What is it you want, Georgiana? Do you know?"

"This beautiful thing between us, this fragile, private thing—it is mine...ours. I don't—"

"Don't what? Don't wish to marry me?"

The very word struck her with horror, and she could see by the look on his face that her horror hurt him deeply.

"I want you. I don't want marriage."

"Let's look at this carefully," he said.

How can he be reasonable and analytic at such a time? She wanted to scream. The horse ambled on, oblivious to her churning emotion, carrying them relentlessly on under darkened skies, the moon having sunk beneath the clouds.

"You said you wish to stay with me. Do you think you could live in my house?" He was as relentless as the horse.

"Certainly not! I mean, yes, but that isn't the point. Of course I would love to be there with you, or in a grand house, or in a one-room croft. It isn't the house." And it wasn't. She would have happily followed him to Spain and lived in a tent. She wouldn't have missed her golden cage.

"Well then. One barrier removed. You should know that, while I'm not a wealthy man in the sense that your father is wealthy, my service and some opportunities it brought me left me well fixed. Many would consider it wealth."

He skillfully maneuvered the team around a rutted part of the road. When she didn't speak, he continued.

"I can afford to feed you, to provide a few servants, and to keep you in muslin and writing paper, while living as a gentleman scholar."

The hard seat of the chaise cut into her back while she struggled in vain for words. The picture he drew tempted her, but she shrunk from it. Marriage meant trading the control of one man for the control of another.

"He can't ruin me." Andrew's voice came to her from far away. He had grown impatient waiting for her reply. "There is nothing he can do to me."

He mistook her silence. She knew that he assumed that she worried about him instead of herself, and the realization shamed her. He offered to marry her, knowing the harm her father could do. He was more generous than she.

"Do you hear me, Georgie? He can't harm me."

"You don't know him. There are many ways to ruin a man." *And destroy a daughter.*

Andrew let out a frustrated breath. "You don't wish me to order your life. Very well, don't order mine. I'm not twenty-two any longer or so easily dismissed." He managed his horse one handed, and ran the other through his hair in frustration.

"Aren't we getting ahead of things anyway," he burst out. "Before we worry about his reaction, I believe the first step is to ask him for your hand."

"No! You mustn't!" Her panic this time had a frantic edge. Her father would become involved. He would demand her obedience. The delicate balance she had struck with her parents gave her the ability to work. What Andrew was asking put all that at risk. She spent too many years avoiding her father's notice to risk it now. "You mustn't do that, Andrew."

"Why ever not? It is a mere formality. We are of age, and he can't forbid it. The worst he can do is withhold your dowry or cut you off from family funds. Is that what worries you?"

She thought for a moment. "No, but I shouldn't like it. I would hate being treated like chattel. It would be ugly. He would make it ugly." She knew that he would humiliate her, that her mother would humiliate her.

"Very well, we can forgo the courtesy of it and simply marry."

"It would never be simple! At first banns they would swoop down and begin to bully the minister and the local magistrate. The entire shire would be in an uproar. They would know immediately. They have eyes everywhere."

She grabbed his arm in her agitation, clinging tightly. "And Andrew, I have nothing but my house. I would come to you with nothing." She would contribute nothing. She wouldn't be a partner. She would be completely dependent on him. Her fragile independence mattered too much to give it up for another man's care.

"Georgiana, your beautiful self is certainly not 'nothing.'" He ignored the horse. "And there is also the work. You have already done me the honor of sharing the work."

She wondered how the work could be enough. Their partnership was too new, too fragile.

"You are correct about one thing: His Grace's eyes and ears." Andrew went on without waiting for an answer. "I wouldn't care to elope, however. I want to pledge my fidelity before God and the world—yes, even in the face of His Grace of Sudbury—not before some blacksmith in Gretna. Your father's reach doesn't frighten me."

"It should. And my mother—"

"Ah. Your mother. Now, she is quite frightening." He said it lightly.

"Perhaps not to you, but you have no idea how much cruelty she can inflict."

"But I do, Love. I saw her at her worst, remember?"

"You saw her aim barbs at me. She ignored you. You were beneath her notice. You have never been on the receiving end of her attacks. She finds everyone's weakness sooner or later and exploits it to cause pain. Sometimes I think she enjoys it."

"We could obtain a special license." His voice reached a new level of wariness. "Once we're married, you would never need to see her."

"Don't be absurd. Don't you understand that his eyes are everywhere? The Archbishop of Canterbury is his cousin. York is my uncle, and Winchester simply a shooting companion but a close friend for all that. It will *not* do."

His refusal to face reality irritated her. Suddenly she felt sick, weary unto death, of men telling her what was best for her.

"Andrew, don't you see, marriage is so very public. I don't want to ruin this beautiful thing we have—the two of us alone."

He pulled the horse to the side with abrupt movements and turned to face her. Her arms hurt where his fingers bit into them.

"What precisely is that, Georgiana? What do we have? What were you doing tonight? Researching Nossis of Locri?" She had hurt him; she hadn't meant to, but she had hurt him.

"No, no, never that," she soothed. "What we have is a precious thing, precious and, and private."

He ran his hands through his hair again, the familiar gesture of exasperation, before he picked up the reins and urged the horse on. "It is never private, Love." He didn't look at her. "Desire may feed on the soul of an individual, but it is never private. It always impacts the larger world. What is it you want from me? What were you asking for tonight?"

She couldn't answer that. She had intended to demand a kiss and gotten more than she anticipated. She could only stare at him, touched beyond measure, but equally confused and riddled with anxiety, wondering what to do with this new reality.

He came to a halt again, and she found herself at the lane to Helsington Cottage. He came round and lifted her to the ground.

His kissed her, a kiss as fierce as it was brief. She reached to pull him back, but he held her away. "We need to settle this."

"I can't talk about marriage, Andrew. I simply can't. Perhaps tomorrow we can piece this together."

"Perhaps." He looked dubious. He glanced up at the dark shadow of the house. "Be careful. If you don't want to marry, you best take care that the world doesn't know where you've been."

In the deep darkness before dawn, she walked up the lane to her house alone.

Andrew nursed his anger all the way to Cambridge. Her proud back, walking unbowed down the night-shrouded lane, had inflamed and infuriated him. Every bump along the route deepened his rage, every slowing of his horse's steps his frustration. She had no idea what she did to him, and in his opinion, she didn't care either. A bitter smile followed that thought. She ought to know now what she did to him—even if she didn't care.

In the public livery where Andrew stabled his horse, a young groom grumbled when Andrew woke him.

"Do as you're paid, damn it. You're not paid to tell me what time of day I have need of you." Andrew slapped the reins against the seat of his chaise and winced. Anger drove him to leap from the vehicle with little thought, and a crooked landing on his weaker leg resulted. Sharp shafts of pain along his irritated nerves sent a wave of nausea through him. He sagged against a stall, breathing heavily.

The groom took his horse with a sullen look and led it back into the stables. Andrew watched him work with quiet competence. The groom was little more than a boy and should have been in his bed another hour or more.

"Sorry lad," he said. "I've had the devil's time tonight. It isn't your fault."

He slipped the boy a coin and limped toward his dark house just as the sky turned a light gray. The house lay silent as a tomb. He labored one painful step at a time, up the stairs to his study where the fire burned low. In the dim light before dawn, he could just make out the shadow of the bed with its crumpled linens through the open door to his bedchamber. *Silent as a tomb but emptier,* he thought.

A serviceable decanter sat at the ready on his window sill. He poured a glass and drank it in one movement. *You're a damned fool, Andrew. This time is no different than before. You present every argument, and they brush you aside. Her family's claws are in her deep. It will never be any different.* He poured another glass and drained it.

Anger teetered toward bitterness. He picked up the decanter and lurched to his chair by the fire, trying to fan the flames of anger, trying to keep the bite of bitterness at bay. "I am not something to be used for your pleasure and tossed aside, my lady," he spat. There was no response from the silent room.

He knew his words were not fair to Georgiana; he didn't care. She never considered the consequences of her actions to him—or to herself for that matter. The Haydens used the entire population of England to suit their comfort. Tonight was no different.

Sunlight crept gradually across the dark planks of his floor. The new day brought no peace and very little clarity.

He heard Harley bang about loudly in the kitchen below. Scorched eggs, dried toast, and burnt coffee. *Damn. I need to hire a decent cook.*

A vision of Georgiana with flour on her nose came to mind. He glanced over at the rumpled bed, and the vision shifted to one of her lying there in that bed, her face transformed with desire. He wanted her there now, wanted to wake up next to her every day just as he told her. Her nonsense about their love—*this beautiful thing...this fragile, private thing*—was a flight of fancy, the stuff of gossamer fairy tales. There was nothing fragile in what he felt and nothing fragile about what they could have together.

Andrew thought about the life they might build together, one with a sheltering, nurturing love, the sort that got two people through a lifetime. *We could, if only she could let go, if only she would let herself, if only—* Shattered glass and the flare of brandy on embers stopped his ragged thoughts.

This is the end. I will leave the blasted woman! he thought and then he sank his head back and laughed bitterly. He would never leave. He should, but he wouldn't.

He wondered what they would do about the work. She might try to pretend that nothing had changed, but he couldn't.

He hobbled to his rugged worktable and found pen and ink.

"Lady Georgiana," he began but crossed it out. Even in correspondence, there would be no going back.

"Georgiana, I'm not able to continue our work." He crossed that out also. This was not about the work. "I'm not able to come to Helsington Cottage in the near future."

He couldn't bear it.

"I'll be unable to keep my commitment." No. He crossed that out. He must finish the work. He owed it to her; he owed it to himself.

"I have sufficient notes here to work on my own." *For how long? Two days? Then what?*

A savage roar and a string of curses filled the air of the study. He threw the crumpled note against the wall. He knew he would never be able to stay away—never.

Chapter Eighteen

He didn't come.

Andrew always arrived at one in the afternoon. Georgiana depended on his punctuality. She needed the dependable, the familiar, the comfort of habit more today than ever. She needed work to restore her balance. She needed to work while they talked, while they reasoned, calmly and logically, through what had passed between them. She needed Andrew. She didn't get him.

Instead, the long form of her brother Richard lounged with sophisticated ease on her gold brocade settee. He had arrived a day early.

Damn you, Richard. She knew with total certainty that everything in Richard's world happened by design. *He invaded my privacy for a purpose, the traitorous swine.*

Georgiana's ormolu clock chimed the quarter hour, fifteen minutes after one and no sign of Andrew. With Richard here, relief warred with desperate disappointment.

"You look well, Georgiana."

She needed Andrew, not Richard. She needed work, not this foolish pretense of civility. What she got was her brother, his silk-clad legs stretched across her fine Axminster carpet, and awkward conversation. She forced herself to respond to his small talk.

"Thank you. Your suggestion of Mr. Peabody was a blessing. He has been a lifesaver in every sense of that word."

Georgiana poured herself another cup of tea. "Your color is excellent," her brother went on, "and you appear more animated than when last I visited." Richard had declined tea in favor of a fine sherry, which he held gracefully in the slender fingers of one hand.

Richard's eyes, so like hers in color, lacked her warmth and revealed nothing. The same could be said of his words—no light and little warmth.

"I take the air with more regularity," she responded. "And Mr. Peabody's regime has had a salubrious effect." Georgiana's mind wandered. *Does last night's adventure show plainly in my face? Where is Andrew? I hope he doesn't come, not with Richard here. I don't want to face them together. Drat it, where is he?*

"I understand you order kegs of water from a particular spring in Yorkshire. Fascinating that iron in water could—"

"What brings you here so suddenly, Richard?"

Her brother raised a well-bred brow at the interruption but didn't comment on it. "There is to be a house party at Murnane House. The Earl of Chadbourn, you may recall, is the Duchess of Murnane's brother. He is to marry a distant connection."

"Will is getting married? I am glad for him. I wish him happiness." William Landrum, the Earl of Chadbourn, was one of a handful of Richard's true friends, his boon companion when they came up from Cambridge before the war—like Andrew.

"Her Grace wishes you to attend, and I have been commissioned to bring you there directly."

"Absurd." Georgiana put her cup down with enough force that it teetered in the saucer.

Richard's cultivated brows rose simultaneously. "I beg your pardon."

"Mother hasn't wished my presence at Mountview these years, much less at a house party."

"She wishes it now."

"She does or you do?"

One of his rare smiles, slight but sure, lit his icy Hayden eyes. "Does it matter?"

"Certainly. If she doesn't wish to see me, she won't see me, even if I'm in the same room."

"That doesn't become you, Georgiana." She noticed he didn't answer her question. "Chadbourn was once your friend, too."

She acknowledged the truth of that; Georgiana genuinely liked Chadbourn, but she was never close to him—unlike Andrew. "Does Will wish my attendance?"

"He is too besotted to know what he wants." Richard's tone spoke his disapproval. "He has succumbed to the most banal and mawkish of sentiments."

"You mean he has the poor taste to be in love with his intended?" It amused her. The Haydens had long savaged those whose sentiments were plebeian, those with sentiments like the ones Andrew expressed last night.

"Who is she?" she asked.

"She is—she is respectable."

"Mother doesn't approve." It wasn't a question. "She is 'no one who is anyone'?"

"That is correct."

Chadbourn has fallen in love with a commoner, how intriguing. Georgiana was stunned to silence. The thought that her mother might wish her to witness the distastefulness of an uneven match occurred to her. She wondered if it was Richard's intention also. Georgiana puzzled over the possibilities. Perhaps Richard wished her to lend support to the bride. She once thought she could read her brother but not now, not now that she knew what he did to her eleven years ago. It clouded her view of him.

"Mother—" he began. She didn't let him finish.

"Why is my presence required?"

"You stay too long in your own company."

"That isn't our noble mother speaking. What is really on your mind, Richard?"

"Chadbourn's wedding and your duty to your station." His chin rose, and his tone became icy. "A lady doesn't avoid the marriage of a peer and a friend when invited."

It was a command, an order to attend, but she still didn't know who had issued the order. The wedding itself might not be so bad. Distantly she heard her brother fill in details of his plans, assuming she would comply.

She might like to meet this respectable-but-common woman Chadbourn had the poor taste to love. She thought she would like that very much. There were other ties, however.

"I can't leave Cambridgeshire at this time."

"What ties you here?" He leaned forward, his look probing.

"Work. I have my work." She did, but it felt foolish to tell him that.

He dismissed her work with a sardonic grimace and a wave of his hand. "Jamie has told me that you continue to work on your poems. There is paper in Devonshire, and ink."

There is Andrew. She couldn't say it. "My books are here."

"I gather you attempted to find some assistance in the University community."

"If you know that, you know I was rebuffed."

Richard raised an elegant brow at her plain speaking. "Yes. Quite."

Her throat tightened. "One goes forward with the work as one can." Her eyes defied him to continue, to put into words what was on his mind.

A light scratch on the door interrupted them. "Mr. Andrew Mallet has arrived, my lady."

"Show him in, Chambers." Georgiana hoped that she showed no sign of discomfort or concern but knew the heat she felt creeping up her neck probably meant she revealed a pink color. She held her brother's gaze. It registered no surprise at her visitor.

"I am sorry, my lady, but I have shown him to the workroom as is your customary practice. Shall I ask him to attend you here?" The butler looked uncomfortable.

"No, that will be all. Please tell him I will join him in a moment."

"Customary practice, Georgiana?" Richard drawled.

"My work, Richard. 'One goes forward as one can.' Your old friend Mr. Mallet is an excellent tutor." *I hope you don't discover how true that is.* "His assistance has improved my work significantly. If you will excuse me, I have a longstanding appointment with him this afternoon. I will see you at dinner."

She crossed the finely polished parquet floor of the foyer with as much dignity as she could muster before turning down a small corridor. She felt her brother's eyes on her back every step, but she forced him from her mind.

Other concerns flooded her, chief among them was deciding how one should greet a lover who has parted in anger in the depths of the night after hours of glorious lovemaking.

It will be simplest, I think, to throw myself into his arms. She made sure she shut the door securely behind her.

He planned to keep her at arm's length, but she flowed into his arms and began to kiss him before he could speak. He wanted to speak to her soberly about the changes between them. Need battered common sense down once again; it pummeled emotion and laid waste to rational thought. Reality was her sweet mouth and the lush body pressed against him. Delicate hands explored the skin under his shirt which had inexplicably come loose from his waist. When those hands began to undo his waistband, he became suddenly, painfully alert and took her wrists in an iron grip.

"What are you doing?"

The triumphant smile of a woman well loved, who knows she is desired, was the only response. She leaned forward to kiss him again, but he restrained her. He pressed her into a chair with elaborate gentleness, but he held her there firmly.

"Stay."

"Shall I bark for you?" Her lips quirked, and he almost relented; but he refused to be drawn in by her nonsense.

"You're making this difficult, Georgiana." He ignored her jibe about barking, turned his back, and moved as far away from her as their small workroom permitted.

"Actually, it seemed easy to me," she replied smugly.

He set his clothing to rights, and bile rose in his throat. "Is this it then? Sex and desire on the workroom floor followed by—what? Scholarly pretense? A return to our proper places for dinner until you can sneak out again into the night?"

That wiped the smugness from her face.

"You are angry."

"Yes. No–confused." That was a lie. Anger built steadily. "We are collaborators. Partners. It is my understanding that you wish for nothing more. One does not undress one's collaborator."

"No, I..."

"You what?" he spat. "You planned a different role for me?"

"No! Us. Different for us."

"How different? We're not equals. Marriage, you tell me, is out of the question. How am I to address you then—my lady?" He could hear his voice rise.

He was entertaining the household, but he didn't care. He couldn't stop goading her. He shouldn't have come. He was still too angry for reasonable conversation.

"I never said that. I never said 'not equals.' I didn't, I can't. That is I—the work is still important."

"Yes, the work, of course. Lady Georgiana's true love," he said bitterly.

"Not fair, Andrew! Not fair by half. I thought you valued it too!"

He ran his hand up the back of his head in exasperation.

"You are correct, of course. Work itself is important." It was true. Work was important to him, but he was no longer sure he needed Georgiana's work. He found it challenging and, until today, delightful, but it would never win him the place his father intended for him.

A message from Geoffrey Dunning lay in Andrew's coat pocket. Geoff had finally been able to arrange the long-sought face-to-face meeting with Wallace Selby. Andrew's father had respected Selby. Selby could offer work—more prestigious work than the crumbs he had sent so far. He could bring Andrew into the highest circles of scholarship.

She appeared to be mollified. She equated "work" with her work. He let her think it. He wasn't going to lay his needs bare to her, not now. He could see her throat working as she gathered thoughts.

"I hoped...I wanted..." she stammered, "to suggest that we finish the work before we try to change, that is, try to discuss or decide—to make something out of—" He let her stumble. *I'll be damned if I'm going to make it easy for her.* "Out of, out of what is between us. When we finish the work."

"The work," he repeated.

"Yes. The work. It brings us together."

"That it does, Love." Mistake that. She lit up like a candle. He couldn't go back to "my lady," but he vowed he wouldn't call her "Love" again. "That it does, Georgiana. It brings us together."

He thought she might be right that they could resolve the rest of it if they finished the work. He wondered if work would give her peace, time to come to terms with his proposal. *Perhaps it will.*

He stared at her. She worried her lower lip with her teeth and stared back with anxiety in her eyes. His own eyes, he thought, must be infinitely sad because sorrow made him mute.

Andrew looked away at last. He limped to the table and picked up the manuscript without enthusiasm. He would think about his other options tomorrow. "We were finishing Nossis, I believe."

"We are finished. 'She whom Aphrodite has not loved...' I understand her better now."

The she-devil! "You still have much to learn." She responded with a hungry look. "Greek," he explained. "You have much Greek to learn. Eros is one thing."

"The longing of one for union with the other?"

"Yes. Union. Physical and spiritual. There is also porneia: the taking of pleasure for oneself, the illicit, the vile." She looked as if he had slapped her. He didn't let her speak. "And rhaidios: behavior that is easy and reckless. Perhaps you wish to explore those also." *If it isn't mutual giving, Georgiana, what is it?*

"I see." She sobered now. Joy had fled, but he couldn't regret his words. He watched her take a shuddering breath and say, "What shall we work on next."

Change the subject, Georgiana. For now. She wouldn't look at him.

"Who is left?" he asked while he searched over the worktable for their index.

"Andrew." An odd note in her voice drew him to look up. "There is one more thing. I am going away for a while."

Away? Where could she go?

"Indeed she is." A familiar voice came from the door. He wondered how long Richard had been standing there. *Damn Glenaire's eyes. Can't he knock like mortal men?*

"Chadbourn is to be wed. My sister is summoned to attend."

Summoned. Normal people were invited.

"Hello, Richard," Andrew said. They were many years past titles and formalities, and not a few years past true warmth. "You look well." *Couldn't you allow me one day to adjust to my lover?*

"I could say the same for you. You found Peabody satisfactory, I presume?"

"More than satisfactory. The healing isn't perfect, but I'll do." He stood erect as if to demonstrate.

"Excellent. I wouldn't want my sister's... Tutor is it? To be incapacitated."

Andrew had no response for that.

"Will is to marry? I wonder why I received no invitation."

Glenaire lifted his well-bred chin. "Perhaps Chadbourn believed you too ill to travel."

And you didn't enlighten him.

Georgiana looked back and forth between her brother and Andrew. She looked as confused and uncomfortable as he felt. Glenaire never looked uncomfortable. He went on smoothly, "If the two of you have things to arrange for your little project, I won't keep you from it. Georgiana and I depart in the morning."

~

"Commentary on Praxilla." Georgiana underlined 'Praxilla,' the last item on the list. Organizing the work gave her a sense of being in control, or it did up until now. Today she needed to feel safe. It felt safe to arrange the work and their partnership.

Once Richard left the room, it took them an hour to sort the notes. Andrew responded to her suggestions and assisted her in packing up their notes with distant care.

He agreed to take two boxes home and work on the commentaries from her notes. She planned to take another box with her. It held assorted research on the two to three authors for whom translations were not yet finished.

"How long will you be gone?" His voice sounded hoarse. She realized it was his first comment on anything other than work in the past hour.

"I don't know. The wedding is in two weeks—just after Twelfth Night. Her Grace may well expect my presence at Mountview for a time. It has been three years." He looked skeptical. "They are my parents, Andrew. I will send you my notes as I finish them."

"That should work. I'll continue to polish the commentaries, make them more consistent in format." She nodded. They had agreed to it; he submitted to her direction meekly. In her estimation he acted much too meekly. She wished he would lash out. She was glad he didn't.

"Do you think Will really believes you are too ill to travel?" she asked at last.

"Perhaps. Who knows what Richard told him. Your brother doesn't want me there if you are to attend."

She felt sick at the bitterness in his voice.

"Some distance to think will do us good, Andrew," she said, side-stepping the issue. "We can finish the work and then we'll talk." She sounded like a pedantic schoolmaster even to herself, but she meant it. She needed distance. She needed to finish her translations. She needed to still the panic in her heart.

Andrew's eyes shot darts at her, but he didn't argue when footmen carried out his share of the boxes. Georgiana felt the darts and the suffocating heat that seemed to radiate from his body. She sighed when he started to follow the footman.

When she thought he meant to pass, he turned so suddenly that he knocked the breath from her body. Warm, strong arms imprisoned her, and he kissed her fiercely. Just as suddenly, he was gone before she could respond.

She believed she ought to be pleased with her perfect control of the situation—up until that kiss, that is. She clung to that thought while misery pooled around her and began to close in. He was gone; empty darkness remained.

Chapter Nineteen

Every hour took her farther from Andrew. Georgiana put her lap desk away hours before the carriage stopped, and she was left with nothing to do but count the miles between them.

Even people lucky enough to be able to read while moving, and Georgiana was one of the lucky ones, find detailed work and concentration difficult in a jolting carriage. With no partner to challenge her ideas, no colleague to share her enthusiasm, work became impossible. Richard rode outside for the last stretch of road, leaving Georgiana alone with darkening thoughts and intrusive, sensual memories.

She rejoiced to see the Crown and Goose in Bridgewater come into view and hours of dirt, awkward conversation, and muddy ruts come to an end. The muddy roads were frightful even in Richard's exquisitely appointed carriage. She sighed in gratitude that she had only one more day of travel to endure and that Murnane House lay a mere one hundred miles from Helsington.

Her brother's staff worked their usual magic. Clean sheets, hot water, and hot tea greeted her. Perhaps she might squeeze in an hour of work.

"Tea is in your sitting room. Dinner will be served in a private parlor in one hour." Richard pronounced. *So much for time to myself.*

"I won't be much company, Richard. Perhaps I'll take a tray in my room." Conversation between them lagged very early in the day. Richard showed no interest in her work and was impossibly closed-mouthed about his own life and his work for the government. Discussion about their family had been perfunctory at best.

"Nonsense. We'll dine together." He neatly ordered her evening, just as he ordered her life.

One hour later, Georgiana entered the private parlor to find a dinner suitable for the Duke of Sudbury's offspring, proper table service (unpacked no doubt from her brother's baggage train), and Richard, looking every inch the Marquess of Glenaire, holding a chair for her.

Georgiana resented his high-handed arrangements in spite of the comfort they brought. She stared at the first course and cast about for something to say that didn't sound petulant. Neither "How are the machinations at Whitehall these days?" nor "Has our lady mother expired of her own venom yet?" seemed appropriate. She chose silence.

Richard directed servants while he maintained what he considered the expected dinner conversation. She heard drivel about the weather, the road conditions, and current fashion. He went on longer than necessary about the likelihood that their sister Eloise would attend Chadbourn's wedding. Monosyllabic answers didn't deter him. His words became one long drone.

"Mm. Quite." She responded to one dry statement. She wasn't sure she heard him properly and didn't care.

"Georgiana! You haven't attended me this entire evening. I just told you Great Aunt Maud eloped with an elderly footman to the Antipodes, and you responded 'quite!' Are you well?"

"Well? Yes. Simply tired." The pudding placed before her revolted her. It would go back uneaten. "I should leave you to your port."

"I hardly think..."

She sat back down. Rebellion flared in her.

Fine. If he wants my company, I shall speak the thoughts that have haunted me all afternoon, and I will expect a real response.

"What caused the scars on Andrew's face?" She heard his

indrawn breath, but it didn't stop her. She was out of patience, and there was no other opening for what weighed on her mind. He would have to endure it.

"That isn't a proper question," Glenaire spluttered. "It's the man's private business." He tossed down his napkin.

His attack was a diversion. Georgiana's next question would be harder to sidestep. She folded her own linen napkin deliberately and set it beside her uneaten pudding.

"He got them doing your bidding." She opened with a statement not a question. "Did you know he was in danger when you sent him there?"

"Really, Georgiana, where is all this coming from?" Richard on the defense was a novel sight.

She refused to be intimidated when he resorted to his familiar glare.

"Did you, Richard?" She repeated.

"Yes. Death is always an option for a soldier," he ground out.

"Capture also?"

"Capture also when one is behind lines. The French were not kind." Richard looked as though he tasted something vile.

"They were brutal," she growled.

"Yes."

"Did you know that then at your desk at Whitehall?" She gave no quarter today.

"Of course. It was my duty to know. Andrew knew also. He volunteered for the mission."

"He volunteered for the mission perhaps but not the army. He never volunteered for the army, did he?" She kept her gaze steady, daring him to deny her words.

An odd expression flitted across his face. It might have been compassion. It might have been guilt. It disappeared quickly and took the gentle face of her beloved brother with it. Only the mighty Marquess of Glenaire remained.

"He made his own choice," he declared, eyes hard as steel, "and he did well. His service made him a wealthy man."

Wealthy? she thought. *Perhaps, but what had war cost him?* She wondered how much he earned with each of his scars.

Richard's eyes were implacable, and it was Georgiana who broke eye contact at last. Andrew made his own choice. Andrew, at least, had been given one. She had no choice at all. Her eyes dropped to her plate.

"Really, Georgiana, none of this is a fit subject for a lady. I won't have it."

Ask me about my work then. "What shall we discuss if not that, brother? How is our esteemed father? How goes the estate?"

"His Grace is well, and Sudbury thrives—as I believe we discussed this morning." He spat it out impatiently.

That was it then for family intimacy. Richard was one more man who didn't care to inquire about what really mattered to her.

"I beg you to excuse me. There is work to do before bed."

She thought he might ask, "What work?" Instead he saw her gone with a bow and relief he didn't bother to hide.

Alone in her room, Georgiana leaned against the door. *'The French were not kind,'* her brother had said. Andrew's scarred body flashed through her mind. The French were brutal. *Richard knew. Richard sent him.*

Emotional collapse accomplished nothing and held no place in Georgiana's universe. She forced herself upright and picked up her inlaid lap desk and the heavy portfolio with it, both thoughtfully arranged on her bedside table by Richard's servants.

She flipped through pages of vellum until she located her most recent translations of Praxilla of Sicyon's fragmentary poems. The work looked adequate, but Georgiana no longer settled for adequate. There was no eros here, merely domestic concerns. She closed her eyes momentarily, forcing her mind into Praxilla's world. Blank walls greeted her in every direction. She knew nothing of Praxilla's world. She damned her lack of education for the thousandth time.

A moment later she picked up her quill and began to write notes for the partner she could no longer see, the colleague she could no longer debate.

She wondered if he also worked alone by lamplight in the house on Little Saint Mary's Lane. It gave her comfort to imagine him there. A slight smile relaxed her face and eased her heart. She listed questions for Andrew and began to anticipate his answers. He would answer. He wouldn't fail her.

Sir Isaac Newton glared down at Andrew from his pedestal on the end of the book shelf. He, Sir Francis Bacon, and marble busts of the other distinguished Cambridge alumni seemed to view Andrew's work with great skepticism. They were cold comfort and no substitute for Georgiana's wit and enthusiasm. He ignored them.

A familiar voice broke into his concentration. "All these wonders and you wish to read Praxilla? Isn't she the dreadful poet who—"

"—dared put cucumbers and the sun and moon on an equal footing?" Andrew capped Geoff Dunning's quote, the well-known assessment of the poet. "Good morning, Dunning. How are you?" Pleasure flooded him. There had been no one to speak to in over a week—not since Georgiana left, taking half the work and all his heart. Company felt good.

"I am well, Andrew, but surprised to see you here. Good to see you working, though." The greeting appeared to be equally sincere. Geoffrey Dunning may be a bit of a fuzzy academic, but he was a kind man and an excellent scholar. "But Praxilla? I thought old Selby had you on the Neoplatonists."

"This isn't for Selby. I finished a passage for him two days ago. He doles his bounty out slowly. I'm still waiting for another."

Dunning nodded sympathetically. "But Praxilla?" he asked. "A diversion?" If Dunning suspected Andrew was helping Georgiana, he didn't say.

"Have you actually read Praxilla?" Andrew asked.

"No, no. Goodness no. Her work isn't much studied," Dunning said, shaking his head. "Zenobius put her in her place two thousand years ago. You just quoted him—cucumbers and all."

"Yes, I know what Zenobius said. 'Only an idiot would put cucumbers on a par with the sun in the same verse.'" Andrew thought Zenobius as narrow-minded as Watterson and the others. They maligned Praxilla as they maligned Georgiana.

"Does seem a bit strong. Perhaps Zenobius mistook her meaning. Did she really write about cucumbers?" Dunning's suggestion stunned Andrew.

"Listen to this verse, yourself, Dunning. Tell me what you think of it.

THE FAIREST THING I leave is the light of the sun
And the next the bright stars and face of the moon
and also ripe cucumbers, apples and pears.

ANDREW POINTED TO THE TEXT. "What do you think it means?"

"Probably not much more than is obvious. She seems to be cataloging pleasures of life—things one would miss." Dunning squinted to reread it. "Perhaps for Apollo in Hades."

Andrew smiled at the man's earnest interest. "It does seem to refer to death, doesn't it? What little pleasures would you miss, Dunning?"

The impassive scholar appeared to give that serious thought. After a moment he said, "Sunlight of course—"

Andrew raised a brow, giving him a schoolmaster's best frown as if to say 'you can do better.'

"—in the morning, on the Cam!" Dunning finished.

"Be honest, Geoff, what would you really miss?"

"Soft sheets, scones and butter, my good leather chair, a delicious beverage I receive at Christmas from a cousin who is a pastor in the glens, deep in the Highlands—but not one of them would be subject for high poetry. Those are domestic things."

That was it then. Praxilla's work—and Georgiana's—dismissed in one blanket statement.

"High?" Andrew's anger flared. "Who is to say what is high?"

Andrew could not think of any poet who wrote of everyday things. Neither the odes of Keats nor the oddity of Coleridge covered tea and scones. Perhaps they should.

"Love, ladies, nature, mythology—who decides what subjects are fit for poetry?" Andrew demanded.

Dunning didn't take offense at Andrew's vehemence. "Good question, old boy. The consensus of the scholarly community one supposes. Interesting question, that."

"Can you think of one who wrote of scones and jam?"

Dunning looked surprised by the question but gave it serious thought.

"Not any of the respected poets. There's that Scots fellow, Burns. He writes of domestic things. No scholars, certainly." Dunning furrowed his brow. "Must be others. 'Pon thought, can't think of any reason why one can't make a verse of homely things. Praxilla did, didn't she?" He smiled at Andrew. "Translating them, are you?"

"My partner is."

Dunning raised his eyebrows as if to ask about the partner but didn't voice it. "How is the work progressing?" he asked instead.

"Well enough. Some questions have arisen though. What do we know of Greek eating habits?" *That is Georgiana's question.* She had asked what was known about the foods and other simple pleasures of ancient Greece.

"You mean, if they had no scones for comfort, what would they turn to?" The thought amused Dunning.

Andrew grinned back at him.

"Might be interesting to find out," Dunning said. "Somewhere in this temple of knowledge we should be able to find that between us, old boy. Shall we have a go? What do you have so far? Old Featheringham the librarian will let us up in the stacks if I ask him."

Georgiana would love this. It was a pity Old Featheringham would never have the pleasure of her curiosity and intelligence.

Hours passed before Andrew finally packed away his notes. Dunning was long gone. Andrew picked up the papers and made his way through the reading room to the gated entrance, passing under brilliantly painted glass of the arched transom, burnished to a dark gold in the setting sun. The students who passed with him ignored its message: Honi soit qui mal y pense. In English, it meant "shamed be the person who thinks ill of another." *They don't often practice it either.*

Old Featheringham scowled when he passed, reminding Andrew how lonely he felt. Dunning's company had cheered him, but Dunning wasn't Georgiana.

God how I miss her! He ached to have her by his side. His dialogs with Georgiana delved layer by layer down into the ideas of the poets, prodded on by her persistent questioning. Together they produced far better work than either of them could have managed alone.

Andrew turned toward the Cam, grateful his improved gait let him walk across the commons to the river. Georgiana's voice, its throaty undertones pitched exactly right to recite the women's works, aroused him even in memory. Memories of her lilac scent were still his nemesis; now they carried the added burden of remembered lovemaking.

He worried that she might never come back. He tried to push the thought from his mind, but fear lurked in the shadows of darkening Cambridge. She had been gone barely a week, but each day felt to him like a thousand years. The first set of questions arrived yesterday; he would have to be content with them. For tonight, he would compose his response. He would give as generously of his mind as he longed to give generously of his very self.

"Ardmore, must you overfill my plate?" Ardmore's countess, the former Eloise Hayden stretched out her nasal drawl but skillfully avoided slipping into a whine that guests nearby might perceive as low-class. "You know my appetite is dainty." She rolled her eyes in disgust and tucked into the plate of delicacies from the Duchess of Murnane's overflowing wedding breakfast.

Georgiana tore her eyes from the bride and groom and smiled up at her brother-in-law. Weak of chin, dim of mind, and plump of pocket, the Earl of Ardmore was perfect for her sister Eloise and harmless enough.

Eloise downed the lobster patties and cheese pastries from the Murnane House chef with more energy than she had exhibited for any other activity. Georgiana let her eyes drift back to the couple making their graceful way among their guests. Chadbourn leaned possessively over his bride, one hand at her back, guiding her. He stooped to whisper in her ear before each encounter to explain every distant cousin and interesting acquaintance. The new countess glowed with a calm joy that clutched at Georgiana's heart.

"How can you stand to watch that performance and still eat, Georgiana?" Eloise demanded. "All that billing and cooing positively turns one's stomach." She popped another pastry into her mouth and licked her fat little fingers.

Marianna, youngest of the Hayden children tittered musically, a carefully modulated titter designed to strike a balance between appreciation of her sister's wit and unseemly laughter. "They are overflowing with nauseating sentiment, are they not?" she said.

Her remark drew a sharp look from her mother. "Young ladies do not remark on the behavior of their hosts," the Duchess pronounced. She shared a knowing look with Eloise and went on archly, "Even if the remarks are true."

Marianna sunk back into her habitual pout. "One can become

quite weary of being reminded of all the things young ladies cannot do," she fussed.

"Catch a husband, Marianna," Eloise said with a smirk in Georgiana's direction, "and then you may do as you please."

Georgiana squeezed her eyes shut for a moment and tried to let the barb fall away. Her armor wore thin after time in her mother and sisters' company. She glanced up at her brother and pondered his remote look. The clockwork efficiency of his mind at work almost shown forth behind ice blue eyes. She wondered if he was busy maintaining the Sudbury estate on his father's behalf, seeing to the welfare of the entire country, or managing the lives of all his friends to suit his own notions of rectitude. All of the above at once, she suspected, while delicately partaking of the wedding breakfast and never once leaving so much as a crumb on his pristine neck cloth.

Glenaire's sudden movement caused her to straighten. He rose to his feet in one fluid motion and bowed over the bride's hand before Georgiana realized the couple had reached their table.

"Lady Chadbourn, my congratulations," Glenaire said, giving her a look that held more approval than warmth, a look that seemed to say he had inspected her and found nothing lacking. He probably had. He and the Earl exchanged an enigmatic look. Chadbourn nodded before turning to the ladies.

The Earl formally introduced his wife to the Duchess as "My Countess." Georgiana's formidable mother gave the woman a perfectly correct nod of acknowledgement, confident that her superior rank demanded no more. The Earl frowned slightly but didn't look surprised.

"Lady Georgiana, what a pleasure to see you," he exclaimed with warmth and (Georgiana suspected) some relief. "It has been too long. Let me make known to you my wife." The word "wife" echoed with pride.

"It is a pleasure to meet you, Lady Chadbourn," Georgiana said.

The lady smiled back. "Call me Catherine, please. Will has told me how much your friendship and your brother's meant to him growing up." She tossed a teasing glance at Glenaire who stunned Georgiana by smiling back.

The Earl chuckled. "I suspect we're long past the need for titles, Georgiana. Can you bear it?"

Georgiana laughed back. "At least you didn't call me Lady Georgie, like Jamie Heyworth did the last time I saw him," she said. "Where is he, by the way? Hiding from matchmaking mamas?" A faint vibration to the table, the sure sign of her mother's sharply stiffening posture, should have been a warning.

The Earl grinned. "Probably, but I actually believe he and some of my rapscallion cousins have gotten up a match in the billiard room where there is more freedom."

"And drinks other than tea or lemonade." The new countess said. More vibrations.

"I see you know our Jamie, already," Georgiana replied. She bit back a grin. *Let my mother be shocked,* she thought.

Catherine smiled at Glenaire. "Not all of Will's friends are quite so wild."

Glenaire bowed in acknowledgement. "Nor so thoughtless. This is your day."

"I'm just pleased Will's friends are here to share his happiness," Catherine said. "Even the less sober ones."

"You haven't met Andrew yet," Georgiana blurted out helplessly. Chadbourn shot Glenaire a speaking glance; Glenaire merely raised one eyebrow. The table quivered ominously. *The Duchess must be ready to explode.*

"The major?" Catherine asked. "No, I have not. Will had hoped to invite him, but Glenaire told Will he still suffered from his wounds and assured us it was kinder not to invite him. I understand he was the scholar of the group, and I am anxious to meet this soldier-scholar. I think I will like him very much."

Georgiana thought she heard an unladylike snort from her mother's direction? *Surely not. Perhaps an outraged puff of air?* Looking at Catherine's intelligent brown eyes, Georgiana found it easy to ignore the Duchess. "You would like him very much, I think," she said. Her voice came out a deep and breathless murmur.

"I have no doubt of it. If we can't get him here, we'll have to come round to Cambridge and invade his solitude."

A few more polite words, then they moved on. Georgiana felt a sense of loss come over her like a cloak. One didn't need to be the only one in a room, she knew, to know loneliness. It was possible to sit among many people and be entirely alone.

As if from a distance, she heard her mother's hiss. "Really, Georgiana. First names with that woman? The title at least gives her the facade of respectability. One must keep climbers like that firmly in their place. And Mallet! Did you have to mention that jumped-up schoolmaster's son?" Outrage shook her jowls and pinched her mouth.

Georgiana watched Catherine smile up at Chadbourn as they floated to another table. The love she saw there pulled at her heart. *"She whom Aphrodite loved."* Georgiana could see with absolute clarity that Catherine knew "what sort of roses the flowers are."

She felt a firm pinch and turned back to the outraged face of her mother. "You're becoming common, Georgiana. It will not do. You've been left on your own too long. You shall come back with us to Mountview for a good long while, long enough to pound some sense of your family's consequence back into you. I shall insist on it." With a flounce, she turned one sturdy shoulder to Georgiana and her face to her other daughters.

"A good long while." Georgiana groaned helplessly. She thought she should warn Andrew. *Will he care.*

Chapter Twenty

"If you ain't going to eat, give a man warning so he don't waste time in the kitchen." Harley yanked a plate away.

I should hire a real cook, Andrew thought. Work absorbed Andrew for the first six weeks since Georgiana had dumped work in his lap and left. He forgot about cooks until now.

"Take it back, Harley. Bread and cheese will do."

"Fine then. Them I can buy. No need to muss the pots."

Or burn the pots. Andrew would fetch lunch at one of the little coffee shops tomorrow, if he felt like eating.

Harley dropped plates in a dry sink. Andrew ignored lunch; he ignored Harley, and he ignored muffled banging in front of his house.

Georgiana's last letter lay spread out on the worn table. She sent two short cryptic notes during her journey to Mountview after Chadbourn's wedding, each scribbled out in haste in a moving carriage. They looked it.

Muffled voices floated into the kitchen with the scent of rain. Andrew cursed the date on the last letter, three weeks past. *Damned woman gets to Mountview, and she forgets the work. She forgets me.* He tipped the paper toward the window light.

Harley's voice sounded more irritable than usual. Andrew reread the letter, looking for something personal. There was none.

Chadbourn and his countess (Will's beloved!) are four days gone on their wedding journey, and the Hayden caravan makes its way to Mountview in slow stages.

Georgiana consistently referred to the young woman as "Will's beloved." The Earl must be besotted. He had hoped Georgiana was as envious as she sounded. Three weeks without word made him less confident. He should have gone to the wedding. Will would have welcomed him.

"Sorry to barge in. Not the way for a proper call." Geoff Dunning stood in the doorway. Rain dripped down his neck and onto the shoulders of his professorial gown.

"Not at all. Delighted to see you!" The delight was genuine. Dunning had promised to hint to Wallace Selby that Andrew waited for more work. He had nothing else to do. The poetry and commentary had been assembled into a manuscript. It wanted only his partner's review and comment. Andrew desperately needed work, something to keep his mind off Georgiana.

"You have work for me?" he asked.

Dunning took the seat Harley offered. "Hot tea wouldn't go awry," he said with a twisted smile to Harley. "Beastly out."

Harley grunted and put the kettle on to boil.

"Sorry, Dunning. It must be urgent to drive you out on an afternoon like this." Andrew's eyes continued to scan Georgiana's letter. She wrote, "I am expected to stay until Lady Day, if not longer."

Lady Day—the March quarter day—another six weeks!

"Not urgent. Going to Gran's for early supper."

Andrew forced his attention to Dunning. "Your Grandmother's? Good of you to stop by."

"Thought you should know soonest." Dunning's neck shown red in spite of the cold rain.

The misery of his expression made Andrew go as cold as the rain. "Know what?" he asked cautiously.

"There won't be work. Sorry to be blunt." Dunning looked away, embarrassed.

"Mallet? Do you hear? Can't dress it up for you. No more work." Dunning's distress increased.

"No work?" Andrew repeated. He looked for misunderstanding. Dunning looked steadily back. There was no misunderstanding, and there would be no work.

"You had better tell me all of it," Andrew said.

Dunning did. He left nothing out, not even the color of Selby's face when indignant—puce. "Murchison wasn't indignant. Fairly gloated. He..."

"Murchison? What did that slimy specimen have to do with it?"

"Didn't I say? That was the worst of it." Dunning reached up gratefully and took a mug of tea from Harley. "He's taken on an assistant. 'An assistant,' Selby called him!" Now Dunning looked indignant.

"Murchison? He took on Murchison?"

"Man's a fool, Mallet. Can't see a grasping mushroom when one ripens in front of him."

Bile curdled in Andrew's belly. Murchison. He wanted to cast up his accounts on the tabletop. "Tell me again exactly what he said. Selby I mean, not that snake Murchison."

Dunning breathed deeply, "I don't see how it would help."

"Tell me again. Exactly."

"'Can't have my reputation sullied. I worked long and hard for it. If the man can't keep his mind above trivia, he shall not be part of my great work.'" Dunning mimicked Selby. He repeated, "'My great work.' Prancing pony thinks he's Plato himself."

"Trivia?"

"Praxilla. Can't say how he found out. Old Featheringham perhaps."

"Murchison."

"How's that?"

"Murchison," Andrew repeated with greater confidence. "I saw him at the library that day. He must have bribed Featheringham."

"Just the sort to do it. Lots of the lazy ones think they can get librarians to do their work for them." Dunning's brow furrowed. "Sorry, Mallet. Selby's a prig."

"Tell me again what he said."

"Which thing? Took an assistant?"

"The rest. Did he really call Praxilla trivial?"

"Puce. Turned puce at the thought."

Murderous rage froze Andrew with ice-cold intensity. Selby dismissed five months of Andrew's work and ten years of Georgiana's life as trivia. Hands clenched as if to squeeze the puce neck of the arrogant old windbag.

Three hours later Andrew remembered Georgiana's letter, carried it to the study, and lay it next to the completed manuscript.

Rereading it didn't improve the words. "It will be more difficult to correspond from Mountview." she had written. She should have said "impossible." *The duchess, that scorpion, has had her in her poisonous clutches for weeks.*

"These are the last of the translations," she wrote. Georgiana declared the translations finished. Andrew thought of the commentaries. His parts were complete, but they needed her approval.

He read the next line. "The work approaches an end, and that saddens me." *Saddens her?* He almost choked on his anger. The end of their partnership loomed in front of him, and all she had to say was that it saddened her?

She told him they would talk when the work was done. It was done, and yet she stayed at Mountview.

Damn it woman, what do you want from me?

He could do nothing without further word from Georgiana. Now he had no work from Selby either, nothing to banish Georgiana's ghost, the ghost that paced his book-lined study, gesticulating and peppering him with questions.

Andrew poured brandy in a glass and drank it down to banish the image, and another image replaced it—Georgiana looking sidelong at his bedroom with another question in her eyes.

Andrew commanded men. He bent unruly partisans to do England's bidding. He outwitted two French colonels and survived the hell of interrogation with honor intact, but he couldn't bend Georgiana. He couldn't even write to her. She was at Mountview, and he sat like a pensioner waiting some scrap of attention from Lady Bountiful.

I'll be damned if I sit here any longer and wait while her miserable family finds excuses to isolate her again. Only one choice remained.

"Harley! You rogue, get up here. We need to pack."

"On the contrary. She is lovely, and quite articulate."

Georgiana's words echoed through the Hayden family's massive dining room. Utter silence greeted it. She regretted the urge to defend Chadbourn's bride from the vicious description her sister had just spewed. Chadbourn's countess didn't need her defense, and it had no impact in any case.

Her Grace the Duchess of Sudbury paid Georgiana no heed. A faint pursing of lips was the only indication that she had heard. She nodded to a footman to serve the evening's pudding, a fine cake with a hot caramel sauce, appropriate for the end of winter. She turned to Eloise, as though Georgiana hadn't spoken.

"You couldn't be more correct. The woman is utterly common, not one trace of grace. The entire wedding was an ordeal." Her fat little hand, heavy with rings, lifted an excessively ornate silver spoon, signaling to the others that they might commence as well. His Grace, regal in habitual silence, sat in the great carved chair at the head of the table. He ignored the women's conversation. Glenaire, the heir, on His Grace's left, took his cues from his father.

Georgiana sat adrift in the middle and wondered what Glenaire found to occupy his mind during these interminable dinners. She thought she ought to ask him, as she could use help learning the skill.

Her mind drifted back to Chadbourn's lovely wedding, and she felt sympathy for the new countess. No, not sympathy. Envy. The bride and groom had glowed with love for one another, and the woman didn't need Georgiana or anyone's support.

"One needed to attend, of course." Georgiana's mother droned on. "Her Grace of Murnane would invite the world to her brother's wedding, and one could not refuse. How she could lend countenance to the bride I do not know?"

"His sister genuinely likes his bride, Mother. Imagine it." Georgiana pointed out. She moved her spoon through the caramel with aimless motions. No one took note of her comment. *I am invisible again,* she thought.

"Perhaps you needed to attend, but really, Your Grace, was it necessary to involve Ardmore and me?" At twenty-nine, Eloise already wore her mother's habitual sour expression. "Attending simply lowered oneself." Eloise's petulant voice clashed with her fine lace dinner dress. She looked as if she had encountered an insect in her soup.

It might have done Eloise good to have actually talked to the woman, Georgiana thought. She put her spoon down, appetite fled.

"Chadbourn always tended to be a bit déclassé—as was his father before him. The man practically doted on his children." The Duchess sniffed as she spoke.

Georgiana's stomach clenched. Loving one's children just was not done. Chadbourn and his lady were utterly besotted and made no effort to hide it, much to her mother's disgust. Longing overwhelmed Georgiana when Will turned to face his bride in the church, love glowing from every inch of him. Once she wouldn't have understood what she saw. Once she, too, might have mocked them. Now, she envied them. Now, she knew *what flowers these roses are.* A very private smile crept, unbidden, to her face.

"Really, Georgiana, if you are going to fidget with your food and smile like a buffoon, you may as well leave the table. I command it." The Duchess sneered down her nose in distaste.

Georgiana began to rise but froze like a frightened rabbit in the face of her mother's disapproval. She despised herself for it.

Glenaire ignored his mother's disapproving glare and rose smoothly to assist his sister. "Are you well?" He pitched his voice for her ear alone. Some of the old affection filled her.

"I am well. I prefer my room. Let it go, Richard." The preference was real; humiliation stung.

Glenaire lifted her hand and kissed the top. "Perhaps tomorrow we can walk."

"I would like that."

"Do get on, Georgiana. Glenaire, you disrupt dinner. A gentleman does not disrupt conversation." Voices faded behind her as Georgiana left the room. She used all her strength to avoid running.

Mountview's air of menace, the constant threat of maternal abuse, followed her up the stairs. She vowed that when she broke free again she would never let them drag her back. She wasn't sure what she would do, but she knew she would do nothing that threatened her fragile independence. Nothing. Ever.

Finely waxed floors and priceless carpeting led the way to an over-stuffed room at the back of the house. She knew it was slightly less fine than the better guest rooms, infinitely more luxurious than the upper servants, and a great deal shabbier than the quarters assigned to Eloise and Ardmore. She hated it.

Nothing there raised her spirits. Her notes, scattered on the table, were days old. The steady stream of correspondence with Andrew that flowed rapidly while she had been a guest of the Duchess of Murnane stopped when she came to Mountview.

Here in her father's house, she feared discovery. Anything sent from this house was vulnerable to prying eyes. She feared that her letters would reflect her love for Andrew. Even if they didn't, fear of censorship made her reluctant to send her questions and ideas. At best, her work would be mocked. At worst, they might trap her here and attempt to prevent the work from going forward.

Georgiana lifted a fine gold chain from around her neck and pulled a tiny key from her bodice. She leaned under her bed and pulled out a strongbox, glad no servant would bother to interrupt the objectionable daughter while the family was still at dinner.

The box opened quietly. Andrew's messages lay like treasured love letters wrapped in tissue. *Fool!* Each was signed simply, "*Yours, A. Mallet.*" Anyone reading them would know them for the business correspondence that they were. No one would mistake them for love letters. Yet, they lay wrapped in tissue and locked in a small strongbox as if she feared discovery.

Andrew had sent no letters in more than a month. She assumed that he was being cautious also or that he was waiting for her to write. Either way, it was safer, she knew, but she missed his letters terribly. She missed him.

She replaced the box in its hiding place and went to the window, as she did every night, and began to count the miles to Little Saint Mary's Lane. She pictured the roads. She could be back in Cambridge in two days. Perhaps Glenaire would arrange it sooner. She would ask him again tomorrow.

She didn't know if the man who wrote those careful, businesslike letters would welcome her. She wondered if he looked out his window and thought of her or if he was absorbed in work. She had hurt him. He might not wish to continue the connection. She did, even if she still had no idea what sort of connection she wanted.

Two days. If she had a carriage. If her father would permit it. If she had the courage to leave. Two days.

Two nights later, Mountview's grizzled gatekeeper informed Andrew with exaggerated generosity that, while his chaise wasn't permitted inside the gate, Andrew might walk to the manor if he chose to try his luck at the servants' door.

Andrew looked at the man's hulking bulk, barrel-shaped legs, and massive arms. He reined in the urge to drive on, dismounted, and began to walk. The manuscript, secure in its leather folio, lay under his arm while wind whipped his coat about. Pain in his back and hip, aggravated by the long ride and the cold, reminded him of how he had felt months ago. The vigor of recent months deserted him, but he soldiered on.

The year had stretched deep into February. March loomed in a few days. The wind still attacked with a bite, but dusk came a bit later. Wind threatened the portfolio with its precious manuscript. He pulled it more tightly to himself with one arm and grasped the silver lion's head on his ebony cane with the other. He leaned his head into the wind that roiled his hair and brought tears to his eyes.

Mountview's massive shape blotted out the sky. Light glowed in every window as if to call out to him, while at the same time the gray stone walls, dark in the moonlight, stood ready to keep him out. It had always been so.

As a boy, he had come here with the heir, permitted in but not welcomed. This time he came as an outright intruder. The impulse to seek the tradesman's entrance flooded him for a fierce moment, but he shook it off. He would enter by the formal entrance.

Night brought no poetic softening to life inside the Hayden household. Georgiana sat stiff-backed in the corner of the family stateroom. Her impeccably correct gown, high-necked and edged in lace, fell in straight lines of navy blue silk, heavy and rich, to the floor. She felt as if her hair, drawn back in a tight knot and covered with an exquisite lace cap, must emphasize the misery lodged deep in the bones of her face. She faded more every week that passed without meaningful work, Peabody's health regime, or word from Andrew. Her will to defy the family weakened daily, and she knew it.

The Duchess of Sudbury held court on a gold brocade sofa before the fire. The Countess of Ardmore, draped her gown artfully around her, tilted her head to catch chandelier light, and gracefully occupied a matching chair. Her husband faded into the shadows of the room, a pale wraith outshone by Hayden splendor. The Duke himself stood in silent dignity to the right of the fireplace. Lady Marianna Hayden sat straight-backed on a small chair just below her mother's.

The room's final occupant, her brother Richard, every inch the Marquess, stood removed from the rest. His posture, while no less dignified, didn't condescend to being part of the carefully arranged tableau before the fire. He sat at a splendid mahogany secretaire and observed his eldest sister.

Georgiana returned Glenaire's gaze without blinking and with little warmth. Neither Glenaire nor His Grace found it convenient to arrange her return to Cambridge after Candlemas or on any day since. She knew Richard couldn't or wouldn't understand her need to return.

They waited in silence for the summons to dinner. The finely carved double doors between the atrium and the family sitting room swung open with a well-oiled swoosh just as the clock in the entrance chimed the hour. All eyes turned in anticipation. The Duchess raised a languid hand for assistance and made an impatient sound. "The announcement, Peters!" she demanded.

The butler's tones were funereal. "Your Grace, I must beg your pardon. A caller has arrived who will not be repelled. He asks for the Lady Georgiana."

Georgiana felt as if air had rushed from the room. Her heart lurched in her breast, beating so strongly she believed the others must see it pounding in her chest. She forced her features to show indifference and her eyes to focus on her father.

"Show the impertinent intruder to the tradesman's parlor." The Duke spoke in bored tones.

The butler looked pained, as if he couldn't bring himself to admit he had tried and failed. The Duke of Sudbury made a gesture of impatience. "Very well. Don't delay dinner. I won't be long."

"Yes, Your Grace. Dinner is served."

Hope warred with confusion. She knew it had to be Andrew, but she wondered what would cause him to come. He hated Mountview.

"Glenaire, escort your eldest sister to the dining room." The Duke skewered Georgiana with a look of command and left the room.

The Duchess chose to overlook the breach of protocol. She sailed through the door alone, with the Earl and Countess of Ardmore following in strict precedence. She assumed her son and his sister would follow in her wake.

The hand Georgiana placed on her brother's arm shook. If he noticed, he didn't comment. He covered her hand with a warm and reassuring one of his own.

Numb feet carried her into the massive atrium. She stopped abruptly. Andrew stood starkly black and vividly alive against the massive white wood and glass entrance. It towered over him, and yet he presented a picture of raw Gothic power. His strong body covered in rich black fabric, his arm extended, one hand on the ever-present ebony and silver walking stick, and his scarred face set in lines of steel radiated strength and will. Only his tousled hair gave any hint of the humanity beneath the surface.

When he saw her, a look of longing broke free from his iron self-control. It transformed his features, only to be masked with equal determination at the sight of the Duke who walked toward him.

Georgiana lurched forward, but her brother's arm drew her to the dining room. She could follow Richard or make a scene that might make things worse. She chose to follow, at least for a moment. Her heart sang. He was there.

~

"We're not accustomed to uninvited guests at the dinner hour. I'll allow you two minutes. You will explain yourself, Mallet, and then you will be on your way."

It wasn't a promising beginning for a marriage proposal, but it was no less than Andrew expected.

"My business, Your Grace, is with your daughter."

"The Lady Georgiana is at dinner. You may convey your business through me."

The Duke, ramrod straight at seventy, had the Hayden height and long years of skill in using it to intimidate. Andrew looked up at the Duke and remembered a time when that ploy had succeeded with him. "I'll see your daughter, Sir."

"You will not. She doesn't wish it. She doesn't wish dealings with a schoolmaster's son."

A flicker of doubt burned like acid at Andrew's heart; it eroded his confidence. He knew that he could lay this man flat and let the devil take the consequences. He would have if he had been sure she wanted him, but he wasn't.

He knew the Duke could be telling the truth. She had refused his hand; she hadn't written in weeks, and she had walked past him in the entrance. In Cambridge she had wanted him badly enough to invade his house. He had no way to know whether or not she still wanted him or on what terms?

He opened his mouth to deny her refusal, but before he could reply, another voice spoke behind him.

"She doesn't wish it." Softer but equally aristocratic, Glenaire's voice cut in. Andrew turned awkwardly, leaning on his cane. He made no pretense of disbelief. The look he turned on his one-time friend held anguished questions and agonized longing. He found no mercy. Richard Hayden stood with calm dignity in the doorway.

"Andrew, whatever affection she may feel or have felt, she understands that it will not do. Go. Don't make this worse for her." His eyes urged compliance.

"Go now, or I'll have you thrashed and removed!" the Duke of Sudbury said in a voice constructed of ice shards. "Immediately."

Andrew's hand itched to lash out in one great sweep of his ebony walking stick. His common sense told him it would do no good. A dozen footmen were at their command. Lashing out would bring only his injury and her humiliation.

"I have something for her," he said.

"I'll see that she gets it." Richard reached for the parcel. Long years of experience told Andrew it wouldn't be wise to let go of the manuscript. The Haydens knew little of Georgiana's skills and her work, and what they did know they despised. He wouldn't entrust this to them.

Georgiana may not want him, but she wanted the manuscript. He hugged the portfolio closer.

"No. I don't think so. I have no wish to complicate her life, Richard. If she is content to stay here, so be it, but I'll keep this."

Andrew couldn't read Glenaire's face. Both men knew they had decided this once before.

"It's for the best," Richard murmured. Andrew nodded. He would leave it for now, but this time he would keep the work they did together.

Andrew turned to go. A vision of wrath confronted him. Georgiana stood just inside the room—her face a mask of rage.

"Have you gentlemen finished arranging my existence, then?"

"It's for the best," Georgiana heard when she slipped into the room. Just as they had before, her brother and Andrew planned to make decisions for her. Rage flooded her veins.

Andrew opened his mouth to speak; she stopped him with her eyes.

"How dare you come here without my consent?" *Never mind that I longed for you every day. Fairness be damned!* "'It is for the best?'" she mocked. "You always know what is best for me, don't you, Andrew? Richard? Did you know that, Your Grace? You needn't stir yourself or worry about my behavior. These two gentlemen have my life well in hand. They always did."

"Georgiana, I–" Richard spoke soothingly. Andrew, she noted, was mute.

"Mr. Mallet was just leaving." His Grace's cold eyes never left Andrew.

"I'm sure he was. Mr. Mallet always does what is best for me, doesn't he?" Her eyes dared him to deny it.

"Georgiana, this isn't the place," Andrew said.

"If it isn't the place, Andrew, why did you come here? You asked for me. You spend five minutes with His Grace, and you change your mind. Why? Because it is for the best? Whose best, Andrew?"

He looked about to speak, but her anger urged her on. "In Cambridge you thought marriage was for the best." She saw her father's face darken dangerously. "In London you thought the army was for the best—and look what it got you. Now what? I stay at Mountview, and you slink back to Cambridge? Then what?"

She wheeled on Richard. "And you brother? Are you satisfied with your investigations? Have my servants reported my every move? Why did you bring me here? To remember who I am? Lady Georgiana Hayden, child of peerage and power, ornament of aristocracy, ivory icon of superior breeding?"

She faced her father at long last. She didn't—couldn't—care about the Duke's stony face. Not this time. "I am sorry, Father, for this scene you so detest. You and Richard believe you can control my very life–with Mr. Mallet's collusion, of course. I won't have it."

The old man's brows rose; his eyes blazed, but she sped on before he could speak. "I will have my life the way I wish it. I won't stay at Mountview one day longer. You can arrange transportation back to my house—the house Aunt Sephronia left me—or I will take the first post in the morning. I should have done it weeks ago."

Words rushed from her, driven by rage and the remnants of fear. "Yes, I know you pay the bills. You needn't worry. I will burden you no longer, and neither will I dance to your tune. All I want from you is to be returned to my life. My. Life."

"As to you, Sir." She looked fire and sulfur at Andrew. "We agreed that when we completed the work we would talk. Very well, we are talking. Here is what I have to say: I find your services are no longer needed. When I return to Cambridge, I expect to find my notes, my translations, and any contributions you made to my work back at my house. Our partnership is at an end. There is, of course, no question of a relationship of any other kind."

She turned on her heels, too angry to say more, and swept past him. She didn't want to see his face, didn't want to know the pain there. She wanted to pack and be quit of Mountview.

Georgiana's heels clattered across the marble floor of the atrium to the broad sweeping stairway that led to the upper stories and the family quarters.

"Georgiana, I insist you return to your dinner. This is insupportable." From the third step, Georgiana saw her mother come out of the dining salon, outrage on every fiber of her being. The Duchess glared fire across the atrium. "Is that schoolmaster's son still here? Has no one thrown him out on his ear? Are there insufficient footmen to remove him?"

Over her shoulder, Georgiana saw Andrew, Richard, and the Duke at the door to her father's office. "You may rest easy, Your Grace. Mr. Mallet is leaving and will trouble us no longer." She looked directly at her mother. "And you will be relieved of my presence also. I won't spend one more day in this house. I am returning to Cambridge. Alone. To live my own life the way I choose. You can finally forget your troublesome daughter entirely."

The Duchess shook with indignation; her mouth moved as if seeking a retort that would not come. Behind the Duchess, Eloise's eyes blazed with hatred.

"You needn't fear, my loving sister." Georgiana said, her words dripping acid. "The life I live may not be to your liking, but it won't disturb your serenity. After tonight, you need never see me again."

"Georgiana!" Her mother's voice echoed in the vast atrium. She ignored it. She ignored them all; she climbed the steps purposefully, one by one. Behind her, Mountview's massive front door opened and closed. He was gone. It was over.

"Do CALM YOURSELF. It isn't like you to enact Cheltenham tragedy, no matter the provocation." Glenaire's habitual mask of hauteur and calm irritated Georgiana. She failed to master that particular Hayden trait. She growled in response.

"He chose to leave," Glenaire went on.

"This time at least he had a choice. He wasn't given one eleven years ago, was he?" Georgiana tossed a hairbrush into her trunk and followed it with a pile of handkerchiefs.

"You refer to his youthful enthusiasms?" Glenaire showed no surprise about the extent of her information. "My dear Georgiana, that outcome was preordained. He had no choice. He understood that. You should also."

"Oh yes, I know he believed that. He still believes it." Her voice dropped to a choked whisper. "I, on the other hand, beg to differ. He was wrong then, and he's wrong now. The two of you never asked me what I wanted, never gave me any choice, never let me control my own life."

"Georgiana, you are becoming hysterical."

The insult impacted her far differently than he intended. "You overreach Richard. I'm not as easily manipulated as the minions who do your bidding. I am a Hayden also, and I will have a voice in my own life."

"You don't—"

"Don't what? Know what you did to me so long ago?" she demanded.

"Remember your courtesy and stop interrupting me," he snapped.

She had no idea how any of them had survived the frigid air that passed for family life in in Mountview. Perhaps she hadn't survived it. Perhaps she was actually dead of the cold. She might have responded differently to Andrew's proposal if life ran in her veins.

"Very well, Richard. Explain to me why you and Andrew didn't give me a say in my own life all those years ago."

"He understood, as you apparently don't," Richard began with exaggerated patience, "that without His Grace's blessing the two of you had no chance to survive. You had no funds of your own—you still don't. He had none. Father would have made sure he never found employment, never earned a shilling. If you had attempted to live in romantic poverty, assuming for a moment the very poverty didn't kill your regard for one another, you would have been humiliated and destroyed, unable to return."

"Did His Grace know?"

"Certainly not. Do you have any idea what they would have done to you if he had learned of your foolishness? I averted further distress only by acting quickly. As a result, you've been able to live an independent life, for a woman, free from our mother's..." His voice trailed off, and a look of understanding passed swiftly between them. "Free at least to pursue your own interests."

"As long as I remained invisible and silent?" She dared him to deny it. "Free to exist in a gray half-world with my books and my garden, free as long as I didn't require companionship or warmth?"

"It is more than most unmarried women have. They didn't force you into the role of maiden aunt, unpaid companion."

"Only because Eloise wouldn't have me. She hired help for their children. She didn't want her impossibly gauche sister in her home. I didn't even have the affection of nieces and nephews to hold on to!"

He looked as though he saw her for the first time. "Would you have wanted the role of charity-dependent in your sisters' houses?" His bafflement almost touched her.

"I think sometimes the children would have been worth it, but no. Neither of them would have given me a moment's peace. It's irrelevant now. I chose my life in Cambridgeshire, and I was content with it."

"Was?"

She caught her lip between her teeth for a moment and chose words carefully. "Lately I have begun to see what I have missed and to desire, belatedly, to put it right."

Glenaire appeared thoughtful. She wished, not for the first time, she could read his mind. "And now?" he asked.

"You heard what I said downstairs. Now I wish to be left to my own life."

He examined her face, reading every detail. "Very well, Georgiana. If it's what you wish, go back to your books and to Helsington. You were at peace there. Go back."

"Oh, I intend to. I'll go back to Cambridge but not to how things were." Nothing would ever be the same. "I am finished with being under someone's control. I will sell Helsington."

"You can't!"

"Sell it? You forget–I own Helsington Cottage, not His Grace."

"How will you pay your servants, your green grocer?" He asked it calmly, but she thought he knew the answer. Helsington was large and well-appointed. Proceeds from its sale would keep her for a very long time, perhaps as long as she lived. She would find ways to supplement those proceeds. She might publish. A chill froze her bones at that. She wouldn't think about it now. Their eyes held for a long time. He knew her plans as though she spoke them out loud.

"Will you take me then?" she asked.

"You'll have the solitude and none of the comfort. Even the garden may not be possible."

"I'll manage. At least I'll have my independence. Will you take me home then?"

"This is—" He meant to say "home," but it wasn't, of course. Cambridge was home, and she was determined to make her own way.

He nodded sadly, but even as he did, she saw his mind at work. She had no illusions that he would stop his interference for good.

Chapter Twenty-One

Despair froze Andrew's heart, and disgust clawed at his stomach. Georgiana couldn't–*wouldn't*–break free of her toxic family. She clung to comfort and her work. She no longer wanted him, and she didn't need him.

Anger drove him in a wild frenzy away from Mountview, down pitted country lanes until he reached the Brighton Road where he turned away from the Sussex coast and north toward Cambridge. Twenty miles of blind rage and bone-rattling speed later, he slowed his chaise. The road led to Cambridge, but it passed through London.

London. The road aimed directly at London. The red fog that choked his mind began to clear, and an idea crystallized in its place. She may not want him, but she wanted her work. *Very well, Lady Georgiana, I will give it to you.*

She told him to send her notes back when he got to Cambridge. She didn't specify the form. Andrew resolved to give it to her as a printed book. *Why not?* He was a partner in the enterprise. It was his work too. Besides, he had burned his bridges with Selby and Cambridge. *It may be all I have to show for my work.*

The idea steadied him. He'd publish the book on his own, and they'd be done. He drove on to London in light of the full moon. By the next morning, Andrew had put up at the Pulteney Hotel, taken a suite of rooms, sent for Harley, and begun to search out printers.

Two weeks and seventeen rejections later, he found himself in the hotel dining room glowering at Jamie Heyworth over dinner, a black mood wrapped around him like a cloak.

"You say you've been in town for over a week? You might have called." Jamie's affront looked sincere, but it didn't hinder his appetite. He reached for another chop at Andrew's expense.

Andrew's glower deepened. Jamie did Glenaire's bidding again. *Damn Richard Hayden.* Even when Andrew turned on a whim to make an unplanned journey to London, Glenaire managed to know about it. Every innkeeper in England must be in his employ. Andrew may as well accept that he would never free himself of Glenaire's interference and stop blaming Jamie.

"You would have welcomed a visitor?" he ground out grudgingly.

"My rooms aren't much, but I'd have been happy to welcome you. Of course, with pockets to let, I'm not much of a host. Perhaps you knew that." Jamie's charm hid a storehouse of insecurities. A deadbeat father and newly acquired bankrupt estate were heavy burdens.

Andrew tried to make amends. "I don't care a fig for the state of your rooms. I'm just preoccupied. Came to town on business, not to socialize. Sorry to neglect old friends."

"Can't blame you, though. The damnable Haydens keep me tied up in their affairs." Jamie looked shamefaced. "I can't blame you if you're angry."

"What does Richard want this time?"

"Naught, I swear it. At least naught that he'll tell me. I think sometimes he asks me things so he has an excuse to give me money, not because he needs my help. Saw him yesterday. He mentioned; he thought you were in town. Didn't ask for anything. Knew I'd track you down, though. I can't afford to lose old friends. New ones are all puppies who don't know what's up or understand what it was like out there."

That much was true. Waterloo and what passed before marked everyone who fought there. Andrew's scars were visible; Jamie's were no less real. The young bucks of London had no idea.

"Andrew! Are you woolgathering or wishing me to perdition?" Jamie didn't sound offended. He rarely did.

"Woolgathering. I warned you I was preoccupied."

"How is your business faring?"

"Doesn't Richard know?"

"Give it over, Andrew. He never said why you're here, if he knows."

"He doesn't." He knew this probably was not true. Andrew took fresh horses at the Frog and Porter and turned directly to London. Somehow, Glenaire knew that much. Jamie's comments made it clear. Glenaire probably had him followed while he searched out every publisher and printer he could locate. He probably knew everything.

"It hasn't gone well–my business, I mean."

"Sorry to hear it." Jamie helped himself to more capon. "You look dog-tired."

Andrew grimaced. "Beyond tired," he said. "I've been searching for a printer for over a week. Most won't touch the work. Not enough popular appeal."

"Scholarly stuff?"

Andrew didn't dissemble well either. Glenaire probably knew in any case or would soon. "It isn't my work, at least not entirely. It's Lady Georgiana's."

"Odd's blood! No wonder Richard has been in a bother. Lady Georgie's scraps and bits are to be made into a book?"

"Most of the major printers won't have it. They say it's too esoteric. That is when they're being kind. When gentlemen want translations, they look for books by University scholars."

"Are they right?" Jamie didn't read enough to have an opinion.

"To a point. This work is unusual. I suggested that ladies might be interested. One said 'novels' were the thing. 'Ladies read Byron, but that's for his good looks and reputation, not his poems,' one said. Damned insulting."

"How many did you see?"

"Too many. One of them demanded to know the lady's name. He said 'scandal sells.' That about did it for me."

"Pity. Lady Georgie worked hard on this for a long time."

"You don't know the half."

"Still, it's not like you to give up."

"I'm not giving up. I found one more printer this morning that may do. I've an appointment tomorrow."

He wanted to be done with the whole ordeal and go home, but pride drove him to continue. He wouldn't let fear that the Haydens might block the printing force him to give up. He knew that the work deserved to be printed. He owed Georgiana that much. He owed himself that much. Tomorrow he would see Mr. Bailey, without question Andrew's best hope.

"If you don't want that fine sweet cake, I do." Jamie grinned at him slyly and snatched the cake. "Told you, Andrew, months ago, what you needed was a woman."

You have no idea how right you were. That thought made Andrew too morose to answer. He would see Bailey tomorrow, and his obligations as a partner would be done. His craving for her might never be done.

Jamie's face took on a momentary look of sheer bliss when he devoured the cake, but something about Andrew must have caught his eye. His face tensed into touching anxiety. No matter how difficult his life, Jamie did care about his friends.

Andrew spoke before Jamie embarrassed them both with it.

"Dinner again would be good, but somewhere other than this place. In fact, I have been given access to a box at the theater. Let's make use of it." It was a lie but an easily maintained one. Jamie couldn't even afford a floor seat; a night at the theater would do them both good.

Georgiana bent again to start the fire, her hands hampered by gloves. When it sparked to life, she felt her mouth spread in a wide smile. Small victories filled her with pride. This particular skill had taken Mrs. Potter an hour to teach her. She returned to her chair and poured a cup of steaming tea for the old woman and another for herself.

"Are you quite certain, my dear?" Edwina Potter's eyes darted with uncertainty. They were sitting in one of the upper rooms of Helsington, the only heated one.

"Quite. Even if I changed my mind, I don't believe there is any going back. Quarterly allowances were due a week ago. His Grace withheld funds. He knew I couldn't pay the staff. He sent them all their notices instead. He assumed I would return to Mountview with Chambers and the upper servants. They'll be absorbed into the Hayden estates."

"Eunice?"

"Is gone, praise God." The memory of poor Eunice torn between relief to be gone from her household and fear for the future brought a smile to her lips. Ridding herself of her forced companion was her first order of business when she returned to Cambridge, the first act of her newly emancipated life.

"I found her a place with my great-aunt's cousin in Wales. They will be good for each other, but I can't imagine just how the world will absorb the mountain of needlework they will leave behind." She sighed. "The rest progresses more slowly than I like. I'm just grateful that tradesmen here are willing to extend credit for fuel and food."

"Well, of course, they are! The Duke of Sudbury's daughter is a good credit risk if anyone is."

"More fools, they." A momentary anxiety so strong she feared her companion could see it wracked her body. "I'll manage. I'm sure of it. In any case, it is too late to go back. The estate agent already has prospects for Helsington. He found a small house in town—a kitchen below and two rooms above. It is at the end of Sheep Street and has a tiny garden, room enough for a rose bush or two. If I get a good price for this property, I think it'll do nicely. The estate agent will have the keys to show the house on Monday."

Mrs. Potter made an unladylike sound. "Really, Georgiana. You have no idea."

Georgiana forced a smile. "I'm beginning to. If the rest of the world manages, so will I, and I have you to turn to when my ignorance confounds me." It wouldn't do to show her fear. She needed Mrs. Potter's encouragement to continue.

"I can't say as I'm sorry you stood up to that family of yours. You're intelligent and strong but alone, dear! I don't wish to discourage you, but you must remember that I have a grandson to look in on me."

"I have friends," she said firmly.

"I won't live forever."

Georgiana patted her hand. "I'll have you for a good long time. I have other friends." The old woman looked at her skeptically. "There is Peabody. And Molly." Mrs. Potter's lips twitched. "I will make more friends. I can do it. I know I can, now that I'm out of my gilded cage."

"Of course you can, dear. If any woman could do it, you can."

"Will you come with me to see the house?"

Mrs. Potter nodded and took another sip of hot tea against the chill. A moment of silence passed companionably before she said, "Have you heard from that scoundrel, Andrew Mallet?"

"My messages to his house came back undelivered. I have no idea where he is." She fumed inwardly. She returned to find her notes in good order but incomplete. He had taken more in her absence and returned nothing. No notes. No translations. No Andrew. With luck, she would move in a few weeks. Without the work, she had no idea how she would fill her days once she did.

Georgiana jumped when a wrinkled hand reached over to pat hers. The naked sympathy in Mrs. Potter's knowing eyes shattered her. Her voice, thick with tears, protested. "Don't weave fairy stories, Edwina. I am angry about my work, only the work."

~

"A woman you say?"

"Yes," Andrew replied. "It's important for you to understand that the primary author of the work is a woman. She did the preliminary research and the final translations."

Bailey's print shop, Andrew's last chance, lay tucked in a small alley, the public mews really, just off Fleet Street. The place proved to be a happy surprise. Windows displayed a number of lovingly printed works. Most of them were poetry and history; there were no gossip rags or caricatures. It gave Andrew hope.

"Y'don't say! Poems by women. Greek. Translated by a woman?"

John Bailey, a small, balding man with perpetually rolled sleeves and an ink-stained nose, looked amused. He grinned infectiously. "Always did believe their minds work as well as ours. Better in some ways. Might make it a novelty to some folks, generate some interest that way."

The little man rubbed his chin doubtfully. Finding him had been a stroke of luck. He asked to see the work and left Andrew to cool his heels while he read it through. He handled the manuscript with care —and the respect it deserved—as he spoke.

"Marvelous work. What's the lady's name?"

"The lady prefers to remain anonymous."

"Pity that. Most of them do. Not that I've seen this work from a woman before. More than a pastime, this."

"The lady is a scholar."

"I can see that. Can't go to those fancy university presses, though, can she?"

"No. She can't."

"Still, if we're to do business, Mr. Mallet, perhaps you best tell me what you're struggling so hard to hide."

Bailey's was a small establishment with two to three books in wide distribution. He relied on small print runs from the aristocracy to stay in business. He might not want to risk the wrath of the Haydens. Andrew owed him honesty.

"The lady is the Duke of Sudbury's daughter."

Bailey's whistle was low and slow. "That bunch won't like the uproar, if there is one, now would they? Might add interest."

"No. The lady will remain anonymous."

"Pity that. And you act as her agent?"

"Yes." Andrew didn't hesitate. They had shaken hands. He was her partner.

"Fair enough. Too fine a work to go by the wayside, Mr. Mallet. Shall we talk business?"

~

"Do you plan to marry, Lady Georgiana?" Peabody beamed at her. Georgiana regretted the impulse that led her to ask him if he had changed his opinion about her ability to bear children. He had been so sure in her first visits, but that was months ago. She felt much better now. Strength and energy filled her. Her monthly problems had disappeared. It seemed pointless now, however. She felt like a fool for asking.

"No, Mr. Peabody, of course not. It is just that my courses have become normal." If anything, they had slowed and were late this month for the first time. "I feel infinitely healthier due to your regime. I wondered, that is all."

The little man's brown eyes warmed with sympathy. "I am delighted to hear that you feel so much better. You are remembering the dark green vegetables, I hope?"

"I had difficulty with some details of your regime while at Mountview, but now that I am home, I am following them to the letter." She wondered briefly how she would manage the Yorkshire spring with few funds, but she put the thought away. The other parts of her instructions would be easier without a high-strung chef to contend with. Henri paled at the thought of brewing tea from nettles, alfalfa, and seaweed. She had learned to do it herself very quickly. It had been easier to brew the tea than to gain access to Henri's kitchen, but she had managed. Beef tea, herbal tea, bushels of dark green vegetables, and iron-rich water—taken together they worked magic.

"Splendid! As to fertility, I can't say for certain. I wouldn't be unhappy to be wrong, but unless you put it to the test, we won't know, will we? Still, I see no barrier to you taking a husband if you wish."

His sympathetic face made Georgiana uncomfortable. She brought their consultation quickly to an end. She found no reason to linger. She wondered briefly if she could ask him to tea but quickly realized that that wouldn't do. She did not know how to go about making friends. She thought that perhaps Mrs. Potter might invite him.

He walked her to the door, chatting about town matters and mutual acquaintances. "Did I hear that Andrew Mallet has traveled from Cambridge?"

"That is correct Mr. Peabody. He is gone. I don't know where he went. Do you?"

"Goodness me, no. I am simply delighted that he is well enough to travel. We seem to have finally corrected his problems also." The little surgeon beamed with pride.

Ten minutes of vigorous walking brought Georgiana to Sheep Street and what was likely to be her new home. The estate agent, a rotund gentleman with jovial manner, sharp wits, and thinning hair, chatted with Geoffrey Dunning.

"Good afternoon, Mr. Dunning. Has your grandmother dragooned you on my behalf?"

"She told me about your dilemma, and I am only too happy to be of assistance." He smiled fondly at his grandmother. If Mrs. Potter needed a man's assurances, Georgiana would let her have it and try not to resent it.

"Shall we be about our business then? Mr. Wilson, what do you have to show me?"

"A trim little house, my lady. You will find no dry rot, no vermin, and no damp." He rocked on his toes briefly. "It is my obligation to warn you, however, that it isn't at all what you are used to."

"I understand, sir. That is as I expect."

"To give much better news, the sale of Helsington may bring even more then we discussed. Colonel Warrington is quite, quite anxious to purchase a comfortable home such as you offer, and you could–"

"Excellent, Mr. Wilson. I will be happy to get more money from the sale, but I am determined to conserve those funds by spending as little as possible on a new residence. Shall we take a look?"

Mrs. Potter, concern in every line of her face, took her arm and entered the narrow blue door behind her. Georgiana was grateful the woman made no attempt to dissuade her from her decision.

The little house didn't disappoint. The lower floor kitchen had stone walls and a stone floor. A large fireplace dominated one wall and a stairway ran along the other, the one shared with the neighbor. She would learn to cook for herself in this place. The upper story had two rooms: a small sitting room and a tinier sleeping chamber. She would bring her work here. She would write and be productive, if not fruitful.

The house, white with blue shutters, was situated farther back than its neighbors, leaving space for a tiny garden in front, one surrounded by a stone wall. It would have fit inside Helsington's stables with room to spare, but it would be enough for her.

Her head almost reached the top of the front door. She watched Geoff Dunning duck his head to go out, and it struck her that this house was even smaller than Andrew's house. It lacked his magnificent study. She suppressed all memory of the man. This house was enough.

"It is exactly as you described it, Mr. Wilson. Thank you." She turned to Geoffrey Dunning who inspected the foundation with earnest attention. She wondered if the amiable University Fellow even knew what to look for, but she humored him. "Mr. Dunning? Do you see any problem."

"No, my lady. If you are determined to take this step, this house is sound enough. The roof, I think, ought to be looked at, but the rest will give you no problems."

"Very well then, Mr. Wilson, I believe we have a contract. You may tell your buyer that Helsington is his as soon as I can arrange to move. Shall we say one week?" The little gentleman beamed at her and produced the documents for signature. He left her in the care of her friends with a key in her hand and a knot in her stomach.

She forced a smile. "Well then, Mrs. Potter. It is done. I need only lay in firewood, sweep the hearth, scrub the kitchen, sort through my belongings, and arrange an estate sale. It is good that I kept the services of at least one footman for the end!"

She looked around her tiny sitting room and fought panic. "Do you think the Colonel might want my furnishings?"

Edwina Potter said nothing. She leaned over and gave Georgiana a hug. Over her shoulder, Georgiana saw Dunning's look of disapproval. He would have to get over it.

Dunning looked at her intently and colored slightly. "Tell me, my lady, have you heard from Andrew Mallet. He is gone over a month now."

"No, I haven't. The knocker is still gone from his house."

"You went by Andrew's house, Georgiana?" Mrs. Potter looked bemused.

"It was on my way to Mr. Peabody's premises, Mrs. Potter," Georgiana's voice sounded tight. "I merely passed through Little Saint Mary's Lane." *And lingered a moment.* "Have you had word from him, Mr. Dunning?"

"Mercy no! Mallet left without warning. His departure was quite sudden. We had spent an entertaining afternoon not long before researching Praxilla's cucumbers and the habits of the Greeks in the library at Trinity."

The image of the two of them pouring over Praxilla in the hallowed halls of the Wren library amused her.

"He quite turned my thinking on that subject. Turned it around completely. Pity others can't see it. Who is to say what subject is fit for a poet? Not I. There was another, too, something about cockleshells and newly hatched chickens."

"Hedyle. We don't have much of hers. She didn't leave enough for us to know her meaning."

"Shame about Selby," Dunning said.

"Selby?" Georgiana's mind raced. "Andrew took the poems to Selby?"

"Gracious no. Old boy found out on his own. Must have been old Featheringham the librarian. Got wind Andrew was—" He colored abruptly.

"Helping me?"

"Translating rubbish." His red face darkened. "His words, not mine. He said he didn't have time for Mallet after that." Dunning's words came in a nervous rush. "Mallet showed me some other epigrams over dinner." He rushed on, "Anyte, was it? Quite well done, quite, I thought. Well worth scholarship. I wasn't aware of them before."

"Enough! I am too old a lady to listen to you talk about literature in a cold house," Mrs. Potter broke in. "It is getting dark, and there are no candles. See me to my house, and I'll feed us all a light supper." The old woman took Dunning's arm and led him to the door. Georgiana lingered. "Are you coming, my dear?"

The house was dark and cold, but it belonged to her. It would be enough. It had to be. She couldn't go back. "I'm coming, Edwina. Supper would be lovely."

She locked the door behind her.

For a man who made his living on the printed word, Bailey was remarkably careless about lighting—or cleanliness come to that. The smell of ink and clouds of paper dust permeated his office. Andrew brushed the latter from his sleeves. Three hours of squinting over newly printed pages in the dim light of Bailey's office left him with a headache. Harley would lecture him again when he went back to his rooms with a sore back.

"Sooner looked at, sooner finished," Bailey said. For his part, Andrew was grateful for any excuse to delay his return to Cambridge and the cold, empty house in Little Saint Mary's Lane. He chose to stay in London to review the first run page by page and correct it as it was set up. He found Bailey's company congenial and Jamie's a distraction. The work consumed him. He wanted to finish it, give it to her, and move on with his life. If he stayed and made corrections, he and Bailey would save weeks of shipping pages back and forth.

He told himself that printing it was the right thing, the only thing he could do. He tossed the pages down in disgust. He hated going through it without her. A book wouldn't bring her back, but he could think of nothing else to do.

Georgiana wouldn't marry him. She made it plain she didn't want him as a writing partner either. He refused to think of establishing her as his mistress. The thought was insupportable. They had been lovers, but she was never his mistress.

She called their lovemaking *this beautiful thing between us, this fragile, private thing.* Andrew knew such a relationship wouldn't stand up to the realities of daily life as long as she lived at Helsington and he lived on the edges. Eros, he thought–that yearning of one soul for another–wouldn't survive if they weren't together. If she wouldn't marry him, he could see nothing left between them except the book. *Georgie might not want me, but she cares about the work.*

"You're making yourself blind. How much more of this are you going to do?" Jamie Heyworth's impudent grin accompanied his welcome interruption. Andrew needed a distraction.

"Not much. Bailey thinks we'll have the first full copy in two days."

"Sorry to hear it. Even blind you're good company." Heyworth ducked a ball of paper flung with expert aim. The two had become regular dinner partners in a few short weeks. Jamie reveled in a free meal every day or so, and Andrew valued the diversion. Jamie's company was far better than his own.

"Shall we dine at Boodles? The company isn't as illustrious as elsewhere, but the food is superb," Andrew suggested.

"Ah, a man after my own heart. Just how long are you going to grace London and I with your company?" Jamie asked.

"In three days—four at most—there will be nothing, your delightful self excepted, to keep me here."

"What then?" Jamie asked.

He didn't know. Once his house had been filled with memories of his father and of family, now it felt empty without Georgiana. He dreaded facing that empty house, the empty town, his empty life, but he wouldn't know if she made good on her threat or if the Duchess had beaten her down again if he didn't go back. He couldn't avoid Cambridge any longer, not with the book finished.

"Back to Cambridge, I presume." Jamie nodded morosely.

Andrew continued. "If I'm to leave this charming..." He gestured helplessly at Bailey's clutter. "Would you join me on the road to Cambridge?"

"The delights of Little Saint Mary's Lane! How can I refuse you, my friend?" Jamie clapped an arm around his shoulder. "Let's discuss it over dinner—and a very good Port."

Chapter Twenty-Two

Jamie's "very good Port" flowed with such abundance that it gave Andrew a slow start the following morning. Snow flurries on a sharp wind hindered his progress further. Andrew knew what actually slowed his steps; the effects of drink and the weather were merely excuses for avoiding the work.

Bailey told him today should be the last of it. In another day, there would be a book. There would be a run of five hundred copies to be specific. Not a large amount, but Andrew thought it sufficient. He would go home to his empty house with only Jamie and Harley for company.

The warmth of Bailey's, even the smell and clutter of the back rooms, was a relief after the winds. "I'm sorry to be late, Bailey, I–"

John Bailey wasn't alone. The Marquess of Glenaire stretched across a wooden chair next to the printer, his long legs and elegant wardrobe gloriously out of place. "Hello, Andrew. Good of you to join us," he said.

Bailey's face registered concern but not alarm. Perhaps Glenaire hadn't threatened him. Andrew removed his greatcoat and hung his hat with exaggerated care while he gathered his scattered wits.

"Hello, Richard. I didn't know you had business with Bailey." If Glenaire thought he could be intimidated out of his mission, he was mistaken. Then again, Glenaire rarely used anything as crude as outright intimidation. He watched his old friend warily.

"This establishment came to my attention quite recently," the Marquess drawled. He looked about with every sign of interest. "Mr.

Bailey and I were just discussing the economics of the printing business. It is difficult for a small business owner, isn't it Mr. Bailey?"

Bailey looked from Glenaire to Andrew and back again. "Difficult, yes, but not impossible."

"You expect me to believe you stopped in to talk business with the shop owner, Richard? Come, come. Surely you have weightier matters on your mind."

"Greek perhaps?"

"Since when do you care about Greek literature?"

"Since it impacts my sister."

"It has always impacted your sister. You simply chose to ignore it."

"Gentlemen, may I speak bluntly?" Bailey interrupted. Clearly the sight of a titled gentleman casually conversing in his office failed to intimidate John Bailey.

"Certainly, Mr. Bailey. What is your concern?" Glenaire managed to convey, "*What concern could you possibly have in the matter of my sister?*"

"If this is about the work I do for Mr. Mallet, then I must suggest you address your concerns directly and not dance around the thing."

"I agree. I understand that you are printing a work for Mallet here."

"My arrangement with Bailey is none of your business." Andrew bit out each word.

The Marquess glanced up from under thick blond lashes. "Oh, I think it is. What concerns my sister is most certainly my business. It is my duty to look after her interests."

Andrew watched Bailey, who went pale. He wondered if he had told Glenaire the identity of the author of the work. He thought not; Glenaire would have guessed.

"I am Lady Georgiana's partner, I have every right—"

"I heard her demand that you return her notes and translations."

"And so I shall—as soon as I return to Cambridge. Her manuscript materials are hers. I will send them directly to Helsington." The Marquess gave Andrew one of his particularly inscrutable looks. Andrew didn't know what to make of it, but he didn't back down.

"But in the meantime, Mr. Bailey will print them?"

"The notes?"

"No. Not in that form. The translations and commentaries as Lady Georgiana and I agreed." Andrew bit out the last words and dared him to object.

"Commentaries? Yours?" Glenaire asked.

"Hers. Mine. It is impossible to separate them."

"And will my sister's name be on this book?"

"No. She didn't wish it." That stopped short of a lie. She wouldn't wish it–if she knew.

Bailey rose while they were sparring and returned with printed sheets. "You can see here, my lord. The lady's identity isn't disclosed."

Glenaire took the pages and read carefully. "'A Lady of Scholarship,'" he said. He turned the page and began to read.

Andrew stood for a while, watching the Marquess. When he appeared intent on reading the entire thing, Bailey gestured for Andrew to sit in the printer's own chair behind the desk. Andrew nodded his thanks, eyes riveted on Glenaire. Bailey bustled out; he had work to do. Five minutes later he returned with four additional pages, the final galleys for Andrew's approval. He left them there, Andrew with his editing pencil, Glenaire reading.

Bailey's clock showed twenty more minutes gone before Andrew lost all patience. He'd be damned before he'd let Glenaire sabotage the project. He rose to his feet.

"I don't need your approval," he insisted.

Glenaire raised an aristocratic eyebrow. "Don't you?" He went on reading. A few moments later Bailey returned, and Glenaire spoke directly to him. "This is quite good, you know. You do excellent work."

Bailey's pride showed, but he was quick to say, "The lady is the one who does excellent work."

"Quite." Glenaire's expression held no surprise. "'With the assistance of A. Mallet'? Quite a bit of assistance?"

"Less than you might think. It is Geo-, that is, Lady Georgiana's work."

"She won't thank you."

Andrew stopped breathing. He couldn't form a clear thought.

Glenaire continued. "She won't thank you for ordering her life."

Ordering her life? Is that what I've been doing? Andrew stared at Glenaire's merciless blue eyes.

"You went ahead without her, didn't you?" Glenaire continued relentlessly. "You gave her no choice about the printing. She won't thank you."

"She'll hate it." Andrew sank back in his chair. He felt all the fight go out of him. Glenaire watched him and waited. Intimidation, one remembered, wasn't Glenaire's style. There were always neater ways to wield the surgeon's knife.

"I did it again, didn't I?" Andrew felt like a bungling fool. Of course she would hate it if she had no voice, no choice. Anger had blinded him. *Glenaire, damn him, is right.*

"You wish me to stop publication," Andrew rasped.

"I wish? My dear Andrew, we're discussing what Georgiana might wish." Glenaire wouldn't have to block publication. He'd get Andrew to do it himself.

Bailey cleared his throat and spoke in professional tones. "You wish to interrupt the print run? The first eighty pages are already printed, and–"

"I'll pay for it." Andrew started to reassure him.

"Finish it." Glenaire's emphatic command startled both of them. "Finish it and bind it." He looked from one to the other. "She may wish it, if you ask her. If she doesn't, I'll pay for it and destroy all the copies."

Disbelief made Andrew mute. Glenaire went on smoothly, "It would be inefficient to lose what is already done. Finish it, Mr. Bailey. Mallet and I will decide its fate after *my sister* makes her decision."

Bailey beamed. "It really is good work. It would be a pity not to publish it."

Glenaire wanted it printed. Andrew couldn't speak. Glenaire's eyes held his, challenging, but Andrew held his ground. Glenaire finally looked away first.

"You seem to have learned more quickly than I did," Andrew whispered at last.

"I had an advantage. She actually discussed it with me at Mountview. I'll leave you and Mr. Bailey to arrange storage of the copies once they are printed. May I request that you send one round to me at Whitehall?" They knew they couldn't refuse. Andrew nodded.

The Marquess rose at last. "You do fine work, Mr. Bailey. I'm glad to be acquainted with it." Bailey would see a steady stream of invitations, cards, and other small jobs coming from Glenaire, Andrew guessed. At least Bailey came out of this fiasco in good shape.

The roof of Georgiana's little house proved to be a much more difficult project than expected. There were workers to hire, materials to select, rafters to inspect, and a carpenter to obtain due to a rotten beam. In a rainy March, the weather factored in. The roofers needed four dry days together to get the bulk of the work done. Even then, she discovered, "done" didn't mean finished. The finish work in her attic and around the eaves would take another few days.

She delayed transfer of Helsington to Major Warrington, but he grew impatient. In three more days, she would have no choice but to leave. Georgiana's head hurt from going over and over the list in front of her. She thought she had been ruthless about packing only what she needed, but she could see that the pile of finished boxes, neatly stacked in Helsington's foyer, would not fit in the tiny house on Sheep Street. William the footman and her maid (the last of the servants, the only two who agreed to accept an extra month's pay from the sale of the house) waited for her next order.

She went over the list again. Her notes and papers must go with her. The little sitting room and half the bedchamber would be lined with boxes, but they had to go with her. Novels and books on gardening could be left for the estate sale. She needed her classics and her Shakespeare, but the rest could stay. With Mrs. Potter's help she weeded six boxes for the kitchen down to one. She wouldn't be entertaining; she would cook only for herself. It wasn't "one bowl, one spoon," but it was simple enough.

"Shall we light the room, my lady?"

"No, William. Leave it dark. I'll close it up. I'll take tea above stairs."

She pulled the doors closed and crossed the foyer where she said goodbye to Andrew the last day. *Perhaps he will come. He has my notes. He must return them. What then?* She had no answer for the mocking voice in her head.

She climbed the stair with a heavy tread, gracefully lifting her pearl gray gown. He was gone. He had left Cambridge without telling her, and he had taken pieces of her work with him. He had taken pieces of her soul. She told him it was finished, but he still had her work.

The dim hallway led to her private sitting room, bright with candlelight reflected on flower-covered walls and the ornate plaster ceiling and fading sun. With the clutter gone, the little workroom looked stark in the fading light. The world outside her window looked gray. She wondered how color could leach out of the world. *Did rainy days dim all color, or had the world bled out all its color as my heart bled out all feeling?* She let the curtains fall shut.

William brought tea she had prepared herself. There would be no need for such service in her tiny house. She would take tea made herself in her own little kitchen. That at least pleased her. She liked feeling competent at something. The ornate tea table wouldn't come with her. It was built more for its dainty appearance than for comfort, and it had room enough for only one person. She drank her solitary tea and fought back self-doubt.

"He said he wanted to marry me!" The empty room didn't answer. She sounded like a spoiled child to her own ears. *He asked, but I refused him.*

She vacillated, she demurred, and she refused him. She sent him away. She thought he would go back to Cambridge. *Where is the blasted man? Where are my notes, my work?*

She forced her attention away from fruitless regrets to her lists and began again. Fill the pantry. Put in firewood. Air the sheets. *Two sets,* she thought, *should do it.* Four boxes were unnecessary. Tag the kitchen table and four chairs.

A discrete knock broke the silence.

"Yes, William?"

"A message, my lady." He handed her a heavy vellum packet.

Richard! What now? He had arranged her travel. She suspected he had arranged the estate agent who miraculously appeared on her doorstep the day after she announced her decision to her neighbors, an honest estate agent at that.

My dear Georgiana,

I trust that all is well with you. I have been informed that Colonel Warrington has acquired Helsington and that the transaction went more quickly than expected. I have arranged for a bank account to be set up in your name to manage the assets from the sale. They have been informed to deal directly with you.

I don't wish to imply that I lack confidence in you, but you must know that if problems arise or you find you regret your decisions, you need only apply to me. Something can be arranged.

. . .

My damned interfering brother just can't stop arranging my life! With a twinge of guilt she realized she should be grateful for his help. He saved her awkwardness at the bank at least.

Her irritation didn't dissipate. She had refused his offer to pay for servants and upkeep so she could stay at Helsington. She didn't want his control any more than she wanted their father's. She would do without his help. No man would manage her life. Still, his concern threatened to weaken her. She put the letter down.

She didn't want any man, especially not one who tried to arrange her life. *Why does independence have to be such a struggle?* She just wished she was not so very alone.

Georgiana crumpled her latest list and restlessly paced to the window again.

Where is Andrew? she thought. *Where is the damned man?* The night didn't answer.

Chapter Twenty-Three

Joy, warm and familiar, surged through Andrew when Cambridge came into view. It would always be home to him. When his carriage rumbled up the cobbles into town, good spirits faded with each turn of the wheel. Georgiana was the heart of his home; without her, he had none.

"Here we are then, home again, and glad of it." Jamie declaimed as he leapt from the chaise. Andrew responded with a nod. The homecoming failed his every fantasy. Quiet, at least, was a relief. Jamie's incessant chatter flooded the entire trip and drained Andrew's supply of conversation to the dregs.

Andrew took a moment to look around at the dark emptiness of his house while Harley saw to the baggage.

"I'll have the shutters open in a trice," Harley's cheerful voice drifted from the back, "and start dinner."

"Good man." Jamie's voice moved toward the kitchen, following the promise of food.

Andrew let instinct pull him up the stairs to the book-lined center of his house. He yanked open the inner sash and the diamond-paned windows. The shutters flew open under his hand.

Soft April light filtered between the familiar narrow rows of houses. It glowed off the deep red brick and fine English stone. Andrew breathed in deeply the smells of river water and cooking fires. No grandeur lay here, merely the familiar and the dear.

Neat pages and an index list remained as he left them, arranged on the worktable. Books on the small wheeled shelf, arranged for maximum utility, stood unchanged, waiting for his hand. He ran a finger over them with a smile and placed another hand lightly on the shelves behind, savoring the feel of leather and the scent of paper. He trailed his fingers along the shelves absentmindedly until he came to the door of his bedroom gaping open. A quick jerk of his hand slammed it shut.

Shutting out memory proved to be more difficult. The room lay dark and cold, like a tomb, like death itself. Jamie could have his room. He would sleep by the fire.

"Dinner will be catch-as-catch-can. Need to see if the markets are open still." Harley broke into speech without preamble when he burst into the room.

"Forget that. I have a delivery for you to make first."

Eyebrows shot up. "No matter to me, but there won't be dinner here tonight if that's the way it is."

"That's the way it is." Andrew reached inside his satchel, pulled out a leather-bound book, and handed it to Harley. He had wrapped it in brown paper along with his hopes and dreams.

Some objects inspire fear and others loathing; the parcel on Georgiana's worktable did both. The notes and papers she expected couldn't be in so small a parcel, and her thoughts were jumbled. *He is back. But where is he? All he sends is this package for goodness sake.*

She paced to the windows looking for wisdom in the brown grass and newly bloomed trees outside. *He didn't come! A parcel. He sent a bloody parcel.* Her eyes strayed to the fearful thing. Some objects inspire hope along with the danger that hope will fail.

"Oh bother. Where's your backbone, woman?" she asked herself.

It took one movement to reach the parcel and another to tear open the covering. A folded piece of ivory vellum covered in a strong dark hand as familiar to her as her own fell out.

. . .

Georgiana,

I couldn't reach you to finalize the draft. I have taken the liberty of obtaining a publisher for the work. All final decisions about the disposition of the work are, of course, yours. I believe the terms of our partnership have been discharged, and that partnership is now at an end.

A. Mallet

Liberty? *Insufferable liberty.* It looked plenty final to Georgiana, bound in gilt and leather, heavy in her hand. The work had been hers to publish, not his.

And the letter–no words of love, no joy of greeting, only business. She threw it down. *Is there truly nothing between us but the work?*

"An end? Who is he to tell me when it is at an end?!" Her words echoed in the cavernous emptiness of Helsington.

She hefted the leather bound book again. It wasn't large, but it had a comfortable weight to it. It felt familiar, soft and warm, in her hands. She ran a finger over the engraved gold letters: *Poetry by the Female Authors of Ancient Greece.*

She opened it and inhaled the clean scent of new paper, heavy linen pages. She admired the watermarked inner lining. That title was repeated on the title page: *Poetry by the Female Authors of Ancient Greece.*

She concentrated on the title before she noticed what was written below in smaller letters: *By an English Lady of Scholarship.*

"'An English Lady of Scholarship.'" A smile played at her lips, appearing and disappearing. It was, of course, impossible to use her name.

Below that she saw written in yet smaller letters, *With the assistance of A. Mallet, gentleman scholar of Cambridge.*

"'A. Mallet, gentleman scholar of Cambridge.'" Anger flared again. "How dare he? How dare he make final arrangements without me? Only a man would violate a partnership in so odious a manner. I had the right to decide. I alone." She chose to forget his message, forget that he said the final decision was hers to make.

She had no issue with him putting his name on it and leaving hers off or even with taking it to the printer, but he ought to have spoken with her first. The more she considered what he had done, the angrier she became. *The beast. How dare he take it to a printer without consulting me!*

Harley had left without waiting for a reply. She knew, without a doubt, that he was in league with the bounder. She sat to pen a reply anyway.

"SHE WAS THERE, all right. Fair put out she looked when I handed her the parcel."

"Put out? Did she open it?"

"I put it in her hand like you said. You never said to watch her open it. She's there." Harley shifted a large crock and two smaller ones in his arms while he talked. "She has the package. Seemed to me like she expected a different messenger."

A long and colorful string of Portuguese curses met Harley's impudent remark.

"He has you there, I believe, Andrew." Jamie didn't pretend not to hear. He lifted an eyebrow helpfully and liberated one of Harley's crocks.

Harley grinned at Andrew. "Haven't heard that language in a while. Would make a sailor blush. One more thing, it looks like the lady is moving."

"Moving? Where?" Andrew felt every sense go on alert.

"Don't know. House stood empty. She opened the door herself." Harley kept speaking, but he followed when Jamie gestured him back to the kitchen. "Boxes piled by the door—a fair number of them."

She opened the door herself. "No servants?" Andrew was forced to follow.

"Looked like they all ran off. Bloody deserters." Harley threw the words over his shoulder.

"Tell me, Harley," Jamie asked, "what are these delicious smelling containers you brought back with you, and what tavern did you rescue them from?"

Andrew followed in silence, his face thunderous. Dinner did little to improve his expression. Jamie's amusing stories did less and neither did the bottle of French wine Harley had miraculously produced. She was leaving. He would send her notes to her, of course he would, but that would be the end.

Jamie savored the last of the wine, and Andrew scowled into the dregs of his glass when a loud knock echoed through the house.

Andrew strode to the door himself and threw it open.

"Damn. Couldn't come herself?" Georgiana wasn't the only one who hoped for a different messenger. A startled and wary William handed him a message. She must have sent him hard on Harley's heels.

"C'mon to th'kitchen. May as well be comfortable while he carries on." Andrew ignored Harley's impudent orders to the footman and Jamie's avid curiosity, his attention riveted on the paper in his hands.

Mr. Mallet,

It isn't for you to dissolve our partnership, particularly after the high-handed and completely unacceptable manner in which you appropriated my work. I will wait upon you tomorrow afternoon to resolve these matters.

Lady Georgiana Hayden

. . .

Andrew felt a grin spread across his face and then fade. She was in a royal snit.

You're very welcome for the anxious and tedious efforts I have made on your behalf, Your high-and-mighty Ladyship.

Wretched woman. The final disposition of the work rested with her decision. He was pretty sure he had told her that.

He figured he probably deserved her temper, though. He overstepped when he got the book printed. Glenaire was right about that. Still, he had hoped for a chance to explain.

He read and reread the final sentence. "I will wait upon you tomorrow." She was in a snit, and she was coming to make war. Andrew spent eleven years learning how to make war. She would come to make war on his home ground. Joy rose in a mighty torrent—joy in the steely control of a man determined to have his way.

When he sat back down to his dinner, his eyes had a marshal gleam.

"Prepare the camp for battle, Harley. We shall have a visitor tomorrow." *Settle matters, we will.*

Promptly at two o'clock in the afternoon, Lady Georgiana appeared at the door. A suspiciously well-groomed Harley showed her to a seat in the front parlor. He bowed respectfully and told her he would announce her before disappearing up the stairs. That alone should have warned her to be careful.

Far too busy keeping the balance between two conflicting desires —the desire to put her lying cheat of a partner in his place and the desire to fall into his arms—she failed to notice Harley's strange behavior. She lost all ability to think clearly.

The sound of two pairs of boots on the enclosed stairs caused the pounding in her ears to get louder and made coherent thought even more difficult.

"Get on with it, man, hurry up!" she snapped.

Her eyes widened at the sight of Jamie Heyworth's toothy grin descending the final step.

"Lady Georgie, glad you are so anxious to see me! I didn't realize you knew I was here."

"I didn't. I thought..." The ludicrous sound of Charles Harley aping a proper butler spared her the need to reply.

"Mr. Mallet will see you."

The declaration forced Georgiana to troop around Heyworth, still grinning like an idiot, to the stairs. With every wary step upward, she reviewed what she should say to the upstart above.

"How dare you proceed without my permission" seemed to her correct but colorless.

"You, sir, are no man of honor." Too pompous.

"You've wounded me, sir, with your perfidy." Too dramatic.

"You are a worm and no man." Too Shakespearean.

By the middle step, she prepared to argue ad hominem. "Your man, sir, is a trumped-up monkey and no proper servant" Not fair to Harley.

"Damn it, Andrew, what were you about?" Better.

"Where the devil have you been?" Definitely not.

"Oh, Andrew, how could you? I thought we were partners." Worst of all. She would not show weakness.

Her last thought just before the door opened on the top step was "You reprehensible son of a horse thief, you stole my life's work!"

"Ah, Lady Georgiana, you didn't have to come to offer your gratitude in person." Andrew stood in the center of the room. He was laughing.

"Gratitude? You insufferable toad! For what should I be grateful?"

"The work, my lady. The fine gold letters, the linen paper, the gilt edges. Didn't you receive it?"

"You know I did. You arranged it without me—and you took credit."

"Arranging your work was, I admit, a mistake." He looked

serious but only for a moment. "No harm done. I came to my senses. Five hundred copies sit patiently in John Bailey's storage room awaiting your decision. Sell them, burn them, give them away. The work, as you say, is yours to do with as you wish. As to credit—" His confusion would have been endearing if it wasn't patently false. "I fear you are mistaken. I'm not a Lady of Scholarship."

"Not that, you fool. Your name is on the cover, not mine!"

She caught the twinkle in his eye. "My dear Lady Georgiana, I didn't realize you wished to have your name on the cover. You gave me the impression you wished your identity to remain anonymous. Does this mean you plan to sell the books?"

"You have Jamie Heyworth running tame in your parlor. You might as well stand in the street and announce my work to my parents."

"Normally, yes, I agree. The very voluble Major Lord Heyworth would serve as a town crier, but in this regard he has been quite mum. He seems to enjoy the subterfuge. I believe he enjoyed tweaking your brother Richard—at least until the latter gentlemen made his own inquiries and inserted himself into the plot."

"Richard knows?" It was a gasp of outrage.

"I fear so. We discussed it and—"

"And the two of you decided what was best for me." Fire roared in her heart. She expected it to flame out of her eyes.

"Am I to understand that you wish to take full credit?" He was trying to change the subject. "That's easy enough to arrange. A word or two in the right ear, and all of London will know."

"No! I, that is, no."

"Well, you may want to wait until there has been some reaction, a review or two perhaps, before you decide to take credit."

She didn't answer.

"You do plan to publish?"

Georgiana stared at the lace on her slipper, unable to raise her eyes from her feet, unable to formulate an answer.

Several silent moments passed before he said, "It is quite good, you know."

She did not look up.

"It is fine work," he went on, his voice a caress. "You can be proud."

She looked up to find him inches from her, uncertain when he had moved so close.

"You did brilliantly." He closed the final distance and took her mouth in a gossamer kiss that barely touched her body, yet seared her to the core.

Names flew to her mind: "Toad," "Wretch," "Traitor," "Thief," but the erratic heartbeat, engendered when his embrace turned her insides to molten iron drowned out the voices in her head. All that reached her mouth was "Andrew. Oh, Andrew."

He pulled away and attempted to speak. She found the puzzled expression on his crooked face endearingly sweet, but she needed him, needed to draw him back, needed his closeness. When her hands began to tug at his shirt, he helped her free it, opening himself to her exploring hands.

She disposed of her pelisse; his jacket landed near it. His waistcoat, and then his shirt were gone. When they reached the bedroom door, strong hands yanked her gown from her shoulders. It slithered to the floor and lay in the doorway. His trousers fell inside the room, quickly followed by his small clothes nearer to the bed. He was gloriously naked, but she still wore her stockings and underclothing when he rolled her under him on the bed. His mouth took her breast through the delicate lace chemise, while his hands found the opening in her pantaloons. By the time she realized he wouldn't wait to remove the rest of her clothing, she didn't want him to.

The fierceness of their joining was as much Georgiana's doing as his. She knew he would pull back if he thought she wanted it, but she wouldn't let him. Weeks of separation and confusion were pulverized by the pounding need of this moment. One shattering moment later

Georgiana lost all sense of her surroundings in the exquisite moment of release.

She felt him continue to move in her, hard and fast, while she slowly regained awareness. She experienced the moment of his pleasure and his own release in full awareness; the joy of it overwhelmed her. Her own satisfaction in watching him transformed by desire rocked her. Tears stung in her throat and rolled down her cheeks. This moment, this private, special moment belonged to them. She wished he could leave it at that.

Chapter Twenty-Four

Andrew took several minutes to come to full awareness. He opened his eyes and began to smile. The smile froze, and his heart stuttered.

"Tears? Dear one, I am so sorry, I—"

"Don't be a damned fool. It was wonderful." She sniffed adorably.

He hadn't intended to kiss her. Harley's performance, Jamie's presence, his preemptive verbal strike, and the solitude of the study all discomforted her exactly as he intended. He forgot to watch his flank. Her very presence had discomforted him more than he anticipated; it overran his common sense.

Here they were, and he knew it was his fault they were in his bed and she was crying. *What a muddle!*

He could not understand the workings of her convoluted female mind. *Foolish woman. She wanted freedom.* He offered his heart on a platter. All she had to do was take it. He watched her quietly for a few seconds too long–long enough for her to hear pots banging and voices below.

"Jamie!" She leapt from his bed.

She ran about his room gathering the remnants of her clothes, and he lay back to enjoy the sight. She was adorable and quite astonished when she turned to see Andrew stretched out on the bed in his nakedness, not moving an inch.

"You're amused? But Jamie!"

"Too late, love. This house is too small to mask the kinds of noise you make."

"I don't! I do? Odious man. You are laughing again."

She slipped into her gown and turned so he could lace it. "Oh, do hurry." Another laugh escaped him; his hands caressed her back, and his lips brushed the back of her neck. "If you insist." He began to dress.

She put on her shoes and recovered her pelisse from the floor of his study, when a thought struck her.

"Was it?" Her eyes were remarkably wide.

"Incredibly pleasurable? Yes." He fastened his waistcoat.

"Not that." She colored brightly. "The work. Was it really good?"

"'Is' not 'was.' It is quite good." He stopped with one arm in his jacket. "Haven't you read it?"

"As printed? No. Too angry."

"Angry. Months of work and you were too angry to even read the blasted book? Five hundred copies sit in Bailey's storage waiting for your decision, but you are too angry to read it. I think it is I who should be angry. It's your work Georgie, and it's damned good. Thank you for allowing me to share it."

"But?"

"But nothing. The work felt good. It's over." He shrugged into the jacket, letting her stew about it.

Tears welled in her eyes. He hoped she wept in sorrow that the work, their partnership, had ended. The sound of voices at the bottom of the stairs brought alarm to her expression. She breathed very deeply, turned her back to him, and approached the stairs, the very picture of a vengeful warrior princess.

"Oh, no you don't!" He reached her in a quick movement and hopped on one foot to ease the cramp it caused. "If the fox truly is in the hen house, we're going down there together." She turned a look filled with a mix of emotions to him. He thought he saw gratitude among them.

"Easy now, head high," he whispered behind her as they descended the stairs. "That's my lady."

Two steps, three, and they were blinking in the bright sun of the sitting room.

Two expectant pairs of eyes, Jamie's vastly amused and Harley's sardonic and knowing waited for one of them to say something. There, by the door, stood another visitor. Geoffrey Dunning had a look of total shock on his face. Georgiana had neither maid nor chaperone; she was utterly compromised. Andrew certainly hoped she understood that. She opened her mouth; what came out resembled a croak. Andrew gently urged her toward the door, his hand on her upper arm.

"Lady Georgiana can't stay to visit this afternoon, I'm afraid. She has reading to complete." He watched the back of her neck turn scarlet.

"Yes, I, that is, I didn't intend to stay. My conveyance is waiting."

Stayed rather longer than she intended, he suspected. Her eyes looked large and unfocused; he had to pick up her hand and place it on his proffered arm in order to escort her out.

He handed her into a hired carriage and spoke softly into her ear as he did. "No partnership, Georgie. I don't make love to business partners. You have to decide what it is, this, this thing between us." He made sure she didn't see his smug smile when he turned away, but he couldn't disguise his sense of triumph. She was his. He knew it. He just needed to help her admit it.

"This thing? Thing? He calls our relationship a thing?" *The smug tyrant!* She nursed anger almost through dinner. Dining alone, however, makes one vulnerable to disordered thoughts. Anger gave way to morose introspection.

"What would you call it then," a voice in her head demanded.

"Can you give it a name suitable for a London drawing room? I image Dunning could give it a name, but it wouldn't be suitable."

"We're partners."

"I think not." The voice grew sardonic.

"He may not think so, but I say we are." *I don't make love to business partners.*

Internal voices, luckily, don't make rude noises. They do conjure images of clean linen sheets, disheveled black hair, and laughing ebony eyes.

The afternoon shook her badly. Jamie knew. Richard's eyes and ears, Jamie, knew. Worse, Dunning knew. *Will he tell his grandmother?* She didn't think he was a gossip, but he was very close to Edwina Potter. How she would look to the people of Cambridge, a woman alone with her books, when rumors about her relationship with Andrew became painfully clear.

"You think he'll stay in Cambridge after this?" Internal voices do ask uncomfortable questions. It was one thing to make a pariah of herself and another to ruin his reputation.

She slammed down her hand. *Damn it. Men aren't ruined by a discreet affair. They are congratulated!* That may be so in London, in her parents' world. She wasn't so sure about Cambridge with its inbred social structure and middle-class values. She had already sullied his scholarly reputation.

And if Jamie runs to Richard, what then?

She looked down the length of gleaming mahogany, empty save for a grotesquely ornate silver candelabrum and her half-empty wine glass. She thought of Andrew's house, full of his friends, his warmth, and his laughter. Soon Helsington and its splendors will be gone, sold to Colonel Warrington who brought a new bride to this place. Perhaps the Warringtons would give this silent mausoleum life.

Georgiana pushed away her dinner, half eaten. Soon she would eat her solitary meals on a smaller, rougher table. She wondered if solitude felt less oppressive when it occupied less space. Yesterday the little house on Sheep Street meant freedom. Tonight, it just sounded empty.

"Do you plan to spend the evening leaning on your chair? You can't avoid the book that way." The voice again.

Georgiana pretended not to notice William who pretended not to watch her. He'd be gone in a week along with the candelabrum and the mahogany table. Her maid had left for her sister's in Surrey the day before. It didn't matter. Her servants were too well trained to invisibility to provide any sort of human comfort.

She began to pick up her plate, but William was too quick for her. As long as he remained at Helsington, she wouldn't carry her own dishes.

Georgiana ran out of excuses. She climbed the steps with feet of lead to the book waiting in her sitting room where she had left it the day before, her life's work in a leather-bound package.

"What are you afraid of? Mockery?" The voice sneered at her now. "It is a book, fool."

She wasn't afraid. Fear was nonsensical.

Gilt letters shown up at her: "An English Lady of Scholarship." It seemed as if her life amounted to nothing else but what could be encapsulated in that neat turn of phrase. The leather-bound volume represented her adult life. *What if it is terrible?*

She picked it up and caressed the smooth cover.

"The assistance of A. Mallet." Andrew. They had done this work together; it was part of both of them. She saw with sudden clarity why she avoided reading it.

Grief terrified her, not failure. Failure could be faced. When they had the work, Georgiana understood what lay between them. She held the finished product, their creation, in her hand. She didn't know what they shared now that they had finished it.

Georgiana brought her solitary candle and the book to her bedchamber. She placed both on the table next to her bed and began to undress. She picked up the book and slipped between the sheets alone.

"Your intentions?"

Black eyes radiated death in the general direction of Major Lord James Phineas Heyworth.

"Honorable," Andrew snapped.

"And?" Jamie continued.

"She won't have me."

"It didn't seem to me that the lady lacked interest."

The look of death intensified.

"Am I correct in my assumption that our Georgie is utterly compromised?" Jamie went on.

"Only if she chooses to be," Andrew replied. It came out as a growl.

"Or if word were to get out," Jamie pointed out.

"It won't. Not from me, not from Harley, and not," Andrew spat, "from you. I would see you dead first, slowly and painfully."

"You would too. Do you plan the same fate for Dunning?"

Mallet's curses would have been at home on the docks of any Mediterranean port. He had tried to overlook the detail that Geoff, though not a malicious gossip, was careless. Georgie couldn't avoid this. She would have to marry him. Still, Geoff had come at the very end. He saw that they had been alone, but perhaps he thought they were working. *Fool! The truth was clear all over Georgiana's face.*

Andrew felt as though a large pole had hit him over the head.

Jamie looked more amused than sympathetic. "Banns on Sunday?"

"Georgiana informed me that banns are tantamount to shouting to her parents. She believes they'll bring hell to pay on the shire."

"There'll be hell to pay, in any case."

"I know that. She knows that. She wishes as little humiliation from her parents as possible. You know the Haydens. Picture the kind of humiliation she fears."

"Special license?"

"To paraphrase the lady, the Archbishop of Canterbury is a cousin. York is her uncle, and Winchester her father's boon companion. Special license is tantamount to banns."

"Gretna?"

"Cowardly, cold, and undignified at our age."

"Common License it is." The little baron stretched his shoulder, an uncharacteristically smug expression spreading slowly across his face. "It will feel good to be of some use for once."

Andrew looked at him quizzically.

"Allow me to introduce you to my grandmother's brother, the Bishop of Ely," Jamie said through a widening smile, "who dislikes Sudbury sufficiently to enjoy thwarting him and is advanced enough in age not to care what Canterbury might say or do."

Andrew greeted this marvelous speech with a hoot of laughter. He hadn't intended to enact his personal drama for an audience, but it seemed there might be advantages. A smile began to evolve deep in his dark eyes.

Jamie's self-satisfied grin answered back. "Shall we leave tomorrow or allow the lady one day to reconsider?"

Andrew's face fell. "Let's allow her a day to get comfortable with it. It has to be her choice. Georgiana's stubbornness might be a hurdle, but she will come around. She has no choice." Andrew shuddered at the thought.

Glasses clinked in agreement. Companionable silence stretched a while before the baron spoke again.

"Hell to pay for certain, if not before then after. I presume your funds are safe?"

Mallet nodded. He was a careful man. "Sudbury can't touch me. I'm unlikely to be considered for a University post in any case, so he can't harm me there. I can afford a wife."

"Humiliation is a Hayden specialty usually reserved for sworn enemies and family members. I can see where she'd want to avoid it. Is that the rub then?"

"That and marriage itself I think. Mostly she is angry with me and with Richard for things that happened long ago."

"Your sudden wish for an army career?"

Andrew didn't expect insight from Jamie. "That, yes. Claims we arranged her life for her."

"Didn't you?"

"There wasn't any choice at the time, but she thinks she should have been given one."

"No logic. Females don't have choices. May not be right, but it's the way it is."

"We don't either, come to that, not all the time. Still, they have a right to their own lives. She has a point. She also has some maggot in her brain about our love being something rare, fragile, and on some illusive higher plane than marriage."

"Isn't it? Passions don't last."

"Fragile doesn't equate to long-lived, I agree, but she can't see past it. I want old age by the fire, care for one another, and work we share—the entire thing, not just a piece of it."

"If she's going by what passes for marriage for her parents and their crowd, she probably doesn't know there is such a thing. Hell, I'm not sure I know there is such a thing. Still, if it is what you want, I'm ready to fetch the license. Just say when."

Richard Hayden, the Marquess of Glenaire, was an orderly man. He arrived at his desk at Whitehall precisely at seven-thirty, just as he did every morning. He reveled in the quiet at that hour, and he used it to read dispatches. By ten, those seeking his good will began to fill the halls, and the importuning began. He listened to most, giving ear to the problems of returning soldiers first and the ambitions of fribbles last.

He left Whitehall precisely at one to walk to lunch at his club.

He stepped out of Horse Guards into the warm spring day and began his familiar walk to Saint James Street, exactly as he did most days.

Today, he skirted the canal along its north edge and noted with disapproval the urchins playing in its dirty water. Saint James was a royal park. Urchins didn't belong there; he disapproved. The walk to the Marlborough Gate, he noted with satisfaction, had been cleared of debris this morning and flowers had begun in the borders. Glenaire was a careful man. All men should be careful about their work. In a world well run, they would be.

He climbed Saint James Street, thin of people as it often was in early afternoon. A small cluster of young men gathered in front of a storefront which was unusual. It appeared to be Franklin's bookstore, just below White's. A modest little store, it never attracted much notice until now. He began to step into the street to avoid the unseemly scuffle when a young man emerged from the store with a familiar looking volume under his arm. His fellows gave up a cheer. "You got one!" One shouted, "M'mother insists on a copy. Say you'll sell it to me."

Glenaire looked more closely at the book with its leather cover and familiar gilt letters. *Poetry by Women. Damn!*

Moments later he was in a hackney on his way to Fleet Street. A very red-faced clerk greeted him. Mr. Bailey was out. The clerk blurted out a confession without waiting to be asked. He incoherently confessed to misunderstanding the situation.

The clerk had put most of the books in storage as requested, but he assumed Bailey only did that because he thought it wouldn't sell. Print copies were never held back. He had sent a small batch to Hatchard's Bookstore and been startled when they requested more copies. Several other stores requested copies the same morning, and he didn't discover his error until he went in to tell Bailey about their success.

"Mr. Bailey was right angry. He said it was my job if the client wants me fired." The man looked at Glenaire with fear. Bailey had already gone to Cambridge. *Prefers to face Andrew rather than face me.* Glenaire smiled grimly. *Wait until he meets Georgiana.*

Glenaire loathed having his orderly existence disrupted, but he had little choice this time. He would assess the situation at Mountview and then go to Cambridge himself.

Chapter Twenty-Five

Georgiana leaned against the crisp linens of her narrow bed. The candles burned low when she finally finished reading and ran her hands along the gilt edges of the pages. She read the gold letters on the cover one more time in the sputtering candlelight, *Poetry by the Female Authors of Ancient Greece.* Her book. Her work. Truly. Andrew hadn't lied.

A small smile teased the edges of her mouth.

Every word in every verse, showcased in Mr. Bailey's exquisite print face, was the same carefully honed translation she had completed. The light of their conversations had finally given her what she needed to bring years of struggle to perfect flower. The choice of words, even Nossis's roses, was left exactly as she had decided it would be.

She recognized the commentary at once. They were her notes, his thoughts, and their discussions tied together with delicately crafted words that sounded like her own voice. The editor, Andrew, made his influence invisible, yet the words reflected their combined wisdom. She could no longer tell where she left off and Andrew began.

Georgiana read the title page out loud to the silent room. "An English Lady of Scholarship." Her graceful finger ran over the words. "Lady of Scholarship." Years of her life captured in three words. "Scholarship." She expected to be filled with contentment. She was not.

Better by far to be "scholar" than "eccentric" or "oddity." Better even than "Lady of Intelligence and Refinement," but she feared that that was how her entire life would now be defined.

She read on. "With the assistance of A. Mallet, gentleman scholar of Cambridge." Without Andrew her work would be a paltry collection of half-baked notes and schoolboy translations, a private eccentricity. Without Andrew, she would still sit alone in Helsington's cold rooms, seeking work to fill her days and hours.

Just as she did now.

The last candle finally sputtered out. She sat alone in the dark. *What a fool I've been!* The book was his gift to her, a labor of love, and the true product of collaboration. It had been their gift to each other, just as making love was a gift to each other. She gave him pleasure. This afternoon she could see his pleasure, and the giving of it brought her tears of joy. She wondered if it was the same for him.

Georgiana slipped deeper under the covers, but sleep eluded her. She turned once and then again, both agitated by and fixated with the thought that Andrew took joy in her pleasure.

Gift and giver, neither was complete without the other. He had given her the book as a gift and with it an even greater gift. He had given her a choice. He presented her with the choice of whether they would sell their book or not. He would allow her the freedom to suppress the work that was as much his as hers.

She ought to be elated, but the quiet pleasure she felt left no real contentment. He also offered her another choice, a harder bargain. He offered her his very self, but he would accept no less from her. Gift and giver, he demanded both. He wanted her life, but he wanted to give her his in return.

Only a fool would spurn the pleasure he gave; only a fool would push away the promise of love and joy, only a fool would—

Georgiana wasn't a fool. She sat bolt upright in the dark, pushed back the covers, and leapt from the bed.

The cold floor brought her to her senses. She couldn't run off to his house this time, not with Jamie in residence. She couldn't be sure of her welcome. She feared she may have waited too long. She didn't know if his offer would still be open. For both of their sakes, it must be.

Georgiana thought feverishly. Memories of their fierce, frantic passion flooded her. He wanted her that much was certain. "I don't make love to business partners." He wouldn't go back to the way things were before, but he hadn't proposed again. "You have to decide," he had said. He wouldn't ask again; she would have to do it.

Shivering in the cold dark of her bedroom, she could almost feel his breath on her neck as it had been when he saw her to the door that afternoon.

"Oh, it's you, is it?" Harley's grin undermined his attempt at severity. Her best glare, calculated to set down all encroachment, caused the grin to spread more widely. "Best come in and join them then." Traffic to old Mr. Mallet's house had been heavy.

Breathe deeply! Georgiana followed her own advice, took a deep breath, and followed him in. She prepared herself for Jamie's curiosity. There would be more where it came from.

"The Lady Georgiana Hayden." Harley's voice did a canny imitation of Chambers. He obviously enjoyed this.

Four gentlemen rose to their feet and bowed in varying degrees of familiarity and respect. She took in the presence of Geoff Dunning, but her attention was diverted by a copy of *Female Authors of Ancient Greece* open on the rough brown table in front of a total stranger.

She hoped she would find Andrew alone, hoped Jamie would have taken himself off to find her brother. She had been certain that she had the only copy of the book. Her eyes made that a lie. Andrew showed the book to Dunning and some stranger. *The wretch!*

Andrew flashed a pained look her way and attempted to speak. "Lady Georgiana, may I present John Bailey. You know Dunning, of course," he croaked in a cracked voice. "Bailey is—

"Honored to make your acquaintance." The little man beamed at her. "Mr. Mallet and I were just discussing this wonderful work and the unfortunate accident. I have come to offer my apologies."

Apologies? Whatever for, and what is he doing with my book? Wonderful! He found it wonderful? Her head spun; she sat down carefully, afraid she might fall. "I'm sorry, I—my book Mr. Bailey? How do you have my book?"

"Sorry, sorry. That's the point, isn't it? I need to apologize."

"Bailey is the printer, Georgiana." She remembered. Five hundred copies in Mr. Bailey's warehouse.

"My clerk, my lady, misunderstood. He thought we held the copies back to gauge the interest."

"He thought there would be none."

"Perhaps." Bailey shrugged ruefully. "In any case, he sent a small batch of copies to Hatchard's Bookstore the morning they were printed. By afternoon the store requested more, and other stores clamored for copies. He sent them all! The poor man was quite proud of his success and most remorseful when I explained what he had done. I set out right away to bring apologies, and warning."

"Warning?" She heard her voice quiver. She was shaking.

"I'm afraid it caused a stir in London. Drawing rooms are full of talk about 'the Lady Scholar.'"

She looked around the room. Andrew looked worried and Dunning puzzled. Jamie's eyes twinkled; he enjoyed this as much as Harley.

"A lady author isn't a novelty, I fear, but scholarship of this magnitude is rare. I'm afraid there has been loose talk and speculation." Bailey looked pained.

Dunning's earnest expression made her apprehensive. "Copies have reached Cambridge already," he said. "Mallet is being given great credit for the brilliance of the work, but he tells me that that is an injustice."

Her eyes darted to Andrew who watched her with inscrutable intensity.

"Am I correct that I have the honor of addressing the Lady of Scholarship who brought us these works herself?" Bailey hesitated, uncertain how to go on.

An electric moment passed; her eyes and Andrew's met and held.

Bailey spoke up in the silence. "Mallet hasn't said, of course. Forgive me if I intrude. I gathered that perhaps you..."

"Yes, Mr. Bailey, I am the translator of the poems. However, without Mr. Mallet they would have remained disconnected notes and fragments. The work as a whole would never have been completed." What she saw in Andrew's eyes turned her insides to jelly and caused her courage to swell.

She looked back at her questioner. He beamed at her; the printer actually beamed. "It is an honor, my lady, a true honor to meet a scholar of your caliber."

"Indeed." Dunning now smiled broadly. "You deserve the praise the literary reviews are unjustly pointing elsewhere. If you were a man, they would not."

"Literary reviews, Mr. Dunning?" She held her breath.

The sad brown eyes filled with sympathy. "I am afraid they fall into two camps. Some—and may I say I am of this mind— believe the translations are exquisite and the poems themselves of great, if somewhat unusual, interest. Generally, those—not me, of course, but some–who take that point of view find it difficult to believe a woman did this work. Andrew has been called a cagey self-promoter who is responsible for an unusual body of work. It's unfair, but there you have it."

"And the other reviewers?" The words had to be forced out over the lump in her throat. There were reviews, good and bad. People were paying attention to her work. In Georgiana's experience, attention caused pain.

"They're of divided mind about the authors themselves. Speculation is that the poems must have been the work of men using female pseudonyms or that the women in question were rare, or different, or —" Dunning shrugged.

"Peculiarly unfeminine?"

"Yes, I fear so." He colored in embarrassment. "Or worse."

Georgiana didn't wish to know what "worse" meant. She took refuge in anger at the narrow-minded prigs.

"I am sorry, Georgiana." Andrew's soft voice sounded consoling. "I should have left my name off the title page."

"No!" She swung around. "No. Without you, there is no book. Without you, there is nothing." She reached out and took his hand, drawing strength from its warmth.

"You understand that all five hundred copies have been sold?"

Thoughts jumbled in her head. "Mr. Dunning, is it actually being read?"

"My, yes. No bookshop in Cambridge could keep it. It has caused a sensation among the undergraduates," Dunning told her.

"As I said, the same is true in London," Bailey added. "I came to apologize, yes, but also to beg you to order a second printing." He looked up at her under furrowed brows, pleading.

She turned back to Andrew who suddenly looked like a proud Papa. He waited for her to speak.

"It's all too much. It's being read? Yes, of course it is, you said that. The women's works are actually being read!"

Jamie finally spoke up. "Even I'm reading it, Lady Georgie. Didn't care to read the commentary, but the little verses are, well, even I can understand them. The ancient ladies must not have been as protected as ours."

She slipped quietly back into her seat, ashen.

Dunning looked rueful. "They are a bit scandalous, I fear, my lady. One can only imagine the London on-dits. You were true to their world in your translations. You shed light on lives many haven't hitherto known about. I am proud to know the scholar of such a work. It is, of course, proper that you didn't wish your name associated with it, but I'm proud to say I know you. Not, of course, that I would breathe your name if you don't wish it. There is speculation enough in town."

"Speculation?"

"Lawrence Watterson is putting it out that Andrew did it alone, when he isn't telling people the works are spurious."

"Scoundrel." Andrew looked as if he had just eaten something rancid. She squeezed his hand.

"No one believes they are spurious. Watterson looks like a fool. You cite the *Anthologia Graeca* and other sources. The works are there for others to find should they wish."

"But they don't know it's my work?"

"No one seems to remember that Watterson spread your request for assistance about." Dunning cleared his throat noisily. "It would be a trivial matter to make sure your scholarship was acknowledged, at least privately among those who appreciate it. I could spread the word."

"I think not, Geoff. Let's give the lady some time to digest what you've told her." Andrew withdrew his hand from hers. "Tell me, Georgie. What do you wish? If we don't reprint, the to-do will die in time."

She couldn't speak; she was numb with shock.

"I am so sorry you weren't able to make the initial decision, but you can make this one."

Georgiana's head spun. Their work was being read. It had reviewers. That reality overwhelmed all other thought. She couldn't make out Andrew's question. Bailey seemed to expect something, but she could only look at Andrew with wonderment.

He took her hand again and drew her to her feet. "I think perhaps she needs to discuss the second printing with her collaborator. In private."

"You were thinking of your parents, weren't you?"

When Jamie described the ancient ladies as less protected than their own, Andrew thought her ashen face might be a prelude to a swoon. He ought to have known better.

She glanced up at him with a deliciously puzzled expression in response to his question. She sat in front of the diamond-paned windows, surrounded by his books, and the vision of her there took his breath away.

"When Jamie raised the more scandalous aspects of the poems, were you thinking about your parents?" he repeated.

"For a moment, yes. I've lived far too many years under the interdiction. No scandal must touch my sisters. No scandal must touch the House of Hayden. I forgot for a moment."

"Forgot what?"

"That I don't have to fear reproach if I don't choose to." The Hayden chin rose. She would battle her own family for this. He let out a breath he didn't realize he held, weak with relief. She would probably have to stand up to the Haydens, and her courage relieved him.

"Let's get down to the root issue quickly here. The milk can't be put back in the bottle. By that I mean, the book is being read, and it is causing talk. I think we are well-served to do a second printing."

"Of course we are!" she responded without hesitation. "Anyone who wishes to read these works should be able to do so. We owe it to the writers."

"That's my girl. More copies won't necessarily fan the flames of gossip. My only question is whether we wish to print it exactly the same or put the name of the Lady of Scholarship on the title page."

"Why would we do that?" She looked genuinely confused.

"To put the credit where it rightly belongs, of course. It's your work. In addition, gossip feeds on speculation. Take away the speculation and—"

"Marry me," she said.

It was the last thing he expected. The look in her eyes knocked the wind from his chest. He groped for words. She misunderstood the look on his face and turned toward the wall.

Andrew reached over and pulled her back to him. He kissed her so fiercely it was as if he could pour his pride, his admiration, and his love into her that way. When at last he gasped for air and began to feather kisses over her brows and cheek, a moan deep in her throat filled him with yearning.

"Repeat it." He whispered. "Say it again." His mouth moved down the column of her throat.

"Marry me." Her voice was husky but sure.

He paused in his progress back up her throat and smiled against the edge of her chin. "My dear Lady Georgiana, you do me great honor, but I must say that isn't the proposal of a young man's dreams." He went back to kissing and would have taken her mouth again if she hadn't covered his lips with her fingers.

"Wretch." She smiled at him.

He grinned into her hand and tried to kiss her again.

This time she pulled away.

"I'm teas—" he began.

"Mr. Mallet," Georgiana shook him off, pulled a few feet away, and struck a pose of mock seriousness. "You must be aware of the high esteem I hold for you and know, as I know, that we suit one another very well." He moved toward her, but she eluded him.

"I am all too aware that I have little to offer," she went on as she avoided his hands. "My fortune is small, but I am compelled to put my suit to the test."

She slipped the book cart between them and whirled it sideways when he tried to pass. "Therefore, with trepidation, aware of my vast unworthiness, I ask if you—"

He reached across for her. A growl rose deep in his throat. "Georgiana!"

She slipped gracefully to her knees, one hand on her heart and the other extended as though pleading. "—would extend to me the great privilege of your hand in marriage."

He stopped in his tracks, sobering. Amusement fled. Georgiana remained. Beneath her teasing, he saw fear and expectation.

"Of course I will, foolish woman," he said while he helped her to rise. He held her at arm's length and went on, "But I think I need to know what you expect from this marriage."

She didn't shirk the question; she stepped away from him and took a steadying breath. *That's my Georgie.* Her courage warmed his heart.

"That night, when I told you I wished to stay with you, you said you wanted it too. I remember you said, 'it's called marriage.' I have thought of it many times. What I wanted was to be here with you, sharing this house, sharing your bed, and spending our days in work. I wanted to have a voice in that work."

She sighed, and he watched her chew her lower lip, that endearing habit she had when she searched for words. He held his peace and waited for her to go on.

"You said 'it's called marriage.' That closeness, that sharing isn't what my parents called marriage, but if that is what you mean, I want it."

"I want it too." He said in a rush. "It doesn't have to be here. We could live at Helsington or anywhere you choose as long as we're together."

"I like it here. Helsington is no longer mine." Her breathless admission startled him. He let her explain. "I sold it. I am, or I was, using the proceeds to support myself without my father's interference. We'll need to manage without it... Father's money, that is. I have no staff. My new house is smaller than this one."

"I can afford a decent staff. We could buy a different house."

"There's more." He waited expectantly, and she went on. "Yesterday, I think I gave you pleasure. I know it."

Pleasure? Mind-exploding pleasure. "Foolish woman. You underestimate yourself."

She held up a graceful hand to silence him. "I didn't realize how it would feel to give pleasure—in bed, when we work, when we're together. It is a powerful thing to *give* pleasure like that."

He frowned and tried to follow her logic.

"It occurred to me that it is powerful to care for one you love in other ways, the giving part." She sighed again, deeply, as if groping to be understood. "I never thought of it, Andrew. You have to allow someone to love you. You have to let them so that they can feel powerful, too."

He took two steps toward her. "You want to let me give you pleasure." He wanted to say it lightly, but he found he couldn't. Something profound shifted around them.

"I think you want to do more than that. And, yes, I want to let you care for me."

He closed the gap between them and pulled her to him, her head nestled on his shoulder. "You trust me with your care?"

"I think." She paused so long he thought she had lost her train of thought, but she finally spoke. "I think caring for someone isn't the same as having power over them. At least it isn't in the abusive sense. If you can take the burden of my love, I can take yours."

He kissed her then, a gentle touch, once, twice, and then more deeply. Her hands went around his neck to pull him into her embrace. He felt her smile against his mouth. "We'll need more work."

He smiled back. "There is plenty to be found. Women poets in Latin perhaps?"

She laughed out loud. It would be well. They could make a life together. Even the sound of Jamie Heyworth at the door didn't interfere.

"So, am I to wish you happy, or to call Andrew out?"

"Go away, Jamie." Two voices spoke with one mind. The passion of their embrace didn't decrease in the slightest.

"Well then, I'll just take myself down and tell Harley to open that fine bottle of wine he has chilling. Bailey will want his answer. Ten minutes?"

Chapter Twenty-Six

They took a full twenty minutes, but the thought of Jamie hovering, aware and protective, dampened passion eventually.

"It's deuced uncomfortable to be interrupted. We best not continue to the conclusion we're both considering."

She blushed brightly. "I can wait, I think. There'll be time to love each other, all the time we want now."

He started to kiss her again but thought better of it. He took her hand and led her to the stairs.

"Possible, yes. Easy, no," he said.

She felt her blush deepen when they rounded the corner to the room. Four pairs of eyes met them: Jamie's dancing, Bailey's warmed by profound emotion, Dunning's kind, and Harley's cheeky as ever.

Harley looked as if he wanted to say, "About time." Instead, he said, "The wine is getting warm. Thought the major was going to have to fetch you."

Jamie reached over to pour. "Am I to toast your happiness then?"

"Certainly. Our book is a success." Andrew gripped her hand as if he feared she would flee.

Jamie lowered his eyebrows. "That isn't what I meant."

Andrew continued smoothly. "And my partner agrees to a reprint. A larger one this time, Mr. Bailey." He grinned down at her. She grinned back like a fool.

"I say! That is splendid. It's a fine work." Bailey beamed.

"As to happiness," Andrew said, pausing to make sure he had

everyone's attention, "yes, you may wish us happy. I have accepted Lady Georgiana's gracious offer of marriage."

Jamie exploded with a loud whoop of laughter and clapped Andrew on the back. Dunning looked a bit puzzled by the wording but offered polite congratulations.

Bailey downed the wine Harley offered and quickly made his excuses. "Can just about make London tonight if I travel light. Best get on it quickly while the demand is there." The little printer rubbed his hands together. "Congratulations again, Mallet. Every happiness, my lady. Every happiness."

Dunning might have left also, but Andrew asked him to stay. "We have a wedding to plan, Geoff, and not much time to do it. You are welcome to help."

A wedding! Things were moving too quickly for Georgiana. She felt her stomach flip and the color drain from her face. Andrew squeezed her hand sympathetically. "Weddings are public things, I know, but they must be endured to get to marriage." He winked again. "I think the sooner we do it the better. Anticipation won't help. Your family—"

"Will object no matter what we do. The sooner it is done the better."

"Good girl. Banns will take too long."

"I can be ready to travel to Scotland in an hour."

Dunning looked distressed, and Harley shook his head. Jamie's face looked insufferably smug. She turned to Andrew, puzzled.

"Actually," Andrew said, "Jamie had an idea."

Georgiana gaped at them. *The rotten men discussed it before I even had a chance to ask.*

"A license, Lady Georgie," Jamie explained.

"That could prove difficult," she said. "Only Canturbury can issue a special license. The archbishops are all my father's relatives or cronies. They'll put a spoke in our wheel without his permission."

"Not Ely," Jamie told her. "Plain bishop, not an archbishop, but he has connections to Canterbury's staff. He can issue a common license. Doesn't give a fig about what Canterbury thinks—too old to care."

"Why Ely?"

"He's my mother's uncle," Jamie said. "If we leave now, we should be back in a few days."

A bolt of excitement shot through her. That would work. She could go with them, and the bishop could marry them. Then she remembered. A common license meant a week's wait.

Dunning spoke up. "Those things take a day. Paperwork, you know." He looked at Georgiana with sympathy. She must have looked like she had been knocked on the head; she certainly felt like it. "Lady Georgiana will want time to prepare, I think, in any case."

Andrew gave her a long look. "Dress, Georgie? Flowers?"

It came to her then. They were discussing her wedding, the wedding she never expected to have. It would be simple; it would be soon, but it should be meaningful.

"Yes, all right. I think so," she said. "And a wedding breakfast, too. Geoff, your grandmother will help, won't she?"

"She'll dance a jig. She's been hoping to see you two make a match of it for weeks now—anything but you alone in that dreadful little house."

Even Dunning's insensitive remark about her house didn't dampen her spirits. *Mrs. Potter will dance a jig.* The idea made her laugh out loud. "We will all dance a jig at the wedding."

Six days later nothing sounded simple.

Where are they? Andrew estimated a few days. They should have been back three days ago.

She wondered if he was deliberately staying away for the required waiting period so she could use his house without added scandal. She wished she had never agreed to a license. She wished they had dashed off to Scotland or at least that she had insisted on accompanying them to Ely.

Georgiana rearranged the flowers in the center of Andrew's worn old worktable (as she had a half-dozen times before) and checked the nosegays on his mantel. Afternoon shadows sank lower with each passing moment and still no sound at the door.

She knew she ought to go downstairs and help Edwina Potter and Geoff Dunning entertain Reverend Parke. He had come to finalize details and wouldn't stay much longer.

She took one more look around. The room would have made a perfect background for their wedding. It was fragrant with memories. They could have wed surrounded by his books and the work they shared. St. Mary's church would have to do, since law and a common license required it.

She took one more look around and sighed. It had everything except a groom. "A few days," Andrew had said, with time for the bishop to complete the paperwork. "We will marry promptly on the seventh day," he had said.

Seven days! We should have dared a special license and His Grace be... She knew better. She feared His Grace her father would have descended with fury. As it was she feared he would get wind of the wedding and interfere.

A knock on the door sent her running. She flew halfway down the stairs before she realized that Andrew wouldn't have knocked. He would have opened the door and flown to her. Another man stood at the door, a slender figure so tall he had to duck slightly to enter. The last apricot-orange rays of sun illuminated impeccably groomed golden hair. Richard.

"The Major isn't in." Harley, not impressed with anyone's consequence, stood with one hand on the door as if to shut him out. Richard looked quizzically at the tableau in the parlor: Reverend Parke had come to discuss flowers with Edwina. He sipped tea companionably and slowly with Dunning and Edwina. Mr. Peabody, who had come for news, sat engrossed in *Poetry by the*

Female Authors of Ancient Greece. Harley waited but gave no ground.

Richard swept his glance inexorably up the stairs to his sister. "Georgiana, I thought I might see you here. There were no servants at Helsington. It is closed."

"Richard, this is a surprise." She forced the words out through clenched teeth. His clear blue eyes, inscrutable as always, scanned her appearance. She descended the final steps and believed he could see her very soul. "Helsington has been sold. The last of the servants left yesterday."

"Is there somewhere we might speak privately?"

For a moment she wanted to insist on the parlor and an audience. Her heart beat erratically, but she wouldn't become a coward now. She wouldn't shrink back.

She gestured up the stairs, gave Harley a reassuring smile, and preceded Richard up. The old batman looked ready for a fight if necessary. She knew he would stay within earshot.

The honey glow of afternoon filled Andrew's study and enhanced the soft crème lace of Georgiana's gown.

"You look well. Your health continues to improve, and that dress, I must say, is stunning." Richard's voice seemed sincere, but one could never tell. "Is there an occasion? I understand your host isn't at home."

"As you see. You wished a word with me?" *Don't be defensive. Stand your ground.*

Richard looked at her more sharply.

"Actually, I have brought you something." He removed a parcel wrapped in paper and unwrapped it on the worktable. She knew what it was, of course.

"I think perhaps you have already seen this. There was a copy downstairs, wasn't there?"

"Certainly."

"Did you know he had it published?"

"Not initially, no. I understand that someone released it accidentally before I could approve. Richard, I would have approved it. The intent was always to publish it. Now that the first run has sold out, we've ordered an additional printing."

"When Andrew came to Mountview, this was his business?"

"Yes." She faced him defiantly.

Richard ran his long graceful fingers over the rich brown leather. "It is quite good, a very fine piece of work. Georgiana, I had no idea. I read it in London, at Bailey's, before it was printed."

The air left her lungs in a rush, as if forced. "I didn't know that. Andrew didn't tell me."

"As I said, it's quite good but not the work of one A. Mallet, I believe."

"Not entirely, no. But without him there would be no book. Is mother in collapse or preparing warfare?"

"Warfare, but not the sort that involves frontal attacks."

"How so?"

"All violence of feeling has been in private. She is more concerned about deflecting any rumors about the 'Lady of Scholarship.' She chooses not to know who it could possibly be."

"Ignore the unpleasant, and it will wither?"

"Exactly. It's quite effective. No one dares to contradict her."

"His Grace?"

"Isn't interested in scholarship."

"I see. If he chooses not to know about it, it doesn't exist. And you?"

"If the Lady of Scholarship wishes to remain private, I have no quarrel with it. I'm proud of you."

She looked away, overwhelmed. He was giving her his approval.

"Are you still set on living alone in a hovel?"

"It wasn't a hovel!"

Damn Richard's arrogance.

A commotion on the stairs spared her from answering any further. Georgiana heard Jamie's heavy steps bypass Andrew's lumbering climb. Jamie burst into the study first.

"Richard! Come to join the wedding party, have you? Too late. Andrew has already assigned the honor of standing up with him to me." He defied the Marquess to stand in their way.

Silence followed that amazing speech. Richard looked over at Georgiana. Whatever questions he had must have been answered, because he gave her one of his rare smiles.

"Don't be foolish, Heyworth. I'm here to give the bride away." He raised her hand and kissed her fingers, whispering as he did so, "Thank God. I feared for you alone."

Tears sprang to her eyes. His concern touched her heart in spite of his managing ways.

Andrew removed her hand from her brother's, a protective glare dark in his eyes. The ferocious expression delighted Georgiana.

"Consider the bride presented, Richard. You are welcome to share in our joy, but I warn you—"

Richard raised a hand to pause, but Andrew overrode it and went on, "—that if you hurt her in any way, if she suffers the slightest humiliation or difficulty, there will be hell to pay."

"My dear Andrew, that should be my speech to you," the marquess replied with perfect hauteur.

"Richard, what about His Grace?" Georgiana asked, suddenly anxious.

"As I said before, he prefers to ignore what he doesn't wish to exist." Glenaire watched her with steady eyes. She would cease to exist to them; she already had. They both knew it.

She reached up and brushed the coarse black hair from Andrew's eyes. "So be it," she said out loud.

Andrew looked puzzled and glanced at Richard suspiciously, but her swift kiss more than satisfied him.

Richard watched them for a moment; his slight smile reached his eyes slowly. He looked around the room as if satisfied with what he saw. "One presumes there is a license. Perhaps the Reverend would like to see it, Heyworth. There's a good man."

"Alas, my lord, it is a common license. What is the date Mr. Mallet?" the reverend asked.

"Six days exactly. We can be married at St. Mary's tomorrow morning."

The next morning, the newly wed couple processed back to Andrew's little house, the bride carrying flowers, their friends marching behind them and crowding up the stairs into the study. If they couldn't marry there, at least Georgiana got her wish to celebrate there.

Georgiana had given both her hands to Andrew and repeated the words that joined their lives as light streamed through stained glass. When Andrew leaned to kiss her, their loved ones clapped in delight.

When they reached the study, Richard peered down at his sister. "Georgiana," he said, "you might want a moment to freshen. Or perhaps not. You are disgustingly radiant already."

"Corporal Harley? Ah, good man! I see the champagne wine is chilled. Cakes and ices as well. Excellent."

Georgiana laughed as everyone did her brother's bidding. They always did. This time no one seemed to mind, and she minded least of all. She had his support and that was all that mattered.

We should celebrate more often. This house was in need of joy, Andrew thought as he stepped around Mr. Peabody and John Bailey deep in conversation on the bottom of the stairs.

He looked at the guests standing in his kitchen door and spilled around his sitting room. They chatted in groups of two and three and happily sipped champagne. He and Georgiana would fill the house with guests often in the future. *Not tonight, though. Tonight is for us.*

That night he wanted nothing except to be left alone with his wife. Glenaire had already begun to hint Jamie away, promising dinner at Cambridge's best inn. Harley announced he would spend a few days in Georgiana's little cottage, ostensibly packing it up, but in reality giving them privacy.

All I want is my bride, who seems to have gone missing.

"Geoff, have you seen Georgiana?" Andrew asked. "She and your mother were deep in some female conversation ten minutes ago."

"Went out back for air," Dunning replied, putting on his cloak. "Mrs. Mallet looked a bit peaked."

Peaked? Andrew looked in the direction of the kitchen. His tiny garden lay beyond it.

"I will bid you good day, Mallet, and give you my congratulations one last time. Mother and I will take our leave in a few moments," Dunning said.

Andrew merely nodded. He headed through the kitchen before Dunning could finish. He heard others making their departures behind him.

"Georgiana, is there a problem?" he asked coming out the door. "Your brother is preparing to leave and—"

He stopped short at the sight of his bride, pale as linen, bent over in the shadowy garden. Edwina Potter sat next to her on a stone bench against the brick wall that surrounded his small patch of green. The old woman had an arm around her shoulders.

Andrew rushed forward.

"What is it, Love?"

"I fear champagne didn't agree with her," Mrs. Potter told him. "She's had a bit of nausea."

He knelt in front of Georgiana.

"I'm sorry," his new wife mumbled. "It should pass."

"Indeed it will, young man. Nothing to be concerned about," Mrs. Potter told him with a smile as she rose to her feet. As if to confirm that, Georgiana sat up straight.

Mrs. Potter beamed at both of them. "I'll leave you two together. You'll want some time alone." She scurried away without another word.

Georgiana leaned her forehead against his. "Andrew, I'm so sorry, but it has passed already. I'll be fine. I won't let it spoil our wedding night."

He kissed her softly. "Nothing could, no matter how you feel or what we do. We have hundreds of nights ahead of us. Are you certain you aren't ill? Do you want me to fetch Peabody?" He stood up. "I'll have to run to catch him."

She grabbed a hand and pulled him back.

"I'm not ill, Andrew. I fear I may have misled you, however. This house is very small."

He looked at her, confused. "I told you we didn't need to stay here," he said, struggling to understand her meaning.

"Mr. Peabody may have been wrong."

His puzzlement deepened.

An impish smile crossed her lips. She pulled him down to the bench to whisper in his ear. "I'm not quite sure, but I think we will have another collaboration to manage in several more months."

Still not making sense. Georgiana just smiled back at him until the radiant look on her face moved something inside him and the light dawned. He felt an explosion of joy great enough to fill their little house.

"Pregnant, Georgie?" he whispered when he could breathe. He covered her belly with his hand. A child grew there, his child. The idea made him tremble.

She nodded, a happy laugh bursting forth. "I've never been so glad to be wrong about something."

He kissed her then, as he wanted to do all evening. "I love you," he said. She didn't answer. She took his mouth with hers and kissed him until they both gasped for air.

Andrew stood and helped her rise. He slipped an arm around her waist, and they walked to the door.

"I think, dear wife, that, no matter what happens, my life with you will be a constant surprise."

Georgiana let out a yelp when he swept her up into his arms. He carried her across the threshold, laughter trailing in their wake.

Epilogue

London, June 1819

Sing, O muse, of the rage of Achilles, son of Peleus, that brought countless ills upon the Achaeans. Georgiana translated in her head as Andrew read *The Illiad* to their son. In Greek.

She looked up from her work and frowned at the pair sitting in a comfortable chair in their shared office. "Honestly Andrew, I'm glad he can't understand it."

Andrew smiled down at the toddler in his lap. "Are you sure? He pays attention. Who is to say he can't understand it?" Andrew retorted.

"Richard is eighteen months old! He likes the sound of his father's voice."

Andrew shrugged. "It gets *Aeneas* used to the sound of the words." Andrew insisted on calling their son by his middle name, if only to avoid confusion with Georgiana's brother.

At the name, Georgiana shook her head. She was losing that battle. The boy would be Aeneas for life. "Will and Catherine are hoping for a cricket team. You're trying to raise a classics department."

"Not at all. Perhaps the next one will be a physician." His smile brought color to her cheeks. The next one would make an appearance in December if all went well.

The little one patted his father's face, rubbing the scar that crossed it, and pointed to the book. Georgiana smiled. "It is a good thing we have a patient child."

A knock at the door interrupted them. Their butler, Simpson, announced, "The earl and countess are here, Ma'am. I put them in the drawing room and ordered tea." He didn't need to specify which earl. It would be the Earl and Countess of Chadbourn.

Georgiana was on her feet immediately. "Have they brought Artie?"

At "Artie," Aeneas wriggled down from his father's lap and started for the door.

"They did indeed bring their lad. Shall I have Agnes take the boys to the nursery?" Simpson's frown, though slight, was obvious. He considered the Mallets failure to employ a nurserymaid a breach of protocol. The Mallets had kept the house in Cambridge, but had settled in a modest townhouse in Bloomsbury. They employed few servants: Simpson, Agnes the maid of all work, and a cook.

"Give us a bit of time, Simpson, but alert Mr. Harley that the boy is here," she replied. Harley, who remained as Andrew's personal servant, managed whatever needed doing, and was the closest they had to a nurserymaid. Aeneas adored him.

Andrew swung Aeneas up into his arms and they walked down the hall together. "This is unexpected," Georgiana murmured.

Andrew nodded. "I expect Will to be tending his fields this time of year; he stayed in London longer this year. It is always good to see them, though." The distance in the men's friendship had disappeared with the arrival of their sons.

A quick glance at the faces of Will and Catherine Landrum, the earl and countess, however, made it clear the visit had a serious purpose.

Before anyone could speak, Aeneas wiggled down and ran to his friend. He and Artie Landrum began marching around the room and giggling in some greeting ritual understood only by toddlers.

Will didn't even watch their antics. "We need to talk, Andrew," he said without preamble.

The arrival of a tea tray with Harley right behind it delayed any response. Georgiana was once again astounded at Harley's quick wit and insight. He sized up the atmosphere in the room immediately, gave a sardonic bow, and scooped up one laughing boy and then the other.

"There are new blocks in the nursery, lads. Shall we see who can build the tallest tower."

Aeneas wrapped an arm around Harley's neck. "Walls o' Troy," he announced imitating his father. His precocious vocabulary never failed to astonish Georgiana.

Harley glanced down at Arty. "What do you think lad? Tower o' London?"

The door closed and silence settled on the room. Georgiana wished her stomach would settle as well.

ANDREW DIDN'T LIKE the expression on the earl's face. Catherine's wasn't much better.

Will glanced at Georgiana. "Maybe we should leave the ladies to their tea."

"I don't think—" Andrew started.

"Don't be ridiculous," Georgiana said at the same time.

"It is about your brother, Georgie," Catherine put in, frowning at her husband.

"Has he finally offered for Lady Sarah Wharton as our parents wish? All London has been holding its breath," Georgiana said.

"No! The gossip is that her father gave him an ultimatum and he declined to offer." Catherine told her.

"That sounds like Richard," Georgiana said. "He doesn't take kindly to coercion."

"Have you seen him," Will asked.

"No. Not— What is going on?" Georgiana demanded.

"He's gone missing."

"Ridiculous!" Andrew said. "The Marquess of Glenaire does not just go missing." Richard would never do anything so thoughtless.

"Have you spoken with his minions, Roger Heaton and Walter Stewart?" Andrew asked.

"I cornered Heaton at Whitehall, and he was evasive," Will answered.

"There you have it. Richard is off on some secret government mischief," Andrew said.

Will shook his head. "Heaton looked nervous. Worse, worried. I don't think they know where he is."

"Are you implying my brother ran off without Castlereagh's directive?" Georgiana demanded.

"That is exactly what I'm saying."

Andrew studied his wife's worried face. "He wouldn't run off to avoid gossip like some men would."

"Never," she agreed. "He's been obsessed with the Volkov business. And Lilias Thornton."

Will nodded "I'm worried. This is not like him.

A disturbance at the door interrupted them and Roger Heaton himself barged in before the butler could announce him. His bow, even to the earl, was perfunctory.

"Forgive my rag manners," he said, hesitating. "I thought—that is —" He ran a hand though his hair.

"It is my brother the marquess, isn't it?" Georgiana said.

"He has disappeared. Is it Volkov? Tell us what you know," Andrew demanded.

Heaton looked harried, but came to a decision. "The Marquess left on the Gibralter packet from Portsmouth yesterday. We lost track of Volkov. He may have gone in pursuit, he's been that determined to stop the man. I thought—that is I hoped he left word with family, but His Grace, your father, dismissed it as nonsense."

"He left no word with us," Andrew said, taking Georgiana's hand.

Heaton nodded sadly, made his apologies, promised to bring word if there was any, and left.

"What do you think, Andrew? Gibraltar?" Will asked.

"I don't like this any more than you do. If the issue is private..." Andrew murmured.

"He may prefer the help of friends over officials." Will finished.

"If he'll take help at all," Andrew muttered.

Andrew turned to his wife. "He may need help, Georgie, no matter what quest he's gone off on by himself. He would—"

"Yes he would help any of us. Besides, Will will go without you if you don't follow him," Georgiana replied. She smiled sadly at Catherine.

Things happened quickly then. Catherine gave Georgiana a swift hug and went to fetch Artie. The Chadbourns left, and Andrew went to pack.

An hour later he stood by the door and took his wife in his arms. The Chadbourn carriage waited on the street. "It may be a goose chase, Georgie. If so, we'll be back in two weeks. If he needs us... Well, I'll be back on time," he said patting her belly.

"Be safe," she whispered.

Andrew felt a tug on his trousers and looked down to find Aeneas lugging their copy of the Illiad.

"Αχιλλέας, γιος του Πηλέα, Papa," Aeneas said plaintively—*Achilles, son of Peleus*. "More."

Andrew grinned at his wife. He knelt and drew his son into his arms. "Papa must go on a trip with Uncle Will. Be good to your mama and perhaps she'll read to you as well. When I come back we'll finish the book."

A swift but powerful kiss saw him on his way.

Author's Note

I hope you enjoyed *A Lady's Honor*. It was a joy for me to bring it back to life, polished up with a new epilogue.

Re-reading and editing this work, first published over a decade ago, revealed some necessary changes. For this edition the timing of the Earl of Chadbourn's wedding was adjusted to conform better with *Family Honor*, Book 1 in this series. That required required a thorough examination of references to season.

In addition, I learned more about English marriage laws in the intervening time. The original edition described a *special license* and immediate wedding in Andrew's study. That, alas, could only have been issued by the Archbishop of Canterbury, something Georgiana was desperate to avoid. The final chapter was rewritten to allow for use of a *common license,* which required a waiting period and marriage in church. It was, at least, faster than calling the bans.

You will find these characters in future books. Jamie's story, *Tattered Honor* is in progress. That one will take us to Rome. Even Aeneas and Artie will have books of their own by mid 2027.

For now, however, we'll pick up the series with Glenaire. His well-intended attempts to manage his friends' lives and interfering ways will continue for years, but I could not resist bringing him to his knees just once. Even the haughty marquess eventually has to ask for help.

Here's a sample: ***An Inconvenient Honor, Book 3, Chapter 1***

Chadbourn Hall, February 1819

If women were as easily managed as the affairs of state—or the recalcitrant Ottoman Empire—Richard Hayden, Marquess of Glenaire, would be a happier man. As it was, the creatures made hash of his well-laid plans and bedeviled him on all sides.

"What did we miss now? I can tell you're unhappy." Will Landrum, Earl of Chadbourn, and one of the handful of men who would call Richard 'friend,' was not fooled by the cool façade and bland expression with which the marquess surveyed his ballroom.

"Who invited Lilias Thornton?" Richard demanded under his breath. His eyes followed a slender young woman who paced out the steps of the Quadrille across the parquet floor of the earl's ballroom.

"No 'thank you for turning your country seat into a diplomatic snake pit for an entire week so the haut ton can mingle with exotic visitors from the East while the foreign secretary manages the fate of Greece over brandy and cards?'" Will demanded.

Richard looked at his friend, one eyebrow raised. "Chadbourn Park fit the need precisely. I thanked your Catherine this morning."

Will grunted. "My Catherine worked miracles when Sahin Pasha showed up with six extra people in his party."

"We can't predict how many retainers the Turks will impose," Richard growled. The Ottomans danced to their own tune; the Foreign Office never knew what to expect. Richard loathed the unpredictable. He went back to surveying the overheated ballroom.

"Who invited Lilias Thornton?" he repeated, while he moved along the mirrored wall of the earl's spectacular ballroom to a position next to a massive marble urn that gave him a better view of his quarry. His eyes never left the dancers.

Will snatched two glasses of champagne from a footman stationed discreetly along the softly flocked wall, tray in hand. He handed one to Richard who took it without looking.

"Catherine also had to scurry when your mother demanded that she invite three more marriageable young ladies and their eager mamas," Will complained.

"I would rather that she refused."

"Refuse the Duchess of Sudbury? Surely you jest."

Richard nodded without taking his gaze from the dancers. "I jest. I have less control over my mother than I do Sahin Pasha." He loathed loss of control even more than unpredictability. He had been forced to sidestep the marriage-minded chits for two days.

Right now only one woman interested him, Lilias Thornton. He watched her throw her head back, send auburn curls bouncing, and laugh up at her partner. *She dances with grace, I'll give her that—grace and unbridled joy. A man could lose his senses over that look.* The last thing he needed was to lose his senses.

Will followed his friend's line of sight. "Beautiful woman," he acknowledged. "Catherine called her dress 'beyond perfection.'"

That dress radiates so damned much continental sophistication she makes the women around her look countrified, my esteemed mother's protégées included. The woman laughed freely again, and Richard felt himself harden in spite of his determination; the surge of attraction irritated him. *I have no time for such nonsense.*

"Who invited her?" he demanded. "It's a matter of some urgency."

Will shrugged. "I believe Catherine included some regular attendees at your sister's literary salon. She must be one of those. You said to invite women who could provide intelligent conversation to members of the diplomatic corps."

"So I did. My men tell me she has been in conversation with Konstantin Volkov three times these past two days."

"You're tracking her conversations?"

"Volkov's. He has no official role, yet he follows the Russian delegation and slinks through society in the shadows. I want to know who he works for, why he sought an invitation, and what he intends."

The entire house party had been arranged to provide a discreet opportunity for the foreign secretary—or more precisely, Richard, his second—to persuade Ottoman officials to moderate their suppression of revolutionary rumbling in Greece. England did not want the kind of chaos that would tempt Russia. Expansionist Russia threatened all of Europe. The weak and floundering Ottoman Empire did not.

"Ask him," Will suggested. "Unless diplomacy requires a more devious approach."

"Lilias Thornton accompanied her father to St. Petersburg three years ago. The crown appointed him to the trade delegation at our embassy there," Richard explained. "She returned without him rather abruptly in early January. I wonder why. Volkov arrived shortly after. It puzzles me." He did not like puzzles.

"It isn't unusual for a young woman of marriageable age to seek London before the Season starts," a woman's voice cut in. Catherine Landrum, Will's countess, reached for her husband's glass and took a sip. She tasted it slowly, seemed to pronounce it fit, and handed the glass back. "Lilias made it clear she's seeking a good marriage," the countess told Richard. "Who is Volkov?"

"She's well beyond the age," he answered. He ignored her question about the Russian.

"Surely not!" Catherine laughed. "Twenty-two may be somewhat older than the norm ..." She paused when a young woman of seventeen pranced by and smiled coyly at the marquess over her partner's shoulder.

"Well, perhaps quite a bit older," she acknowledged when they passed.

"She served as her father's hostess in his postings abroad since she turned sixteen. She has shown no interest in the marriage mart until this year," Richard said. "I don't care about the gossip. I want to know about her connection to Konstantin Volkov."

"Ask her," the countess suggested.

"I intend to," Richard said as the last notes of the dance faded. He set out in the woman's direction.

About the Author

Award winning author, Caroline Warfield, grew up in a peripatetic army family, and the need to travel never left her. After a varied career (largely around libraries and technology) she retired to the urban wilds of eastern Pennsylvania to be closer to family and to write. She remains a traveler and adventurer, enamored of owls, books, history, and beautiful gardens (but not the act of gardening).

Caroline calls her books family-centered romance, and this one is no exception. Family makes her characters what they are, for better or worse. She takes them as they are, scarred and wounded, and sets them on their path to their own happily ever after, because *love is worth the risk.*

Soli Deo Gloria

Website http://www.carolinewarfield.com/

www.ingramcontent.com/pod-product-compliance
Lightning Source LLC
LaVergne TN
LVHW091117080826
845145LV00008B/1952

* 9 7 8 1 9 7 2 5 9 0 0 1 0 *